Set Apart:
The Sanctified Sisters of Belton

A True Story

Enjoy Belton!

D. Ligh

Set Apart:
The Sanctified Sisters of Belton

A True Story

Debra Lufburrow

Set Apart:
The Sanctified Sisters of Belton

A True Story

DEDICATION

To the people of the City of Belton in
celebration of our sesquicentennial
anniversary.

1850-2000

INTRODUCTION

This book is the result of many months of careful research and reflects all possible accuracy in the depiction of a few citizens of Belton, Texas, and some of their experiences during the years 1855-1898. Deliberate alteration of known facts includes the changing of Ada Haymond's youngest daughter's name from Emma to Emily, and changing Agatha Pratt's daughter's name from Ada to Anna to avoid confusion in telling the story. Although technically fictional characters, Sarah and Tennie are based on the personal journals of several Belton women who knew and interacted with Martha McWhirter and her family. Sadie is patterned after accounts recorded in the Bell County ex-slave narratives. The Sisters did employ a Black female worker for several years in Belton who later moved with them to Washington, D.C. All other names in the book represent actual Bell County residents and visitors, each portrayed with love and respect.

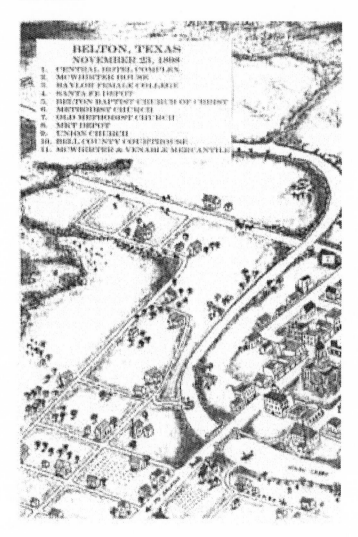

BELTON, TEXAS
NOVEMBER 23, 1893
1. CENTRAL HOTEL COMPLEX
2. McWHIRTER HOUSE
3. BAYLOR FEMALE COLLEGE
4. SANTA FE DEPOT
5. BELTON BAPTIST CHURCH OF CHRIST
6. METHODIST CHURCH
7. OLD METHODIST CHURCH
8. MKT DEPOT
9. UNION CHURCH
10. BELL COUNTY COURTHOUSE
11. McWHIRTER & VENABLE MERCANTILE

CHAPTER 1

Belton, Texas, November 23, 1898

"Fibe o'clock, Mistus Miller?" the driver asked as he slowed the buggy to a stop in front of the Central Hotel.

"Yes, that's right, Moses," Sarah patiently responded as she stepped from the rig to the wooden sidewalk. Every Wednesday for the past nine months the faithful servant had dropped her off in front of the hotel at half past two and had come back for her promptly at five o'clock, yet each week he asked the same question. Thankful that he was so dependable and too kind to even consider reprimanding him, Sarah just smiled. "Five o'clock. Oh, and tell Sadie not to bother with supper tonight," she added. "Mr. Miller won't be home until tomorrow evening."

"Yes'm, Mistus Miller," Moses replied, shaking the reins and muttering to himself as the buggy began to creak forward. "Fibe o'clock. No supper."

Glancing over her shoulder at the clock on the courthouse tower, Sarah saw that she had plenty of time before the three o'clock meeting. Then brushing the road dust from her new dress, she gathered her skirts and started up the front steps of the hotel. Tapping across the broad porch on tightly laced, high-heeled boots, she pushed open the heavy wooden door. Every time Sarah entered the hotel, she was impressed by some aspect of its design, decoration or maintenance. Today she noticed the sparkle of freshly cleaned windows offering a clear view of all that was happening on Main Street.

The Central Hotel had become the place to be seen in Belton, and the attentive, well-considered touch of the women who ran the hotel was evident in every detail. At times, Sarah thought about how curious it was that the town had finally come around to respect the women and their successful business. For so many years the group had earned nothing but hostile disapproval from the townsfolk, but now the Central Hotel was well supported by the collection of prominent citizens who chose to dine or even live at the popular boarding hotel

Stepping inside the congested lobby she greeted her friends briefly and threaded her way through the noisy assembly of well-dressed women. Heading toward the front desk, Sarah was looking forward to her weekly visit with the hotel manager as much as she was to the meeting of the Woman's Wednesday Club.

Sarah's invitation to membership in the literary club confirmed her as being among Belton's best-educated ladies. Since the group's first meeting just nine months earlier, twenty-five prominent women of the town had met weekly to "breathe and haply institute a course of ingenious study," according to the club motto. The fact that the new organization had chosen to meet in the fashionable Central Hotel made Sarah's good fortune complete. For there at the front desk, she had been able to re-establish contact with her friend, Ada McWhirter Haymond, from whom she had been estranged for a number of years. The growing maturity of both women enabled them to appreciate the relationship they once shared, and Sarah's weekly visit had become a cherished time of reunion.

Her anticipation turned to dismay, however, when she reached the front desk and found another woman sitting in Ada's chair. "Why, Mrs. Rancier! How nice to see you again," Sarah greeted the stern-faced matron as she covered her disappointment with her usual cheerfulness. "I didn't expect to see you here."

"Good afternoon, Mrs. Miller," Josephine Rancier responded as she rose from her seat and stepped up to the counter. While Sarah's fashionable costume may have made the plainly dressed woman feel self-conscious at one time in her life, years of donning simple work attire had completely erased her awareness of style. Of course, the dark, unadorned dress, sensible shoes and muslin apron identifying her as one of the owners of the hotel had, in Belton, become a style unto itself. Before her scandalous divorce years earlier from the town jeweler, the attractive and popular Mrs. Rancier had enjoyed all the advantages of Belton society, yet now seemed content in a very different role. "Actually, I didn't expect to be here today, either. You must be a member of the club," she said, politely returning Sarah's smile.

"Yes, I am," Sarah replied as she discretely surveyed the area behind the desk for an indication that Ada might soon be on her way back to her post. "But I usually get here early enough to visit with Ada for a little while before the meeting. Has she stepped away for a moment?"

Although she was accustomed to some degree of disrespect from townspeople, Mrs. Rancier's normally placid expression registered a ripple of distress at hearing Sarah use Ada's first name. "*Mrs. Haymond* isn't feeling well today. I've been assigned to the front desk until her replacement arrives."

"Oh, goodness," Sarah said, alarmed to find out that Ada was sick again. "I'm sorry to hear that. Well, then, I suppose

SET APART

I'd better go on to the meeting. Good afternoon, Mrs. Rancier." Turning away from the desk, Sarah pardoned her way through the groupings of women and entered the well-appointed parlor, where she hurried to take a seat next to her stepmother, Mrs. Tennessee Edwards. Time had all but erased any visible trace of the six-year difference between the women's ages, so that they now simply appeared to be middle-aged friends. Tennie's calm, gracious demeanor, her finishing school education and the fact that she had become the stepmother of a half-grown girl when she herself was but nineteen, however, had always defined her position in the relationship.

As Sarah settled into the seat beside her, Tennie reached out her properly gloved hand to smooth the fabric of her stepdaughter's skirt. "Did you see Ada?" she asked, mindful of Sarah's enjoyment of the weekly visit. "You're in the parlor earlier than usual."

"She wasn't at the desk," Sarah answered, a look of concern clouding her face. "Mrs. Rancier told me she's sick again. You know, Tennie, Ada's had a great deal of trouble with her health. I hope it's nothing serious. She was just beginning to look better. And happier than I've seen her in a long time."

As Sarah spoke, she watched the familiar motions of her stepmother delicately straightening the seams on the fingers of her gloves. Then opening the reticule that matched her tailored gray suit, Tennie retrieved her Wednesday Club program and a pencil from the drawstring handbag. She always took careful notes on each lesson.

"Poor Ada," Tennie sympathized. "She's been working so hard at managing this hotel by herself since her mother went to Washington, D.C., and I'm sure there must be extra duties involved in their decision to move the business up there. It doesn't surprise me that she's ill. She must be terribly disappointed at missing this meeting, too. Did you remember that she was going to show us the orchids she brought back from Mexico? That surely would have been the highlight of Mrs. James' report today." She opened her program to locate the information and made note of the change.

"Oh, yes. I was looking forward to her colorful addition to the meeting, if you know what I mean. I enjoy the lesson each week, but some of the meetings can get a little tedious. Ada's good humor would be more than welcome. Perhaps I should go to her room and see how she is," Sarah suggested aloud to herself. "That's what I'll do. I'll run upstairs to say hello and be back before Mrs. Tyler begins the roll call. Don't let anyone take my seat." Leaving her program on the chair, Sarah collected her handbag and made her way across the plush, patterned carpet to the hotel lobby.

As she exited the main part of the three-story building, Sarah strode past Ada's cutting garden in the center of the hotel complex, which she noticed was surprisingly well tended for so late in the year. At the sight of her friend's handiwork, fond memories of the time she had spent with Ada's family came to mind. She thought about the encouragement and loving discipline of Ada's parents, Martha and George McWhirter, and recalled how she had fit so comfortably between Ada and Ada's sisters, Emma and Nannie, in the girls' big feather bed. She remembered tolerating the mischief of John, and caring for the babies, Merlin and Douglas, as though they were her own little brothers. It seemed that her happiest growing-up memories included the busy McWhirter family.

With an involuntary shudder, Sarah acknowledged that contrasting with those pleasant memories was the stark reality that Martha McWhirter, the woman she had often called

17

"Mama," had also rocked the very foundation of some of the town's most beloved and respected institutions. It was Ada's aging mother who was singularly responsible for the path of destruction that had torn apart so many Bell County families in the previous twenty years.

Sarah could recall a time, not too many years earlier, when not one of the ladies now assembled for their exclusive meeting in the comfortable parlor would even have acknowledged the presence of the women who owned and operated the Central Hotel, much less set a well-shod foot inside their establishment. She found it remarkable that time had somehow begun to mend the rift between the townsfolk and the women of the hotel. When several pious women left their homes and families to follow Martha McWhirter, resulting in the formation of a unique religious community, unsuspecting families, her own included, had suffered permanent damage. The separation had been a painful part of Belton society since the 1870s, and despite the appearance of healing, she and everyone else knew that sensitive scars still remained.

Reaching the end of the walkway, Sarah climbed the stairs on the outside of the laundry building to the upper story where Ada shared a suite of rooms with her nineteen-year-old daughter, Emily. At Sarah's soft tap, Emily opened the door at the end of the balcony and welcomed her inside with a sincere smile that made Sarah glad she had sought out Ada's room. "Oh, hello, Mrs. Miller! How nice of you to come up here to see Mama. She's asleep right now, but I know she'll want to visit with you when she wakes up. Can you stay awhile?"

"Stay?" Sarah hesitated for a moment, then reached out and patted the young woman's arm. "Well, of course, Emily honey. I'm here for the club meeting, but I don't mind being a little late. You know, sometimes I think I enjoy talking with your mother more than I do attending the meetings."

"Mama's told me how much she looks forward to seeing you every week, too," Emily replied warmly. "I'm sure she'll be up soon."

Since Sarah and Ada were in the habit of visiting at the front desk, Sarah had never had an opportunity to see her friend's comfortable suite. Although earlier in the year Sarah would not have been bold enough to invite herself to Ada's room, the moments the two women had shared together since February had helped to restore the familiar relationship they once enjoyed. Beginning as a stilted greeting as they stood at the front desk, the weekly encounters had evolved into heartfelt conversation as Sarah was eventually invited to sit and visit behind the desk, despite disapproving looks from folks on both sides of the town's divided, but now largely unspoken, loyalties. Over the months, Sarah had been able to learn more about Ada's life during the years of their estrangement, and without passing judgement, gain a better understanding of Belton's unique society of women.

Glancing around Ada's sitting room, Sarah was pleased to find it so stylishly decorated. The walls were carefully painted and wallpapered, and delicate, dotted Swiss curtains hung at the windows. Arranged in an intimate grouping, an oak settee upholstered in dark blue velvet faced two matching chairs. A treadle sewing machine and sewing cabinet placed beneath a window, and a lamp on a table near the settee completed the furnishing of the cozy room. Yet Sarah couldn't help but notice an assortment of boxes, trunks and clothing that had been strewn hastily about.

"Please excuse the mess," Emily apologized as she cleared away some of the clutter that lay on the chairs. "I don't know if Mama told you, but the Central Hotel Company has just bought a house in Washington, D.C. Six of us have been up there since July, looking for a place big enough to hold twenty-five women, and we finally found one. It's on Kennesaw Avenue." Emily moved a stack of linens from a chair to the sewing cabinet.

"Now that we've found a house, we're anxious to find a buyer for the Central Hotel, so we'll all be together again," she said happily. "Grandma had to come back to Belton for a few days to take care of some business, so I came with her to visit Mama and help her start packing. She seemed to be feeling fine yesterday, but this morning she started coughing. Since she went back to bed, I haven't gotten much further than making this big mess. Oh, well. Let's go see if she's awake yet."

Sarah followed Emily through the sitting room into the adjoining bedroom. In the papered room, two matching beds stood against the back wall, separated by a marble-topped washstand, complete with bowl and water pitcher. A large dresser, mirrored wardrobe, and a lamp table were tastefully arranged on the other side of the room. The lone chair in the room had been positioned beside the sickbed.

Standing at Ada's bedside, Sarah looked down at the sleeping woman whose form was barely a rise under the crisply ironed white sheet. Her thin face was pale, except for the dark circles beneath her eyes, and strands of black hair, just beginning to show streaks of gray, clung to her damp forehead. Emily sat down in the chair beside the bed and wiped her mother's feverish face with a washrag she had dipped in the bowl of cool water.

"Is she very ill?" Sarah asked cautiously, trying to hide her rising sense of concern for Ada's frail appearance. Her friend's condition certainly seemed to be more serious than the "not feeling well" reported just minutes earlier by the woman at the front desk.

"Mama's just about worn herself out coughing, and she hasn't eaten anything all day," Emily sighed heavily. "At least she's getting some rest now. The doctor said he'll stop by later today to check on her."

"Goodness! I just spoke with Mrs. Rancier. She didn't say that Ada was sick enough to have to call Dr. Ghent."

"Well, that was Grandma's doing. You know that Mama's had trouble with her lungs for some time now. When she got up this morning, she looked just awful. She insisted on going down to work at the front desk, but that only lasted until she couldn't control the coughing. I went to Mr. Austin's store for a bottle of cough medicine and then put her to bed before lunch. She's been asleep ever since. You know how those elixirs can put you to sleep, especially if you haven't eaten. After Grandma came up to check on Mama, she called for Dr. Ghent. She must be really worried 'cause you know Grandma doesn't call for the doctor unless someone's birthing or dying."

"Well, your mother's too young to die and we know she's not giving birth," Sarah said, forcing a laugh to reassure Emily. "Surely Dr. Ghent can give her something that will help. You're right about your grandma and doctors, though. The first time I can remember her calling a doctor was when your Uncle Samuel was born, which was not long after the family moved to Belton," Sarah explained, deciding that a conversation with Ada's delightful daughter would be a pleasant way to pass the time until her friend awoke.

"You know, Emily, back in those days, most women just called the midwife, but your grandmother wanted a doctor to be there. She was forty years old the summer Sam was born, and that doesn't make childbirth any easier on the mother or the baby."

Emily rewet the rag in the bowl of water on the bedside washstand and gently placed it on her mother's forehead before she turned to face Sarah. "I knew that y'all were old friends, Mrs. Miller, but I didn't know that you've known Mama since before Uncle Sam was born. He's probably over thirty by now."

Sarah smiled at the young woman's remark. It certainly didn't seem that long ago, and as she studied Emily's face and in it saw the image of young Ada, the years vanished. "Oh, I'm an older friend than you think, Emily. We grew up together, your mama, your Aunt Emma and I. And we all went to Salado College when we were girls, back when it was the only secondary school close by."

After another look at the woman in the bed satisfied Emily that her mother was resting comfortably, she turned again to face Sarah. "Salado College? Mama never told me she went there. Well, that would explain the paper fan. Come see what I found," Emily invited as she stood, hastily drying her hands on the muslin apron that covered her dark skirt. Leading the way back to the sitting room, she went straight to where a hatbox lay open on the settee. Placing the big box on her lap, she moved her full skirt aside to make room for Sarah as she began to rummage through its contents.

"When I started packing for Mama's move to Washington, I came across this box of things she must have been saving for years. It's full of newspapers, postcards, letters, and all sorts of interesting papers and photographs. Here it is. This is from Salado College." She held up a sheet of stained paper, folded back and forth in narrow, irregular pleats to make a fan.

"Oh, my word," Sarah exclaimed, taking the fan from Emily. She smoothed out the page to read, "Visit Salado

College in Beautiful Salado, the Athens of Texas. Picnic and Bar-B-Que. July 4, 1860." An engraving showed the college building as it would look when completed. Under the picture, the schedule of the day's events and the college's Board of Trustees were listed. On the other side of the yellowed paper were advertisements of the merchants who sponsored the picnic.

"Goodness! Your mother must save everything. This is where I met her for the very first time. The McWhirter family was living in Salado back then. The college was being built that year and the trustees decided to use the occasion of the Fourth of July picnic to lay the cornerstone of the college building. I'll have to say, it sure didn't look much like this picture on that day. Let's see . . . I was about to turn thirteen that summer, and Ada, I mean your mama, was ten years old."

Ada McWhirter
Salado, Texas, July 4, 1860

When I woke up that morning, I knew it was a special day, but just for a second, I couldn't remember why. It wasn't my birthday, because I had my tenth birthday a few weeks ago. But I woke up with that same special-day feeling.

It's hard to think with the sun in your eyes. When we sleep on the back porch in the summer, the sun comes up right in your face. That's because when Mama and Papa built the house, they wanted the back porch to be in the shade in the afternoon. I was only five years old when the house was built, but I remember wanting to sleep on the porch before it was even finished because I was so tired of sleeping all bunched up in the wagon: Mama, Papa, me, Emma and John.

SET APART

We came here to Salado, Texas, with the wagon train from Tennessee where I was born. Almost right away, Papa and the other men started cutting down trees to build houses. Me and Mama and my big sister, Emma, helped the mamas look after the babies and small children. Our little brother John was two years old, and we had to keep him away from the fires that were set to clear the brush away.

We've built a room on to our house since it was finished that spring. Now there are six of us kids: Emma, me, John, Nannie, Merlin and Baby Douglas. Mama loves little babies, and it still makes her sad when she thinks about the two that died in Tennessee. Maybe that's why she keeps so busy with the church.

Mama and Papa have belonged to the Methodist Church since before they were married. They met at one of those summer camp meetings where the families would get together in the mountains and go to tent meetings at night when it got cool. Mama says that going to church in Texas is like having summer camp meetings all year.

Traveling circuit preachers come on different Sundays to preach outside in the grove under the brush arbor when the weather's nice. That's probably what reminds Mama of the camp meetings. There aren't any church buildings in Salado, so the Methodists, the Baptists and the Campbellites all built a Sunday School building together. Mama teaches there, and she likes everyone learning about Jesus together. That's why she's happy that the new college is not being built by any one church.

The new college. That's what was causing my special-day feeling. We always have a big celebration on the Fourth of July, but this one was sure to be even better because of the college. Salado is a busy stagecoach stop, and that week lots of folks got off to stay at the Shady Villa Inn just to come and

24

see the new college. I wish I was old enough to go to school
there in the fall with Emma.

She's gotten so difficult since she turned fourteen. She says
no girl who goes to the college will be wearing her hair down
in braids. When I woke up that morning, she was already
inside the house, brushing her hair and waiting impatiently for
Mama to finish nursing Baby Douglas so she could put up her
hair like the older girls wear it. Mama just shook her head and
handed the baby to me when I walked in. She knew that if she
didn't fix Emma's hair right then, Emma would never leave
her alone.

'Don't go running off with that book when your hair's
done,' Mama told Emma. 'We have breakfast to fix, a picnic
lunch to pack, and chores to do before we leave.' Mama gets
real annoyed at Emma for reading so much when she's
supposed to be doing her chores. I don't know what it is with
her and books. Once, when she was supposed to be out
feeding the chickens, Mama found her sitting by the well,
reading a book. Instead of giving Mama the book like she was
told, she threw it into the well. That night, I found her reading
the last chapter of the book. She had torn it out and hidden it
in her apron pocket before throwing the book in the well.
Anyway, the college will have an auditorium, a science lab
and a real big library. With all those books to read, we may
never see Emma again once she starts school there. That
would be just fine with me except that I would have to do her
chores. She gets up early to help Papa milk the cow, and I'm
not big enough to carry the milk pail without spilling half the
bucket. (Besides, I'm afraid of the new cow we got after Papa
sold Bluebell because she wasn't giving enough milk.)

Emma's hair is lighter brown than mine and much longer,
since she cut mine real short when I was six years old. It was
the first spring after we moved into the house, and Nannie had

just been born. Emma thought it wasn't fair that there were three girls now and John was the only boy. She convinced me that if my hair was cut real short, I would be a boy, too. That was back when I believed everything she told me. She got two whippings that day: one for cutting my hair and one for using Mama's good sewing scissors. It seems like she's been looking for ways to be disagreeable with Mama ever since. I think its easier just to do what Mama says.

Mama finished putting up Emma's hair and went into the kitchen to pack the food we had already cooked. She had made extra biscuits the day before for the picnic so she wouldn't have to light the oven again. I changed the baby's diaper and put him in the cradle in the kitchen, close to the back door where it's the coolest. Pretty soon, he'll be too big to sleep there.

In Tennessee, Grandpa White made the cradle for Mama's first baby, Mary. She died of a fever when she was two years old. Mama once told us that Papa used to call her his little red robin because she had Mama's red hair and she could sing before she could talk. A brother named Andrew died when I was a baby. Sometimes I think it's strange that Mama still talks about the dead babies. I wonder if other mothers do, but I don't ask. I know that our neighbor, Mrs. Wells lost a baby last winter and Sarah's mother lost two babies before she died herself. That's what the mothers say, 'she lost a baby,' and that really used to confuse me, and I wondered how anyone could lose a baby, but now I know it means that the baby died.

We met Sarah at the picnic. Our family walked all the way to the fairgrounds with our basket full of food. Papa said that there would be too many wagons and carriages on the road with all the visitors that were coming to see the college, and he didn't want to put another stick in the logjam. There were also wagons leaving from the fairgrounds all day to take folks up the hill to see the campus. Sarah's family had come on the stagecoach from Belton, about one hour away. They had a room at the Shady Villa Inn, where the stage stops. We met Sarah because Merlin almost drowned. When we got to the fairgrounds, John wanted us to put our quilt near the creek so he and Nannie could go wading and catch turtles and stuff. So that's what he did as soon as the quilt was spread out. 'Stay with your brother,' Mama called to Nannie, as if John's shadow could ever come aloose of his heel.

Papa and me and Emma went off to put our cakes on the long table of food the townsfolk had brought to share, and then we stood in line for the barbeque. Mama put Douglas and Merlin on the quilt and started unpacking the basket. She said she hadn't but turned her back and Merlin was gone off after John and Nannie. He tripped at the edge of the water and fell right in where it's real shallow. Mama screamed for help and Sarah's family just happened to be walking by. Sarah's father is a doctor, Dr. Edwards, and he ran over to see what he could do. Of course Merlin didn't really almost drown, he just scared Mama half to death. In fact, he was laughing when we walked up with the barbeque, wondering about the crowd gathered around our quilt. That's when me and Emma first said howdy to Sarah.

She'll only be thirteen when school starts in the fall, but she's already finished all her primary work and passed the tests, so she'll be in Emma's class. Wearing braids, I noticed. Papa invited them to share our barbeque. Mrs. Edwards had carried a pie all the way from Belton.

Our parents visited while we were all eating together, and they decided that Sarah would live with us while she goes to the college. That's one reason there were so many visitors at the picnic. Since there are no dormitory buildings built at the college, families came to find homes for their children to live

27

in while they go to school here in Salado. Emma taught me that word dormitory. It's a house where students live while they go to school.

I think I'll like Sarah living with us. She was dressed so pretty for the picnic, with hair ribbons that matched her dress. You could tell right off that she had never worn anyone's hand-me-downs. I was glad I had on the new dress Mama made me for my birthday, even if I didn't have ribbons to match.

Me and Emma and Sarah carried our plates over to sit together on one of the big, flat rocks at the edge of the creek. Mama would tell us that it wasn't nice manners, but the first thing we asked Sarah was 'why does your mama look so young?' Sarah told us that it wasn't really her mama at all, but a new stepmother who was only six years older than Sarah herself. Well, no wonder she looks so young! I'm six years older than Nannie. Even though she talks like a mama and dresses like one, that stepmother could be Sarah's big sister. Sarah told us that if it hadn't been her own mama's plan for her to go off to school when she finished primary, she would have thought she was being pushed aside by this new mother. As it turned out, though, Sarah really likes Tennie, the stepmother. She's very pretty and nice and we were surprised to find out that she didn't come here from Tennessee, which is her real name, but from St. Louis. Sarah told us that she had decided she wasn't going to leave Tennie alone in Belton with her father. Until she met us, that is.

She told us that her father tends to be a little gruff and sometimes makes Tennie cry when she thinks no one is watching. He's also gone a lot, and she and Tennie are often left at home with just the servants who live behind the house. She said that she hopes Tennie will have a baby soon and not be so lonely when the doctor is away and she comes to live here. That's when Sarah told us about the two babies that died, and how the last one had been buried in the same coffin as her mother. I wonder if Sarah knows where babies come from. I tried to imagine being just nineteen and married to a mean older man. Papa is nine years older than Mama, but he sure doesn't seem like it. They do everything together: farming, teaching Sunday School, chopping wood. He was so pleased when she named George Merlin after him. We call him Merlin.

After watching some of the fireworks at the fairgrounds, we said goodbye to Sarah and then walked home. Emma and me and John and Nannie changed our clothes in the house, grabbed the pillows and quilts we use to make a pallet, and dragged them all back out on the porch. Inside, Mama was putting the babies to bed as Papa told her of the talk he heard at the picnic about a war starting soon, back close to where we used to live. I don't know much about wars, but I felt happy that our family was safe in the sturdy log house, so far away from the trouble. I know my Papa will never let anything happen to us.

CHAPTER 2

Lost in thought as she studied the paper fan, Sarah was startled by a knock. Ada's older sister Emma peered from behind the door. "May I come in?"

Sarah's eyebrows disappeared under the brim of her new hat as she recognized the woman who had been effectively exiled from her own hometown.

"Aunt Emma!" Emily put the hatbox on the floor and jumped up to embrace her mother's older sister. "How did you get past Sister Rancier at the front desk?"

"You mean your grandmother's posted sentry?" Emma asked in a mildly sarcastic tone. "I heard that Mother was back in town, and I know she's around here somewhere. Even though she won't speak to me, I'd like to see her try to keep me from tending to my little sister and visiting my niece," Emma stated with exaggerated defiance, determined to mask the pain she still felt after almost twenty years of forced estrangement from her mother. "Or my friend Sarah. Hello, Sarah. I know y'all will excuse me, but I must see Ada right away. How is she?" Not waiting for a response, Emma walked straight into the bedroom with Sarah and Emily following close behind. Lowering herself into the chair at Ada's bedside, she leaned forward to study her sister's pale face. Tenderly, she picked up Ada's limp hand and held it to her cheek for a moment, then removed the washrag to feel the sick woman's forehead.

"Her coughing was terrible earlier, but she's resting now," Emily reported. "Dr. Ghent should be here soon."

"Good. Her health has had me worried for quite some time. She's lost so much weight since . . . well, in the past ten years or so." Relieved to hear that the doctor was coming, Emma returned Ada's hand to the bed and stood to give Sarah a belated hug. "At least my other little sister looks to be doing well. How are you, Sarah?"

"I – I am doing well, Emma, thank you. It's nice to see you, too. It's been a long time, hasn't it?" Sarah stammered. "I understand that you and Mr. Pond have moved back to Belton, but I surely didn't expect to see you here at the hotel. Perhaps we can visit for a bit while we wait for Ada to wake up. I mean, if that's all right with you, Emily. I don't want to be in the way, with the doctor coming. And I know you're trying to pack. I can't stay very long, anyway. I should be getting back to the club meeting, of course."

Emma almost laughed to see Sarah so shaken at her unexpected appearance. But touched by her remembrances of Sarah's tendency to chatter when excited or nervous, Emma just smiled and nodded, then looked to Emily.

"Of course it's all right. You both stay, please. I can do some more packing for Mama tomorrow before Grandma and I board the train for Washington. Y'all go on back to the sitting room. I'll be there in a minute. I want to straighten up in here before Dr. Ghent comes. I didn't realize I had made such a mess," Emily said quietly as she motioned the women toward the doorway. "We'll leave Mama to rest. I'll just be a minute, then maybe you can tell me some more about Salado, Aunt Emma," she whispered as she shut the bedroom door behind them.

SET APART

The women made themselves comfortable in the cluttered sitting room "Salado? What's she talking about?" Emma asked.

"Just wait until you see what Emily found," Sarah teased. "I'll let her surprise you. But first, you must tell me what you're doing here at the Central Hotel, Emma Pond. All of a sudden I feel like we're children again, and fixing to get in trouble. So far, your mother's never walked into the hotel when Ada and I are visiting at the front desk. I don't know what she'd do if she caught the two of us in Ada's suite! What will she say if she sees you here? Aren't you afraid you'll run into her?"

"Oh, Sarah, I stopped being afraid of my mother a long time ago, and she can't hurt me any more than she has." But the look on Emma's face said otherwise. "I just can't believe she's moving everyone up to Washington, D.C. It won't be long until they'll all be up there, and when Ada's gone, she's gone. That's one reason why I rushed over to see her. I'm glad the two of you have been able to get back together, though. It's ironic that it was the Woman's Wednesday Club meetings that reconnected y'all."

The door to the bedroom creaked open and Emily tiptoed into the sitting room. "I think I'll leave the door open in case she wakes up and wants something." She crossed the room and joined the women as they sat. "Have you shown the fan to Aunt Emma?"

"Not yet. I was waiting for you, Emily."

"Fan? What are y'all talking about?"

Sarah leaned over to the hatbox and handed the fan-folded sheet to Emma. "Oh, my word! Where'd you get this old thing?" Emma teased as she took the familiar, but long-forgotten, page from Sarah. "This was about a hundred years ago!"

"It was in this old hatbox I found when I started packing for Mama," Emily said as she picked up the box from the floor and set it beside her on the settee. "She's never told me anything about Salado, Aunt Emma, and I'm just full of questions. Can y'all help me with some answers?"

"Salado! I'm sure we can tell you a thing or two about Salado, honey. Let's see . . ." Emma mused, studying the fan. "We moved to Salado with the wagon train from Tennessee in -- oh, it must have been 1854 -- no, '55," Emma told her niece. "At least it was called Salado, but there really wasn't a town yet. When our wagon train got there, it was nothing but a trail through the woods. There were no stores, telephones, water towers, or electric lights. No schools or churches. Just beautiful trees, that clear creek fed by natural springs, and all the wild game you could shoot. Why, you can't even find a buffalo anywhere around here anymore. Or a bear! Sarah remembers the bears."

Sarah made a face and nodded her head as she recalled young John McWhirter bringing home two orphaned bear cubs one afternoon.

"The wildflowers were beautiful that first spring. We'd never seen anything like it. An ocean of bluebonnets; then the Indian blanket, verbena, larkspur, goldenrod. Your Aunt Nannie was born in May, and that's what I wanted to name her, May McWhirter, but Mother thought differently."

"You mean Grandma had another baby as soon as y'all got to Texas?"

"Oh, there was always a baby in the house back then. There were two more by the time the college was started, which was the reason for the broadsheet this fan's made from. We had been in Salado about five years when Colonel Robertson, the founder of the town, decided it was time for us to have a secondary school, so he donated the land at the top

33

of the hill to build the college. I had just finished my primary classes and was wondering whether I'd get to continue my schooling. The Methodists had a college and the Baptists had Baylor University, but for some reason, Mother didn't like the idea of sending us to church schools."

"Sounds like Grandma had her strong ideas early on," Emily commented.

Emma nodded. "You know your grandma pretty well. She and Papa belonged to the Methodist congregation, and they were very involved in the Union Sunday School in Salado. There used to be one in Belton, too, and in most other small towns at the time. Mother's always liked the idea of everyone worshiping and learning together. I'll have to admit that I think probably the Lord liked it, too. But as soon as each congregation got big enough, the plan was for them to build their own church buildings and go their own way.

"Salado College was different from any of the other schools in the area. From the beginning, it was organized to accept pupils of any denomination and not to teach specific doctrines. It was all spelled out right in the charter, and Mother approved highly. The limestone college building you see in the engraving on the fan was started in 1860. By summer, it was time for the Masonic ceremony to lay the cornerstone, so the college trustees hosted the big picnic at the July Fourth celebration to advertise the college. Everyone in Salado was there, and hundreds of people came by stagecoach from Austin and Waco and all over Texas to tour the new campus. Some families came to buy homesites. A lot of folks moved there over the next few years so their children could attend Salado College. And that was the day we met Sarah." Emma smiled warmly at her childhood friend.

"I was just telling Emily about that when you walked in," Sarah said. "I was never so happy to make new friends as I was that day. My mother had died the winter before, and right after Christmas, Tennie came to be my new stepmother. When we heard about the college opening, my father made plans to go to the picnic and find a place for me to board. Emily, when I met your mama and Aunt Emma, I knew I was in the right place. Almost immediately, I felt like I was part of the family."

"Tell me some more about the picnic," Emily urged as she pointed to the old fan in Emma's hand.

"It was a perfectly beautiful day, with a clear blue sky," Emma began. "Hot as blazes, of course. The picnic was held at the fairgrounds on the banks of Salado Creek. We had a quilt spread out under the trees near the creek so the babies could nap in the shade. You know those grass bracelets your mama likes to braid? She made those for George Merlin. One on each arm and two around his neck. Then she folded this program into a fan to keep baby Douglas cool while he slept on the quilt."

"Remember when Merlin fell in the creek?" Sarah smiled as the memories returned.

"Excuse me, Aunt Emma," Emily interrupted. "I'm already confused. Douglas? George Merlin? Who are they? I've never heard of them."

"Why, they were two of our brothers." There was a strained moment of quiet before Emma could continue. She was beginning to realize that her niece was missing some very basic family information. "You see, Emily, over the years Mother gave birth to twelve children, but lost six of them before they were four years old. Douglas and Merlin were among those six who died. I've always thought that their deaths had something to do with how much Mother has changed from the way she was back then. She's quite . . . *different* now."

"Oh, poor Grandma. It's always sad to lose a child, but *six* babies . . . I had no idea. And now Grandpa Mac is gone, too."

Remembering that Emily had only known her grandmother as a beloved and respected leader of the community of women in which the girl had been raised, Emma decided it would be best to keep her opinions about her mother to herself. "Yes, Mother's had her share of sadness. But I don't think I've ever seen her happier than she was that day at the picnic. The ladies from the church came by our quilt to see the new baby, little Douglas. Merlin was two that summer. It was amazing how well he talked already. He could call each visitor by name. That child would eat almost anything you put in front of him. Even vegetables. He was such a sweet little boy," she added wistfully. "Mother loved Salado, and I think we would have stayed there if it hadn't been for the war."

"What happened?" Emily asked.

"Well, not long after the picnic, Texas went ahead and jumped into the War Between the States with the rest of the fool South," Emma said with disgust. "It didn't seem to matter to anyone that General Sam Houston himself, the hero of the Texas revolution and the first president of the Republic of Texas, had come to Salado to make a speech warning us how dangerous it would be for Texas to get involved in a war the South couldn't win. You know what a lot of good *that* did. About a year later, troops started leaving from Bell County to fight in the war. I remember that Mother and Papa had an argument about him joining up with the Confederacy. After all, he was over forty years old and had already fought in the Indian wars in Florida. Mother thought his place was at home with the family, but Papa insisted on going. When he left the next spring, we were all sick in bed, even Sarah. Her father came and doctored us. Then he took her back to Belton with him until school started the next fall.

"Papa had no way of knowing how seriously ill we were, but that's when George Merlin and little Douglas died, despite Dr. Edwards' care. Mother had been expecting again at the time, and when the tiny baby boy was born right after Merlin died, she named him George Merlin, the second. He died before Papa got back from the War. Of course he came right home when he found out what had happened, but he hadn't gotten Mother's letter until several months after the babies died. By that time, she was more than ready to leave Salado. We ended up moving to Belton before Robert and William were born in 1865."

"More babies! Now, I do remember hearing that Uncle Robert had a twin brother," Emily said. "His name was William? What happened to him?"

Emma was quiet for a moment as she pictured her tiny brother in a casket no larger than a soapbox. "William was so small when he was born, Mother could slip her wedding band all the way up his arm to his shoulder. He lived about a year," Emma said, shaking her head sadly. "We really thought he might make it, but when he got sick in the spring, he was just too small to fight."

"Oh, that's awful, Aunt Emma. I'm sorry. When I asked about Salado, I didn't know it would bring back such sad memories. But I do appreciate the information; I didn't know any of that. I hope you don't mind my questions," Emily said as she put the hatbox on her lap and retrieved a faded photo. "The things in this box have made me so curious. Now, here's something I do remember: Grandpa Mac's store on the Avenue. I used to love going in there when I was little."

"Oh, yes," Emma said as she peered at the photo. "McWhirter and Venable. That's a very old picture of the mercantile. Your mother and I worked there with Papa for a time. And so did my brother John. Did she ever tell you about that?"

"No, never."

"In fact, right there in that store is where I met your Uncle J.J."

George McWhirter
Belton, 1869

It has worked out well for the older children to be helping out in the store. John is a strong young man and does a fine job of unloading the merchandise from the delivery wagons and keeping the shelves well stocked. Emma is friendly with the customers and can make a quick sale, showing each customer exactly what she's looking for. Ada is as organized and practical as her mother, knows just what to order, and can almost run the business of the store on her own.

Working here also helps keep their minds off their mother. It's going on two years now that my Martha has been under this delusion, as Dr. Ghent calls it. He told me that it was something that women often experience after the birth of a child, but little Sam is almost two years old now. I suppose I have to give her all the time she needs. I reckon it's just the Lord's way of teaching me to be patient.

Maybe she's just had too many babies. Or lost too many. Little William died not long before Sam was born, so her problems may have started back then. Or even before that. She has said more than once that a little piece of her died each time she lost a child. I don't know if she's ever forgiven me for not being there when she had to bury three little boys in less than a year. I should have been with her.

When she first told me that the Lord had spoken to her that night after the church meeting, I have to admit I wasn't surprised. From the start, I've always known that my Martha was special.

We met at a Methodist camp meeting when she was just seventeen. Even though I was nine years older, I was quiet around her, like I'd always been around girls. Martha never noticed; she could talk enough for the both of us. She would talk about anything and everything: raising chickens to lay bigger eggs; the secret to making the lightest biscuits you ever tasted; figuring out what God is saying to folks in their dreams. I still remember one thing she said that first day I met her: 'I wonder if blind people dream in color . . . or even in pictures. Do they dream about things they can't see?' She certainly gave me something to think about.

Everybody listens to Martha, whether they agree with her or not. She can make folks take interest in any topic she brings up. It's fascinating to watch as she gets them to agree with what she's saying, even if they started out on the other side. I'm as much in love with her as the day we met. I reckon I can wait as long as it takes for her to come out of this delusion.

It was just about two years ago after we came home from a church meeting that she told me she had heard the voice of God asking her if the meeting was the work of the devil. We, the Methodists, had met that night to talk about separating from the Union Church and putting up our own church building on the Pearl Street lot, now that the congregation is getting so big. Naturally, they expected Martha's help. But she stood up in front of everybody and reminded them that Jesus' last prayer before He died was a plea for the unity of all believers. She said, 'Remember, brothers and sisters, that in the gospel of John, Jesus prayed: "Holy Father, keep through thine own name those whom thou hast given me, that they may be one as we are one." I don't believe He wants us to divide the Union Church,' she insisted. 'It's His True Church.' When the motion to build the new building passed despite her testimony, she stormed out of the meeting. It was on her walk home alone that she said she heard the voice.

I know I should have been embarrassed to have my wife speak out in the church meeting like that, but I thought she had a good point. What if, after almost nineteen hundred years, it was time for Jesus' prayer to be answered? What if, as Martha suggested, the time for the unity of all believers had finally come, and was starting right here in our little town? I've read in the Bible how the Lord often used women to do His will, and I believe that my Martha is just the sort of woman He would use.

The next morning was when she had her 'vision'. She told me that was how she knew for certain she had been sanctified by the Spirit of God. Afterward, she locked herself in our room for the next several days and fasted and prayed and studied her Bible until the pages were falling out. I moved into the downstairs bedroom with John and little Sam, and have been there ever since.

My Martha's a very busy woman these days. I know she has to be the best cook in town. She's always bringing a meal or a cake to sick folks or a new family. Everyone asks for her recipes, especially her biscuits. Her housekeeping is so well organized, you'd think that she was the army officer in the family. She continues to teach at the Union Sunday School where I still serve as the superintendent.

She also leads a weekly prayer group made up of ladies from all the churches in town, as she has for years. Some of the women in the group have recently withdrawn from fellowship with their husbands for fasting and prayer, following Martha's example, I suppose. Even though she has lost a few former friends due to her outspoken opinions, she still goes out calling on the ladies of the town several times a week and receives visitors on the second Thursday of each month, the same as she's always done. She has the front parlor dusted and a pound cake and fresh tea and coffee waiting for her callers. It confuses me that, despite her delusion, so many of the things she does appear so normal.

One night not too long ago, I couldn't sleep and left my bedroom to find something to eat. Martha was awake as well, reading her Bible in the kitchen. It seemed so natural, so familiar to see her sitting there in the lamplight, that I started to put my arms around her. Then I remembered. 'Martha, do you have to believe this way?' I asked her. 'Can't you find it in your heart to have some other religion that won't divide us? If you were in your grave, you couldn't be further from me.'

'I wish I could, Husband,' she told me, and I believed her. 'You know I've prayed and prayed, but the revelations keep coming, and I have to follow them.'

I am learning to be a very patient man, but I am praying for the revelation that will tell her to come back to the husband who is waiting for her, the one who loves her.

CHAPTER 3

"So, are you going to tell me about how you met Uncle J.J.? It may be my only chance to learn something about the forbidden side of the family," Emily teased.

"You may be right about that," Emma said, regretting the truth in Emily's words.

"You'd like your Uncle J.J., Emily," Sarah added, trying to lighten the tension she heard in Emma's voice. "He's a very interesting man. I'll bet you didn't know that he was a cowboy for a while."

"Really? A cowboy? No, I only remember hearing that he taught at Salado College before it closed."

Emma smiled at her niece. She wished she had been given the opportunity to be a proper aunt to the curious young woman. Although she had made many trips to Belton over the years to visit her father, Emma had always been prevented from having any contact with Ada or her children. It seemed a shame that her own children had never gotten to know their cousins, even though they had grown up just a few miles apart. Ever since Martha had declared that the women were to have no casual contact with outsiders, even relatives, Emma had relied on reports from her father for information about the rest of her family. Of course, along with the rest of Bell County, she followed their more public activities in the newspaper, but it had always been difficult to hear the hateful stories that continued to surround the eccentric group headed by her mother.

"Yes, that's right, Emily, your Uncle J.J. taught at the college. Literature, as a matter of fact. But when the cattle drives started coming right past Salado and Belton, he joined up with the cowboys right after classes were out one year. He saw it as an adventure, a chance to see the country and make some extra money, but he also found out that it was very hard work. I think most of all it made him appreciate his job at the college. I remember the day he walked into Papa's store. He had just joined up with his first cattle drive as it came through Salado, and even I could tell he didn't have any idea what he was getting into. He was quite a sight: a schoolteacher in brand-new cowboy clothes. His new work pants were so stiff they would hardly stay tucked down in his shiny boots. He was wearing a blue chambray shirt that I could tell had been *ironed*, and a bright red bandana. I wondered how long it would take him to look like a *real* cowboy. But, my, he was handsome in that hat," Emma said with a stir of affection and pride as she recalled the day. "And colorful, too. He bought a yellow slicker before he left the store.

"One of the things I enjoyed most about working at the mercantile was meeting all the new folks who came into town. The cattle drives brought trail bosses and cooks who needed supplies. The courthouse brought lawyers and their clerks looking for paper and ink. And of course, there were plenty of regular customers buying household goods. My brother John was about fifteen that year. His job was to keep the shelves stocked with merchandise that Ada ordered. He'd sweep the floors and load and unload wagons. We were quite a team." Emma smiled proudly as she remembered the successful family business.

SET APART

"But you wanted to know more about Uncle J.J. Well, he walked into the store that day with John and immediately we found out we shared something in common: Salado and the college there. He had come to teach the literature classes not long after Sarah and Ada and I matriculated. The three of us went back to Salado so often, though, I was surprised we hadn't met him at one of the college's many reunion parties. That's how Sarah met Mr. Miller, by the way." Emma paused to share a sly smile with Sarah.

"Anyway, Mr. Pond told me he worked at the college during the school year and mentioned that he had taught the Riggs boys. Sarah remembers the story of the Riggs family, I'm sure. We all went to school with Rhoda Riggs. Everyone knew the story about their family, but no one ever talked about it."

"What story?" Emily asked. "What wouldn't anyone talk about?"

"Well, Indians. In fact, I still find it hard to talk about . . . Indians," Emma replied, clearly distressed at the thought of doing so. She coughed to clear her throat and spoke a little louder. "You know they used to be *all* around here. Friendly ones, usually. But you never knew what would set them off to start . . . killing folks." She cleared her throat again and shook her head, an anxious look on her face.

"Are you all right, Aunt Emma? Can I get you a drink of water?"

"Oh, no, honey. I'll be fine," Emma responded, forcing a laugh and swallowing hard. But when she put her hand to her cheek, she realized she was perspiring. "Well, on second thought, I would like some water, Emily, thank you."

As Emily hurried into the bedroom to pour a glass of water from the pitcher beside her mother's bed, Sarah leaned toward Emma. "Emma, what is it? Are the Indians still bothering you?" She tried to disguise her amusement with a look of concern. She and Ada and John had always been surprised at how easily Emma trembled at the mention of Indians. "That was almost forty years ago, honey."

"I know it, Sarah. I haven't even thought of them for ages. Isn't this silly? My hands are shaking. What am I going to do? She'll want to hear that horrible story about the Riggs family, and I can't tell it now. You know I'll be ill, right here in Ada's room. I already feel as sick as a dog at a butcher shop."

Sarah pressed her fingers to her mouth to stifle a smile, then reached out to pat Emma's arm. "I'll tell her. Don't you worry about it, Emma. Do you need to leave the room?"

"I'll be fine," Emma responded as Emily returned with the glass of water. "Thank you, sweetheart."

"Is there anything else I can get you? You're not getting sick, too, are you, Aunt Emma? You're quite pale." Emily declared.

"Oh, no, I . . ."

"Perhaps some fresh air would help, Emma. I don't mind telling Emily about the Riggs."

"That's a fine idea, Sarah. I believe I will step out on the gallery for just a minute."

As Emma set her glass down and rose to leave, Sarah turned her attention to Emily. "You know, Emily, we used to hear lots of accounts of Indian raids when we were children, but it wasn't often that we actually knew the folks involved. That's what makes the one about the Riggs family so extraordinary. You have to remember that the story's been passed around for so many years, now, you may hear it differently the next time it comes up, but this is what Rhoda told us when we first met her.

"It was not long before the college picnic we were talking about, in 1859, I believe, that Mr. Riggs was outside, working

45

on a fence near the house. It wasn't unusual to see Indians in those days. Normally, they wanted to trade for something they knew the settlers had, or sometimes they just rode up to ask for a meal. They had different customs, you see. Nobody knows what happened between those two Indians and Mr. Riggs, but they ended up, well, killing him." Emily's eyes opened wide in surprise and disbelief. Indians had not been a threat in Bell County for many years.

"There must have been a commotion or a warning of some kind, because Mrs. Riggs thought she had time to get her four children to the safety of a neighbor's house nearby. She was wrong. They killed her, too, and left those poor little boys for dead. John was an infant, and William couldn't have been more than two or three years old. Then the Indians plundered the house and carried off Rhoda and her little sister, Margaret."

"Oh, my goodness! I'll bet they were taken so they could be turned into Indian girls like Cynthia Ann Parker," Emily said.

"I'm sure that was the intention," Sarah agreed as she wondered whether the story of little Cynthia Ann's capture was one of the reasons for Emma's deep-seated fear of Indians. The ten-year-old girl had been taken from her home and became fully integrated into the Indian society after attempts to rescue her were unsuccessful. Although reunited with her own family as an adult, separation from her Indian children made the remainder of her life miserable and lonely. It was believed that her early death was the result of a broken heart. Obviously, the very real possibility of Indian abduction in years past had a lasting effect on Emma.

"When Rhoda and Margaret weren't found with the rest of the family, neighbors immediately set out to look for them. Later that evening the Indians stopped to eat some of the food they had stolen, and spotted the search party. Although the savages fled with the girls on their ponies, Rhoda and Margaret managed to jump off and escape. They started back toward home, and when it got dark, they spent the night in an empty cabin, where they were found the next morning. All four of the Riggs children were taken to live with relatives in Sugar Loaf, but moved to Salado during the war so the girls could go to school, and that's where we met them."

Emily relaxed visibly. "So the little boys weren't dead after all."

"No, they were just fine, thank the Lord. As Emma mentioned, they grew up to become your Uncle J.J.'s students," Sarah explained.

"My goodness, that's quite a story!" Emily exclaimed. "I'm glad we don't have Indians to deal with anymore."

Emma opened the door and peeked inside. "Ah, that fresh air has done wonders, Emma," Sarah observed. "Come sit down. Was there anything else you wanted to tell Emily about her uncle?"

"Well, only that when your Uncle J.J. went off to be a cowboy he took my little brother John with him. They both promised to write to me from the trail."

John McWhirter
Belton, 1870

I can't believe that Mama's taking this religion thing so far. Papa keeps telling me that she'll get over it and get interested in something else, but she's been acting strange since Sam was just a baby. She talks a lot about her dreams and visions. Papa says it's just a temporary delusion that will go away when the

47

baby is a little older. Well, Sam's not a baby anymore. He's three years old now, for crying out loud! I'm ready for her to start acting like a regular mother again.

One night Mama came home from her prayer meeting real angry. Because most of the ladies in the group still belong to the Methodist Church, they wanted to have their meetings in the new church, the one Mama made a big fuss about them building. One night they found the door locked, but they were able to get little old Mrs. Henry in the window to open it for them. The preacher apologized the next day, saying that since the cattle drives were starting to come through town, he had to lock the door to keep the drunk cowboys out. But the next week, not only was the door locked again, but the windows were nailed shut, too. Mama was so mad. After that the ladies went back to meeting at our house.

Last year after I finished my primary classes, I started working at Papa's store from real early in the morning to real late at night. I had to do something to get away from Mama's crazy preaching. Of course at the store I have to put up with nosy neighbors wondering what's going on at our house, asking why there are so many women over there all the time. Some of them stay overnight, but since I'm not home much, I can honestly tell them that I don't know anything. I do know one thing: I will never be able to call my mother, or any of those other women, 'sister' like they're doing now.

The day Mr. J.J. Pond came into the shop was my lucky day. J.J. is a cowboy working with an outfit that was fixing to bring a herd through town the next day. He came in with a fancy saddle that needed some repair, so I took him over to see Mr. Potts. As we walked across the Courthouse Square toward the saddle shop, J.J. mentioned that he was looking to replace their wrangler, too. That's the cowboy who handles all the extra horses on the drive. He said that when they were camped outside of Salado the other night, a quick thunderstorm came up and all the men grabbed their bedrolls and waited it out under the chuck wagon. In the morning, one cowboy was still asleep under the tree. But when they got closer, they saw that he wasn't sleeping. He'd been killed by the lightning, and everything on him that was metal was plumb melted. Belt buckle, buttons, coins in his pocket. All melted. I felt real sad for the wrangler, but right away I volunteered to take his place.

When we got back to the mercantile, I told Papa the whole story. I could tell from his eyes he was unhappy that I wanted to leave home and set out with the trail drive, but it hardly took a minute for him to decide it was an opportunity I really couldn't afford to pass up. He told me that even though he would miss me working at the store, he thought I would actually be better off in the company of strangers than in my own home He said he was afraid that it could be a while before our household returned to normal. That made me wonder if Papa was losing hope that our family would ever be the way it was before Mama had her 'vision' she keeps talking about. It doesn't seem like she even sees what she's doing to our family. The younger kids have never known what it was like before all this started happening. Papa's right, I just have to get away. Maybe things will be different when I get back. As I was leaving the store to run back to the house and get my stuff, Papa said that he would pick out a good bowie knife for me to take.

That's when Emma walked in with our lunch. I introduced her to J.J., and they both looked at each other kind of funny. I thought it was strange when they started talking about Indians. That's one subject Emma always avoids. I've only found two things that make my big sister get all shaky: Indians and snakes. One time she actually got sick when I showed her some arrowheads I found down by the creek.

When I told her I was leaving to be a cowboy, she didn't say a word against it. She did insist that I write to her while I was gone, but I noticed she was looking right at J.J. Pond when she said it.

CHAPTER 4

"So are you saying that Uncle John was a cowboy, too?" Emily asked, eager for more information about family members she had never known.

"Oh, yes," Emma replied. "Mother never knew it, but he read all the cowboy dime novels he could get his hands on when things got slow at the store. He was a young man ready to see the world beyond Bell County. Both he and Mr. Pond wrote to me while they were on the trail. I remember working at the store and going to the Post Office every day after they left, hoping for a letter. And when the first one finally came, I had to wait *all day* to read it. That busybody Mrs. Henderson was in the store and she just would *not* leave."

"Oh, yes, Mrs. Henderson," Sarah recalled as Emma began an animated description of the friendly farmwife, using broad hand gestures to accompany sharply emphasized words. Sarah chuckled to herself at the endearing sight and sound of Emma's monologue. It had been years since she had given any thought to the peculiar way her friend talked when she was excited about a subject. With no concern for how much time was passing, Sarah sat back in her chair, basking in the warmth of fellowship with Ada's sister and daughter.

"Mrs. Henderson was a farmer's wife, Emily. A very nice woman, and very friendly. It was just that she only came to town twice a year. That meant she had to shop and *talk* enough to last her six months." Emma explained. "Now, I like to visit as much as anyone, but I had this *letter* in the pocket of my

51

apron. The Hendersons had about ten or twelve children, and when she set out on her shopping trip each year, Mrs. Henderson always brought one of the older daughters with the newest baby. Boy or girl, every baby looked like the one from the year before, redheads every one. We talked about the children, then we talked about the weather and who was new in town. That sort of thing. And *then* she was ready to shop.

"She had to buy calico for all of the girls' dresses, muslin for their aprons, coveralls for the boys, and flannel to sew winter underwear for everyone. *Then* we went to the cookware rack and the hardware section to find everything else her family would need for the next six months." Emma paused to take a breath. "*Then* after we double-checked her list, I had to wrap everything in heavy paper and tie it with string and help her load it all into the empty trunks she had on the back of her wagon. I remember she showed me how she had traced the children's little feet on newspaper so she could buy their Sunday shoes from Mr. Hammersmith down the street. When she *finally* left, I asked Ada to please step out of the office for just a moment, in case another customer came in, so I could read my letter."

"Didn't they both write to you, Aunt Emma?" Emily asked.

"Oh, yes, but two letters were in the same envelope, so at first I thought it was just one *awfully* long letter from my brother. John told me all about his new life as wrangler of the cattle drive. He was in charge of the remuda. That's the herd of extra horses for the cowboys. Although he was at the tail end of the drive, where it was the dustiest, he loved it. I thought it sounded like *dread*fully hard work, but John welcomed the responsibility. He wrote about how the cook always led the way in the chuckwagon, so he could pick the place to stop near some water and have a meal ready for the rest of the outfit when they arrived. Sometimes John helped the cook, who wore a beautiful pair of snakeskin boots. He wrote a whole page telling the story of those boots: the rattlesnake roundup, the rattlesnake stew, taking the skins to the bootmaker . . ." Emma shuddered.

"Then I was surprised to find a short letter from Mr. Pond. You know, I don't remember a thing he wrote except that he said he would be coming back through Belton and asked permission to call on me formally. He was so old-fashioned," Emma recalled with a bemused smile.

"Maybe that's because it was such a long time ago, Mrs. Pond," Sarah teased.

"That's okay," Emily said quickly. "I think it's a sweet story. A love story."

Emma sighed and nodded her head, lost in the recollection. "It really took me by surprise to think of myself having a gentleman caller," she continued. "Ada and I often talked about how we could see ourselves working together in Papa's store for years and years. Two old maid clerks. Neither one of us was interested in having any part of what was going on with Mother, and we knew there was no way a man would ever be interested in us after what Mother had done."

"Which was?" Emily questioned.

"Oh, Emily. I'm sure your mother's told you about Grandma scaring off every young man in Bell County."

Emily shook her head, a baffled look on her face.

"Honestly, Emily, I can't believe your mother never told you any of this," Emma said with a sudden, sharp edge of resentment to her voice. She was clearly irritated at having to be the one to explain the painful events of the past to her niece. "Well, you remember that years ago, Grandma heard 'the Voice' on the last night of revival week."

SET APART

Sarah stiffened at the sarcastic tone Emma used in referring to the vision Martha McWhirter never tired of recounting through the years, but if Emily was offended, she hid it well. "The next evening, a party was planned for all of the young people of the Methodist church. Your mother and I were supposed to go with two young men we knew. We were so excited, but . . ." Emma's face reddened as she recalled the humiliation of that night more than thirty years previous.

"Ada and I were in the kitchen fixing each other's hair with the new curling iron that was heating up on the stove when Mother came in and announced to us that the party was, in her words, 'the work of the devil.' After spending all week decorating our party dresses, we were *mad*! She *knew* how much we wanted to go. There was a *terrible* argument. Then she left the house and went to tell our young men not to come over to pick us up." Emma pressed her lips into a tight line. "We were mortified." She sat quietly for a while, somewhat surprised that relating the story had clearly awakened the long-buried feelings accompanying the incident. "One of those young men was . . . Ben Haymond," she added with an uneasy look at her niece. She had no idea what the girl's reaction might be.

Emily's face broke into a smile. "My father!"

Encouraged, though somewhat surprised by her niece's response, Emma continued. "Yes, your father. And in the five years between that horrible night and the invitation to the Cotillion, you probably know that he and his brother, W.P., we called him Dub, had opened a very nice grocery store in town, Haymond Brothers' Grocery. Ben was the one who finally persuaded your mother to go."

"Cotillion?" Emily asked as she watched her aunt take the hatbox and begin to dig through its contents.

"If Ada kept everything, she surely must have the invitation to the Christmas Cotillion hosted by the town merchants that year. Ah, here it is," Emma said with satisfaction as she displayed a pale green card lettered in gold. "I can't believe your mother never told you about the Cotillion. Mr. Pond and I were already married by then and living in Salado, but Ada was still working at the store, even though she never felt comfortable with the customers. She didn't care for the socializing that comes with working out front like I was telling you about Mrs. Henderson. She preferred to stay in the back office to do the bookkeeping chores. When this invitation came, she was reluctant to go to the Cotillion, even though all of the businesses on the square had sponsored it and were expected to support the event. I'm sure she still saw herself as that old maid store clerk. But then one day Ben Haymond came into the store."

Emily took the invitation from Emma's hand and gently touched the gold lettering. She looked through the open door of the bedroom where her mother lay sleeping soundly. "Please, Aunt Emma," she urged wistfully. "Tell me about my father."

Ada McWhirter
Belton, 1872

Working at the store got so much more difficult after Emma and John left. Papa hired another girl to help me with the customers, but she doesn't know everyone in town like Emma did, or everything about the merchandise, like John did. I'm so much better at just taking care of the inventory and invoices. That way I don't have to be out front to answer questions about what's going on with Mama. She wants me to spend more time with her and the ladies in the prayer group, but that's not how I see my life right now. I've always wanted a family, like the one we had before Mama had her vision. I'm only twenty-three, so it's not too late, even though I know all the men in town assume that I will follow Mama's path. But that's not what I want.

I want Ben Haymond. Even though he was one of the fellows that Mama ran off the night after she heard the voice, he came into the store and invited me to the Christmas Cotillion. I refused, of course, but Ben is very persuasive. Charming, I think, is another word for it.

I hadn't had any new clothes in so long, but after Ben's invitation I hunted down the bolt of green watered silk that had come to the store in the last shipment. I sewed a new party dress, my first one in years, and I think I used every ribbon and trim left in the store. When Ben came to pick me up, the smile on his face told me that I was beautiful. The way he kept looking at me, I really believed it. I had never seen him in anything other than work clothes, either clean or dirty, so I was very impressed with his new suit and his blond hair all combed back away from his handsome face.

That night the courthouse looked, well . . . heavenly seems too nice a word to describe an old building that needs to be replaced, but that's how I saw it through the lamps that lined both sides of the front walk. Inside, we were greeted by the members of the invitation committee, including Ben's brother, Dub, and his fiancée, Jo. At the end of the main hall, both staircases leading up to the courtroom were draped with greenery, making the whole building smell like Christmas. The big upstairs courtroom was lavishly decorated as well. Two long tables were filled with every kind of food, but I was too excited to eat a bite, even though Ben was so sweet to bring me a plate of Mrs. Denney's crystallized fruit. I think we danced to the Silver Cornet Band all night. Polkas, waltzes. We learned the Schottische. Ben's a wonderful dancer. On the way home he held my hand. I could feel the electricity of his touch right through my glove. As we walked up Main Street chatting about the dance, the subject came up of the party five years ago and the scene Mama had made to keep us apart. It was embarrassing to even think about it. Ben was well aware that no men had come calling at our house for several years, but he was happy for the way things had turned out for Emma. He told me he was proud of her for making the decision to move away from here when she married Mr. Pond, even though he knows I miss her terribly. 'It was a good play on her part,' he said. His statement puzzled me.

But I understood what he meant when he began to tell me how he often compares life to a game of cards. 'Every day's a new game, Ada. That's what makes life so unpredictable. Sometimes I go for what looks like a sure thing, and sometimes I take a risk. There's an exciting line between chance and strategy. The whole outcome of a game can be completely changed by the decisions made in a single hand. For example: how would tonight be different if other cards had been played, other choices made, that night five years ago? What one person does affects the next player's move, and so on. I have to tell you, Ada, I was afraid to call your mother's bluff back then,' he laughed. 'If I ever find myself in a game with her again, I'll make sure I'm the dealer. I think my game has improved over time.' Then he laughed.

We walked a little farther up the hill on Pearl Street, and he continued. 'I'm always very aware of what I'm holding, of course, but I don't know what anyone else has - - until she shows me her hand, that is.' We stopped at the picket fence in front of the house, and he lifted my hand to his face, touching his lips to my wrist just at the edge of my glove. 'And I call that playing with a partner.' He smiled and then he winked at me. That's when I fell in love with Ben Haymond. He swung open the squeaky gate and we started up the front walk. When we reached the porch, he leaned very close to whisper in my ear, just in case Mama was standing near the door. I had never been that close to a man before, and he smelled so delicious, I could have eaten him with a spoon. He told me he wanted to call on me when he got back from Houston in the spring, and I was disappointed that I would have to wait so long before I could see him again.

It was a very long three months, but when he returned, we talked about marriage. He said he wants to start a business in Fort Worth and take me far away from Mama and all the trouble she's caused. Right now that seems like a good idea to me.

CHAPTER 5

"Well, Emily, I can tell you that your father was the most handsome, most popular bachelor in all of Bell County," Sarah announced with enthusiasm.

"And she would know, because she knew every bachelor in Bell County," Emma teased. "In those days, Sarah was quite the coquette."

Emily eyed Sarah and Emma curiously, trying to see them as young women. Mrs. Miller, a coquette? Although Sarah had retained her slim shape, Aunt Emma had, by her own admission, gotten so heavy she could "just as soon roll one way as the other." As Emily studied the women, it was a challenge to imagine them as young girls.

Sarah narrowed her eyes. "You hush now, Emma. We were talking about Ben Haymond. Surely you'd agree that he was the most charming man you'd ever met," she sputtered, embarrassed by her own initial outburst and Emma's remark. Like Emma, Sarah wondered what Emily had been told about her father, though she had little doubt the girl had been led to believe that he'd never been anything but a hostile husband and an irresponsible father. In Sarah's opinion, Ben had made some very foolish decisions regarding his family. His plans to remove his children from what he considered to be an unhealthy situation had failed horribly, with disastrous results. Still, she had always liked Ben and saw him as a victim of his own poor judgement.

Emma, too, admitted to having had a soft spot for her brother-in-law. "Oh, Sarah, I would never deny his charm. *Everyone* loved Ben Haymond, not just Ada. You couldn't help it. In those days, Emily, he was a teamster, driving an ox team and heavy wagon back and forth between Belton and Houston several times a year to pick up merchandise for the Haymond Brothers' grocery store in Belton. That's how the stores were stocked in the days before the railroad came to Bell County," Emma explained. "After the Cotillion, Ada saw Ben for a short time between each of his trips. He brought her a gift every time. And a story. Your father was a born storyteller, Emily."

"I'll say he was," Sarah interrupted. "I'm sure you never heard the one about the Indian squaw he and another teamster rescued from drowning when they were trying to cross a flooded river one spring." Sarah focused on Emily's attentive expression, and ignored Emma's horrified look at the mention of the word 'Indian.' "The woman was from one of the friendly tribes, and after her rescue, her family just about killed Ben and the other teamster with kindness every time the two of them passed by the village. They were given all sorts of interesting gifts and an invitation to a tribal feast each way. It sometimes took several days out of their travel schedule. They finally had to find another place to cross the river just to avoid those friendly Indians. Of course, their relationship with that tribe came in handy once when they ran into an unfamiliar band of savages, but that's a whole 'nother story."

"Oh, I'd love to hear more," Emily begged.

"Maybe some other time, dear," Sarah said, conscious of Emma's critical gaze. "I'm afraid I changed the subject."

The Indian interlude safely past, Emma discretely patted her neck with her handkerchief and continued with the story of Ada's courtship. "I'm sure there's plenty more to that tale.

Let's see, where was I? Oh, yes, the Cotillion. They saw each other whenever Ben was in town, and about a year after the Christmas Cotillion, your mother and father were married at the house on Pearl Street."

"I remember how your mother tried her best to talk Ada out of the wedding, Emma." Sarah added. "I'm sure she expected that Ada would remain unmarried and be content to join her prayer group. The old-maid life you were talking about, I suppose. But Ada had always wanted a family. Ben was so nervous the day they were married. He could hardly wait for the ceremony to be over so he and Ada could leave Belton and be on their way to Fort Worth. He didn't want to stay one minute longer than he had to. They left so quickly that afternoon after the wedding, we weren't able to have a shivaree for them."

Emma shook her head as she recalled Ada's wedding. "I don't think I've ever seen a bride as uncomfortable as Ada on what was supposed to be the happiest day of her life. I'm sure she expected a fight to break out between Ben and Mother at any moment. There was just enough time for 'I do.' Never mind the shivaree. We were disappointed about that, weren't we? It's one of the *best parts* of a wedding! A time to have a little *fun* after the seriousness of the ceremony. It's too bad they're not as popular any more.

"I remember it was you and your Mr. Miller and Ada who put together the one after Mr. Pond and I were married. All of that *yelling* and *singing* and banging pots and pans outside the window of our room at the boarding house. I don't know why I thought we'd escape being given a shivaree by going straight to Salado. When I heard all the commotion, I just about jumped right out of the nightgown I was trying to put on, nervous as I was about being in that room alone with Mr. Pond," Emma admitted with a hearty laugh. "Whoever made up that silly tradition? Ada and Ben were probably not sorry to miss it."

"Did my father open a grocery store in Fort Worth, too?" Emily asked, anxious for more information about the man she hardly knew.

"No, honey," Emma said gently, wishing the girl could have known her good-natured father. "He became a salesman. Since he was starting his own family, he had an idea to start his own business, too. But things didn't work out in Fort Worth."

"What happened?"

"I'm not sure exactly what happened, but the business didn't go well. There were money problems, legal problems. I remember that I was real surprised to hear about it. Your father was so charming, he could sell dirt to a gravedigger." Emma was quiet for a few moments as she reflected on the facts surrounding the early days of the Haymond family. Knowing Emily's loyalty to her grandmother, she was hesitant to place too much blame on Martha for the breakup of Ada's marriage.

"He really loved your mama, Emily, and wanted to do everything he could to keep your family together. I know one of the main reasons he went to Fort Worth was because he could see how dependant Ada was on Mother, how she still craved Mother's approval. When a young couple marries, they have to learn to depend on each other. But being away from family can create problems, too. Your sister, Hattie, and your brother, George, were born in Fort Worth, and frankly, I think Ada was homesick. Being a young mother is a very difficult job, especially in a strange town. When Hattie got scarletina, your mother was so worried about her that she brought her all the way back to Belton to see Dr. Ghent."

"That's odd. Didn't they have doctors in Fort Worth?" Emily asked.

"Oh, yes. That's where your mother met Dr. Scheble. You know, Sister Gertrude Scheble's husband. He treated both Hattie and his own daughter for the same illness. But when the little Scheble girl died, Ada brought Hattie to Belton. Although your sister received medical care from both Dr. Scheble and Dr. Ghent, Mrs. Scheble was convinced that Hattie's life was spared because of Mother's prayers and those of her followers," Emma explained.

Dr. Adolphus Scheble
Fort Worth, 1878

I have always considered myself to be an educated man, fully capable of making decisions with all appropriate wisdom. The death of our darling Malinda, however, has left me uncommonly distraught. I treated several children in a similar manner during this most recent outbreak and our child was the only death, causing me to question my skills and calling. I have been in correspondence with several colleagues and instructors at my medical institution to learn the reasons why I lost my beautiful daughter to scarletina.

One of my patients, little Hattie Haymond, was also treated by her mother's family physician in Belton. After Hattie's complete recovery, I asked my wife, Gertrude, to please travel to Belton to find out all she could about the child's treatment. This turned out to be one of the worst decisions of my life.

Gertrude went to Belton as I requested and stayed all night at the home of the child's grandmother, Mrs. Martha McWhirter. It turns out that Mrs. McWhirter is the leader of a holiness movement. She has separated from her husband and devotes her time and energy in separating other wives from theirs. During her stay, my dear wife was introduced to the mysteries of this peculiar religious spasm.

The trip to Belton was the beginning of a transformation in her character, which seems to have developed into a confirmed mania in the months since she returned from that accursed town. She has withdrawn from her once-enthusiastic participation in church activities, and her deportment suggests a quietism carried to the point where she wishes to disengage herself from all worldly relationships. Listlessly and mechanically, she somehow manages to perform the domestic duties required of a wife and mother.

I learned, quite by accident, that Gertrude was in correspondence with Mrs. McWhirter. It appears that my wife intends to ask for a divorce 'at the proper time' when her vile leader has determined that I have accumulated enough property to make her an asset to their commune. At that time, she is encouraged to 'throw off all restraint, bring the baby,' and join them. I have no idea how to explain to my remaining son and daughters what has happened to their mother. What can I anticipate but disaster for my marriage and this family of children?

CHAPTER 6

"Do you think the Sisters' prayers saved Hattie's life, Aunt Emma?" Emily asked.

"Oh, honey, the Lord hears all our prayers, but I have to tell you that I can't believe He was pleased with some of the things your grandma started teaching."

"That's because you're not sanctified," Emily said defiantly, quick to defend her grandmother.

Ignoring the remark, Emma continued gently. "Some of the things Mother believed and taught have caused a great deal of trouble in this town and have affected a lot of people, not always in a good way. Like I told you, the prayer group began before your mother got married and moved away, but while she and Ben were in Fort Worth, the group began to grow. The women listened to everything Mother had to say and became very devoted followers. At first she taught straight out of the Bible, but then she started teaching what she said were her own revelations about holiness and sanctification, and how a believer should not be yoked with an unbeliever," Emma explained.

"But that's in the Bible," Emily interjected.

"That's true, dear, but so are the teachings about marriage commitments and about divorce not being pleasing to God, not to mention instructions on how Christians are to live in *peace* with other believers," Emma insisted. "I think it's safe to say that Mother left out some of those points. Now, I know it's a fact that many of the women lived with drunken or

65

abusive husbands, but Mother taught that it was *God's* will for them to leave an unpleasant marriage if their husbands were not sanctified, at least to her satisfaction. Her requirements became very different from what was taught in the other churches, different from what is written in the Bible. Most of her followers had been members of the Methodist Church, but as far as I know, that body never took any formal action against Mother or what she was teaching."

"That's what I remember, too," Sarah agreed. "Back then, about twenty years ago now, the Methodist Church always had two preachers. We kept the same circuit preacher for years, but the town preacher changed every year after the Methodist Annual Conference. I don't know why that was, but we never got to know any of them very well. And the truth is, your grandmother talked almost every one of them into seeing things her way. Except for Reverend Alexander. He was the revival preacher, and he knew exactly what was going on here. He never mentioned names in his sermons, but you could always tell who he was talking about when he preached on marriage and divorce, or communal living or nihilism."

"Nihilism?" Emily asked. "What's that?"

"It's the total rejection of an established institution like the church," Sarah explained. "Basically, that's what you grandmother did. I remember one Sunday when Reverend Alexander quoted a scripture from First Timothy. It refers to the rejection of the church in the latter times when some shall depart from the faith, 'giving heed to seducing spirits and doctrines of devils.'"

Emily frowned. "You're not saying that Grandma is following the devil, are you? Because if that's what you're saying, . . ."

"I'm just telling you what Reverend Alexander said, Emily honey," Sarah interrupted gently. "Except for the Methodists' official denouncement of the Union Sunday School she used to teach, his sermons were the only reaction I ever heard from the Church about your grandmother's departure from the discipline.

"Of course, the Methodist Church was having other trouble at the time. The church was divided right down the middle on the idea of holiness, or Christian perfection. Most folks were calling it 'sanctification.' All over Texas, many sincere people gained a new experience of God's grace and love and then insisted that every Christian must have the same experience in order to be sanctified. Many a congregation split over the issue, and new churches were formed. You can see how the Methodist Church may have considered your grandmother's group to be nothing more than another expression of this holiness emphasis, especially when the folks in Belton started calling your grandmother's group the 'Sanctificationists.'"

Sarah wasn't sure if Emily was absorbing the information about the church background from which Martha's teachings had deviated, but somehow, she felt obligated to share with the girl what she knew to be true. "On the other hand, the five ladies in the prayer group who had come from the Baptist Church were actually charged with heresy and removed from their church roll. It was quite a scandal."

"Heresy? I never heard that mentioned before. Why heresy?" Emily asked, puzzled.

"Well, you know that your grandmother believes that established churches have no authority over God's people and, as a result, the sacraments recognized by the church have no meaning. The Baptist women who joined her went along in proclaiming that the practices of baptism in water and participation in the Lord's Supper were simply spiritual lessons not to be taken literally. In other words, they no longer supported the celebration of baptism or communion, two of the most basic practices of any Christian church. You can imagine the protest among the preachers and church members," Sarah said.

"I don't know anything about what you're saying. Grandma doesn't talk much about such matters anymore," Emily admitted. "I can remember when we used to have regular Bible lessons and prayer meetings. Now Grandma says that all the members of the Sanctified have the Spirit of God and that living our sanctified lives is our worship. It's strange to be reminded of how the community began because now it really seems more like a family business than a church. Maybe the keeping of those traditions and rituals are part of what keeps a church going in the same direction."

Rev. Martin Vanburen Smith
Pastor, Belton Baptist Church Of Christ
Belton, March 15, 1877

I have been dreading this day ever since I first heard about the situation and realized that I would have to take action. It is the first time in my almost twenty years of pastoring that I have ever had to deal with a church problem as severe as this. Since coming to be the pastor of the Baptist Church in Belton two years ago, I have delighted in the growth of the church in this busy town. The wood-framed house that was constructed for my arrival has recently been enlarged to accommodate the meetings of the growing church body, so we no longer have to use the Union Building. With church membership steady at around one hundred believers, my wife, Cornelia, and I feel that we know each member personally. It is an exceptionally close-knit and friendly congregation. Since I am the first full-time pastor, the church members are used to looking out for one another.

Belton being such a small community, I learned almost immediately after my arrival of the trouble that the Methodist Church has had with its former member and popular leader, Mrs. Martha McWhirter. While I did not know exactly what doctrine she espouses, I did know that most of the women who have followed her away from the traditional teaching and practices of Christianity have been her friends from the Methodist Church. Only recently have I learned that five of Mrs. McWhirter's followers are on the roll of the Baptist Church.

Our Baptist deacons meet on the second Thursday of each month to conduct the usual business of the church. In the event that a member has to be reprimanded for an unchristianlike behavior, he or she is called to the meeting to be officially cited by the governing body of the church. Last night, however, a special meeting of the deacons was called to discuss what action should be taken in regard to the behavior of these women. It was finally decided that we had no choice but to charge them with heresy, defined as a practice or belief that is contrary to the fundamental doctrine or creed of the church and specifically denounced by the church as likely to cause schism. If what we have heard about these women is true, schism may be the least of our concerns.

This morning I had the task of locating the women and delivering a copy of the heresy charge and a written summons to the four o'clock meeting. All I knew was that they had been living in Mrs. McWhirter's home for the past year. It was a cool and clear morning as I set out down Pearl Street, and I noticed that the green was just beginning to return after the typically drab Central Texas winter. I prayed that the beautiful day would brighten the dreaded task.

As I approached the McWhirter home, I was surprised to see so much activity. Women were walking up to Mrs. McWhirter's house with their young children and disappearing inside. Other women had loaded a handcart with laundry supplies and were heading down the road. Another group was putting axes and hatchets in a wagon. They wore plain muslin aprons and heavy leather gloves. Although I had seen them peddling the firewood in town and knew it was how they supported themselves, it alarmed me to actually see these young women preparing for a day of work like common darkies. I understand how their behavior causes much distress and embarrassment to the husbands they have left. I walked through the gate behind a young mother with two small children. She opened the front door of the house and walked inside as I reached the front porch. As another woman drew near, I asked her about Mrs. McWhirter and was invited to come in.

Once I removed my hat and stepped into the house, I could see that the women were taking their children to a classroom just inside the front door. Benches and desks filled the front parlor to the left of the entry. Chalkboards, maps and charts gave it the appearance of an ordinary schoolroom.

My first impression of Mrs. McWhirter was that she was a very gracious, well-born lady, perhaps fifty years old. I introduced myself and told her the reason for my visit. Almost as if she had been expecting my arrival, she took the notes I had brought to give to the five women, assuring me that they would be delivered. I had the impression that she was about to show me to the door when she invited me to sit down.

We sat in the formal parlor to the right of the entry where I told her that I appreciated the opportunity to meet her personally and, perhaps, clear up some misunderstandings involving the ladies in question and their reported beliefs and behavior. Heresy was indeed a serious charge, I said, and it was possible that, as in most small towns, things were not always accurately reported. I told her that I sincerely prayed that this was the case.

Mrs. McWhirter made it quite clear, though, that there had been no misunderstanding. 'The Scriptures are all written in figures,' Mrs. McWhirter explained. ' Jesus told his disciples that it was done that way so they might understand things by His Spirit, and the world would be blind to His truths. That's why he taught his lessons to them in parables. He was training them to look beyond the obvious.' She believes that the Lord speaks directly to her through dreams and visions and by His Spirit. 'Only those who have been sanctified can understand what the Scriptures truly say,' she insisted.

I was speechless. I could tell that she sincerely believes what she was telling me, and I also detected the charisma with which she has convinced the others of the same. She has obviously exchanged the truth of God for a lie, and I could not give her the impression that I condoned her behavior.

How can she say that they are following the Scriptures if she ignores or twists His words? 'Either Scripture is God's truth, or it's not,' I told her as calmly as I could manage as I began to explain what the Bible clearly said about baptism and the Lord's Supper.

At that point Mrs. McWhirter stood up and invited me to come to her Bible study on Wednesday night. She didn't want to talk about what she called 'old-fashioned church rituals' and insisted that the Bible was now more or less a 'dead letter' in these modern times.

Dead letter? Dead letter! I felt my face grow red, but before I could protest, Major McWhirter walked into the room, and

SET APART

Mrs. McWhirter acted as if she never noticed my distress. She graciously introduced the two of us and excused herself to her work.

I walked out of the house with Major McWhirter, himself a remarkable man. He told me that he has the greatest respect for his wife and believes her to be under a mysteriously consuming, but temporary, delusion. In spite of everything, he intends to honor his marriage vows and remain by her side. I have to admire his commitment to the Lord in this matter, but I wonder if it isn't he who is being deluded.

I shared with him that I've lived with a redheaded woman myself for many years, but I don't believe I have half the challenge that he does. May God bless him in his dedication to his marriage and his devotion to his wife.

CHAPTER 7

"That's a very interesting thought, Emily, what you said about the traditions and rituals holding the church together. People will come and go. Times will change, but church practices like baptism and communion have continued, probably in a similar way, for almost nineteen hundred years now," Emma remarked, somewhat surprised that although she seemed somewhat overwhelmed, Emily appeared to be digesting the new information. "Of course, we're talking about more than just traditions and ritual. It was Jesus himself who said, 'Do this in remembrance of me.' And most of us still do. That's just plain obedience. Some things shouldn't ever change."

"I couldn't agree more," Sarah added. "Those practices have stayed in the church for more important reasons than tradition." Sensing a disagreement in Emily's tight-lipped silence, Sarah quickly steered the conversation forward. "But speaking of change, I'll bet your mother was surprised at how different things were when she and Ben moved back to Belton with your sister and brother. As I recall, that was late 1878, just before you were born, Emily. Twenty years ago! By the end of that year, we were surprised to find out that the prayer group had grown to about twenty women. Even though your grandmother began to put less emphasis on the unity issues that had originally separated them from their churches, she was still teaching about holiness and sanctification in ways not found in the Bible."

Emily opened her mouth as if to defend her grandmother, but closed it when she realized that she actually had neither the knowledge of what Martha used to teach nor even of what was in the Bible to be able to debate the topic of sanctification. Judging from the perplexed look on Emily's face, Emma could tell that the girl knew little of the background of the women by whom she had been raised. "Mother had clearly defined ideas regarding Christian perfection. I'm sure you realize what caused the most trouble, though, was when she claimed to have received a revelation that declared the sanctified life to be purely celibate."

Sarah's jaw dropped at hearing mention of Martha's most unusual requirement for her followers, but Emma purposely ignored her as well as Emily's own stricken face and stiff posture, refusing to allow the two women to make her feel uncomfortable. It was a fact, not gossip, and in a discussion about the beliefs and practices of the Sanctified Sisters, it was probably the celibacy of Martha's group that had most severely affected the town.

"The husbands of the ladies in the prayer group were none too happy about it, of course. Not surprisingly, several of the women left their homes and moved into the big house on Pearl Street. And since quite a few children came along with their mothers, the women started a school in the house -- the one you, Hattie and George went to."

"The 'sanctified school' is what the townspeople called it, and not in a nice way," Emily recalled with a scowl as she remembered the teasing she and the other children endured. "Sister Rancier taught us our primary subjects, and Grandma taught us from the Bible."

"Yes. As a matter of fact, Mrs. Rancier's contribution to the group went far beyond her role as teacher," Sarah added quickly, anxious to move the conversation away from the delicate subject of celibacy. "The women who brought their children to the classroom in the parlor paid her the same as they would have paid any other teacher. When she turned the money over to your grandmother, it became the beginning of the common fund of money that made it possible for the group to begin to support themselves and their children financially.

"I know that you've lived in this environment all of your life, Emily, but just think how strange it was for us to see these women, our friends, actually *working* to support their families. They were the wives and mothers from the best families in Belton. None of them had ever made a bed or even snapped beans before, since we all grew up with servants in the house. And it was simply unthinkable to imagine a lady ever working for money." Noticing Emily's slightly amused expression, Sarah saw that it was almost impossible for the girl to picture the privileged life the older members of the church had abandoned. All Emily had ever known was life as a worker in an efficiently run hotel business. Sarah had learned from her conversations with Ada that although the women occasionally found a way to set aside time for short vacations, the days at the hotel were long and the work exhausting. They had discovered that the only way to get away from their work was to leave town, a fact that Sarah suspected might have had something to do with their decision to relocate to Washington.

"But by the time your family moved back to Belton, Emily, all of the women were contributing to the common fund by selling eggs and dairy products to the grocery store, taking in other folks' laundry, and chopping and selling firewood. These were physically demanding jobs that the Negroes who lived on the other side of the creek continued to do after the war. It was, well, so *common*. You can see how your grandma's teachings and her group's business practices caused trouble in the homes as well as the churches."

"But in those homes, there was trouble before the women came to Grandma," Emily argued, glaring at Sarah and Emma. "I grew up with stories of drinking and arguing and . . . trouble. That, I know." Emily's eyes filled with tears of anger and confusion. She may have been uncertain about the early teachings of the church, but criticism was a familiar field. Having been taught that all persecution was to be endured and even expected as part of living the true Christian life, she had always considered the church and its members to be above the petty faultfinding and vicious gossip so eagerly handed out by the townsfolk. Emily was grateful that the town had grown more tolerant of the peculiarity of the women of the Central Hotel, but if her grandmother was right in describing their sanctified lives as 'perfect,' why did Sarah's words seem to make so much sense?

Sarah looked to Emma in dismay before responding. "Yes, I'm certain you do know more about this than I do, Emily, honey. I'm sorry. I didn't mean to upset you. It's not really my place to talk about some of these things. My goodness, I don't know what's gotten into me. Perhaps I'd better go now. I should be getting back to the club meeting, anyway." Self-consciously, she straightened a seam on her glove, afraid that she could have jeopardized her relationship with Ada by speaking so frankly. But when Sarah stood to leave, Emily surprised her by springing up from the settee and throwing her arms around the older woman.

"Oh no, please don't leave now. I'm sorry, Mrs. Miller. I'm the one asking the questions, so I can't get upset if the answers aren't what I expect to hear. Please stay with me and Aunt Emma until Mama wakes up."

As she returned the girl's embrace, Sarah was reminded of her own daughter and the close relationship she shared with her children. Filled with compassion, she thought about

Emily's fractured childhood and realized that the girl was making a plea for more than just company. She was searching for the pieces of her life that lay hidden at bottom of the musty hatbox, pieces of a complex story that perhaps Sarah could help Emily put together. She raised her hand to smooth the girl's hair and looked into the eyes that seemed so familiar. "Well, all right. I'll stay, dear. I'm sure I've already missed roll call, and I've always suspected that I only come to the club meetings so I can see Ada, anyway. Of course, I'll stay with you until your mother wakes up."

Just then there was a tap on the outside door and Tennie peeked in. "Excuse me, Sarah," she said. "The club meeting has been dismissed, and Moses was waiting out front. I told him to go on home. I hope that's okay."

"Oh, my! I suppose that means I've missed more than just roll call. Is it really that late?" Sarah asked, rising to greet her stepmother. Intent on the conversation, the women hadn't noticed that the light in the room had grown dim as they visited. "Come in, Tennie. You remember Ada's sister, Emma, and this is Emily Haymond, Ada's youngest daughter."

Tennie greeted Emma, then turned to Emily. "I know you, Emily, but you probably don't remember me. I'm Mrs. Edwards. How's your mother? Sarah told me that she was ill."

Emily looked through the bedroom door at Ada who was still soundly asleep despite the conversation in the sitting room. "She's not well. Thank you for asking, Mrs. Edwards. We're all waiting for her to wake up. Dr. Ghent should be here soon." She looked gratefully at Sarah who had moved to the side table to light the lamp. Although the entire Central Hotel was equipped with new electric lights, the rooms were also furnished with old-fashioned lamps, since the electric plant at the Leon River shut down every night at nine o'clock.

Although fascinated by the new convenience, Sarah often found herself lighting an oil lamp out of habit.

Going into her sister's bedroom, Emma lit the lamp on the washstand beside Ada's bed and turned the wick down to provide a gentle light. The glow cast dark shadows beneath the sick woman's eyes and in the hollows of her cheeks. As the others joined Emma in the bedroom, no mention was made of Ada's alarming appearance, though it weighed heavily upon them all.

"Dr. Ghent is a fine physician," Tennie assured Emily gently. "I know he'll take good care of your mother." She was determined to encourage Emily despite her misgivings about the sound of Ada's labored breathing.

Seemingly oblivious to the comment, Emily took the washrag from her mother's forehead and, once again, refreshed it. Then turning back to Tennie, she asked casually, "How do you know me, Mrs. Edwards? Are you a friend of Mama's?"

Tennie looked inquiringly at Sarah. It had been years since she had even thought about her own involvement with the Sanctified Sisters, and she never talked about it. Considering it a lesson learned, she was intensely thankful for the way her life had been changed. It was a marvel of irony that Martha McWhirter was partially responsible for the favorable way things had worked out for her and her family.

Nodding reassuringly, Sarah put her hand on Tennie's shoulder, acknowledging her stepmother's obvious discomfort. "It's all right, Tennie. Emma and I have been answering Emily's questions about her family history. I know she'd be interested to hear how you fit into her story, if you don't mind sharing with her. But let's go into the other room to talk. Ada should sleep until the doctor gets here," she said, leading the way from the bedroom into the sitting room where the four women took their places on the chairs and settee.

Unsure of where to start, Tennie looked from Emily to Sarah and back to Emily again. "Oh, this is so hard to talk about. So much has changed since then. It's been almost twenty years, now," Tennie said uneasily. "Well, Emily, I first went over to your grandmother's house many years ago because I was . . . lonely, and there were so many friendly women there," she told the girl. Then, turning back to Sarah, she asked, "Are you sure you want me to tell my story?"

"Yes, Tennie, please. Emily grew up with women and children who left lonely or hurtful relationships," Sarah reminded her. "You were there in the beginning and saw how they were convinced that they had found God's answer to their prayers. I don't know if Emily has ever talked to anyone who found a different way to solve her problems."

I'd like to hear about it, Mrs. Edwards," Emily encouraged. "Really, I would."

Tennie took a deep breath and looked down at her hands clasped together in her lap. "In the beginning, I was wary about visiting Mrs. McWhirter. I had heard the stories about her that were going around town, but she had been out to the house to call on me several times, and I found her fascinating to talk with. Quite different from anyone I'd ever met. When I finally got up enough courage to ask her help with a difficult hexagon quilt I was trying to piece, I paid a call to her house on Pearl Street.

"We had a delightful visit, and she asked me to come the next day to her prayer meeting. I surprised myself by accepting the invitation. When I met the ladies in the group, I soon discovered that many had stories very similar to mine. Not every one of them had left their homes, but I immediately understood how the town could be suspicious of the close-knit

79

group. Of course, once a woman made the decision to follow all of Mrs. McWhirter's requirements of sanctification, she was totally supported by the band of women, both financially and emotionally. That dependency drew them tighter and tighter together. They loved each other very much. I saw a kind of loyalty among the women that was, somehow, attractive to me. I regularly attended the meetings and got very close to actually joining them myself, but something always held me back." Tennie paused as she considered what that might have cost her. At the same time, she thought of her former friends from those days who were still in the church, their lives forever altered.

"One time when I was over there, your grandmother told us that God communicated with her though dreams. In one dream she saw the Bible as a big, beautiful clock with two places to wind it, one for the Old Testament and one for the New Testament. She sensed that there was a hope in each part and that she had been given the key to showing us the hope to be found in studying the Bible. According to Mrs. McWhirter, sometimes the dreams explained scripture, but the dreams never contradicted scripture. From then on, the interpretation of dreams became a part of our regular study time together."

Wondering whether to continue, Tennie shifted self-consciously in her chair to realign her posture and looked at Emily. The girl's attentive expression encouraged her to go on with the story.

"Once I became comfortable in the group, I kept going over there because I was left alone at home so much of the time. Dr. Edwards traveled from sunup to sundown attending to patients, and he regularly went away on extended trips to medical meetings. Sometimes he was gone for weeks at a time. He never took me, and after our daughter, Beulah, was born, it was pointless to even ask. When he was home, he was often cruel and critical about my cooking or housekeeping, sometimes bringing me to the point of tears. I loved my husband, though, so when he did offer a rare bit of praise, I lapped it up like a hungry puppy.

"When I started going to the house on Pearl Street, it was like finding an oasis in the desert. Suddenly I had a whole group of friends who cared about me. They truly enjoyed my company and valued what I had to say. Each time I visited I became increasingly enthralled with Mrs. McWhirter's brilliant illumination of the Bible and the deep spirituality of the prayer meetings. It was an experience I know I'll never forget. It's hard to find the words that would describe how much we all loved her and enjoyed being together. Of course, you know what I'm talking about, Emily. You've no doubt experienced it for yourself." The girl smiled and nodded her head. Not much had changed, she realized. After more than twenty years, the women of the church continued to adore her grandmother.

"When Dr. Edwards was gone, I took Beulah over there every day. Just before he was due to return home, one of the Sisters would help me clean my house and prepare a delicious meal. This went on for more than two years."

"So what happened?" Emily asked.

"Well, it was in the late spring, not long after you were born, Emily. That's why you don't remember me," Tennie added with a reassuring smile. "Dr. Edwards had just come home from a long trip to Galveston. After supper we moved into the parlor. He complimented me on the coffee, and I eagerly poured him another cup. Then I sat down and picked up a collar from the sewing cabinet beside my chair and began to embroider. On the floor, Beulah was looking at the new picture book her father had brought from his trip." Tennie paused, sighing. "I can still see that scene as though I'm looking at a photograph card on the stereoscope. Even though I was thoroughly satisfied when I was with the Sisters, this is what I really wanted, my family. This was what I had prayed for. At that moment I was truly happy.

"Then my husband spoke to Beulah. I remember his words like it was yesterday. 'Tell Papa what you did today, Beulah,' he said. I held my breath because I knew what she would say. Even though he was gone much of the time, I knew that my husband still shared the town's opinion that Mrs. McWhirter and her followers were dangerous to the fragile fabric of Belton society.

"'I learned the Lord is my shepherd, Papa,' she told him. Then, basking in her father's attention, my three-year-old daughter recited the entire twenty-third Psalm to her astonished father. He was absolutely amazed and asked her if she had learned it at Sunday School. You know, of course, what she told him," Tennie said, confident of Emily's response.

"Oh, I know where she learned that," Emily said brightly. "The twenty-third Psalm was one of our earliest memory pieces in Sister Rancier's class. What did he do when she told him?"

"As you can imagine, he immediately lost his temper. I sat there taking the full measure of his angry, hurtful words as I had for years. But this time I didn't cry. I prayed. When his tirade was over, I knew God had answered my prayer because suddenly I had all of the words I needed to speak honestly to my husband.

"It was a very strange feeling. I had been raised the same way as most girls -- to be a good wife and mother by never complaining or arguing or even voicing an opinion. But now I had the words to say out loud what I had told him in my head a thousand times. I had the boldness to talk to him with the same confidence I had when I talked to my friends at Mrs. McWhirter's house. So when he finished shouting, I calmly told him about the loneliness I felt when he was gone and the love and acceptance I had found at your grandmother's house. It was a frightening and liberating feeling all at the same time."

"What did he do?" Emily asked, intrigued at the thought of this delicate woman talking back to her angry husband. She was all-too familiar with such situations ending in violence.

"Dr. Edwards was stunned, I'll have to say. He had never once heard me respond so openly and honestly to anything that he had to say. He had certainly never known how I craved his attention, his approval and love. I tried to make him understand how much the prayer group meant to me, but that I would give it all up for him, for our family. He didn't know what to say.

"After a long, uncomfortable period of silence, I took Beulah upstairs to get her ready for bed. I remember how much trouble I had unbuttoning all those tiny buttons on the back of her dress because my hands were shaking so badly. Then in her sweet little voice, Beulah asked, 'Didn't Papa like my Bible verse?' After the tension of the evening, I simply wept." Tennie wiped away a tear, remembering the moment. "Poor little Beulah. She probably thought the twenty-third Psalm was a very powerful verse to cause so much commotion. But I know the Lord was being my shepherd, for that night was the turning point in our marriage."

"What changed?" Emily wanted to know, curious about the unexpected turn the story was taking.

"Well, a few days later, when I failed to show up at her house as usual, Mrs. McWhirter paid me a visit. Having decided at last to spend more time at home, the doctor had canceled his next trip and was there to meet her at the front door."

"Oh, no! What happened then?" Emily asked, anticipating a familiar answer. Angry husbands rarely won a confrontation with her grandmother.

"I was inside the house and I knew they were arguing. I couldn't understand much of what was exchanged, although I did hear Dr. Edward's final words to your grandmother, 'Shame on you, Mrs. McWhirter, for taking advantage of the women of this town. You give them what they need and they become your slaves. I've seen them peddling wood on the streets like darkies! My wife is no longer your slave.'

"My husband said nothing further to me about her, but it was quite clear that he wanted me to have no contact with any of the Sisters. Although I missed my friends at first, I came to realize that I no longer needed that type of fellowship. More importantly, I recognized that it would destroy my family as it had so many others. I was fortunate in that my marriage was restored. No . . . it became the marriage I had longed for but never had before. Beulah and I began traveling with Dr. Edwards, and he spent more time at home. He even started going to church with us. The Lord means for families to stay together, Emily. I'm convinced of that."

The room was quiet for a time. "What about my family?" Emily asked plaintively. There was no response. From outside, the courthouse clock chimed the half-hour.

"We don't have to talk about this anymore, honey," Emma said, breaking the silence and the tension as she reached over to her niece, patting her on the knee. She put the lid back on top of the hatbox and moved it aside. "It's all water under the bridge now."

"But there's no one else to answer my questions, Aunt Emma. Mama won't ever talk about Ben Haymond. You know, that's the way she refers to him: Ben Haymond. Not 'your papa' or 'my husband' or even just 'Ben.' And you know Grandma always blames everything on him, which is ever so convenient now that my father is *dead,"* the girl said bitterly, unexpected tears stinging her eyes.

"I'm sorry I upset you, Emily," Tennie said, struggling to hold her own emotions in check.

"Oh, no, Mrs. Edwards, it's not you. I'm just finding out that I've lived my whole life in the dark. No one ever tells me anything. I suppose I'll always just be 'Ada's baby girl,'" Emily responded, quickly wiping her eyes.

Tennie stood up. "I really must be going now," she said as she placed her gloved hand on the young woman's arm. "I'm glad I got to see you before you leave again, Emily. I hope things go well for you in Washington. I'll be praying for you."

Emily rose and followed Tennie to the door. "Thank you for sharing your story, Mrs. Edwards. I appreciate your honesty." Her shoulders slumped as she closed the door and turned back to Emma and Sarah.

CHAPTER 8

Suddenly realizing that Tennie had probably intended to offer her stepdaughter a ride home, Emily became flustered. "Goodness. Mrs. Edwards said that your man, Moses, has left. How are you going to get home, Mrs. Miller?" Emily asked as she returned to the settee.

"That's all right, Emily. I'll just hire a hack from the livery stable across the street. I told you I would stay to hear what Dr. Ghent has to say. I'm worried about your mother," Sarah said with genuine concern.

"Please don't talk like that, Mrs. Miller. It frightens me. I don't know what I'd do without Mama. The Sisters are my family, but not like Mama is family. Grandma calls that being 'fleshly,' but I can't help feeling that way. I couldn't bear to lose Mama . . . again," Emily said, her voice lowering to a whisper.

Sarah sensed the girl's fear. "I'm sorry, Emily. I didn't mean to alarm you. I want to find out what treatment the doctor recommends for her cough and what I can do to help. She's come to my aid in the past. Please don't worry, sweetheart. Your mother's a strong woman. She's been through a lot."

"Been through a lot," Emily repeated thoughtfully, her eyes searching Sarah's face for clues. "Please tell me what you mean. Since Mama won't answer my questions, there are gaps in my life that I can't seem to fill. I just have to know more about my family. About myself. Things no one else will tell me." She turned and gave Emma a pleading look.

"I really wish I could help you, Emily, honey." Emma told her niece. "But when your parents moved back to Belton before you were born, Mr. Pond and I were not around very much. We were living in Salado and seldom came to Belton after Mother announced that she and her followers would have no contact with family members who weren't sanctified. Based on her definition of the word, that is."

No longer feeling the need to defend her grandmother's teaching, the girl looked back to Sarah, tears of frustration and hopelessness brimming her dark eyes.

"Well, I can only tell you what I know, Emily. When your mother came back from Fort Worth, I didn't see her right away." Sarah paused as a she felt a stab of regret over the circumstances of Ada's return. "You see, your grandmother's prayer group had become very organized, and I assumed that your mother had joined them. The egg and butter business was well underway and they were all so busy with their work that they started to isolate themselves from the other women of the town. I'm sure your mother's first concern was to do what was best for her family, but between your father starting a new business and your grandmother talking to her about joining the Sanctified, she was left in a difficult situation."

"That's another thing I've heard before," Emily interrupted. "Left in a difficult situation."

"Yes, I'm sure you have. It was a *very* difficult time for your mother," Sarah said. "But from what I understand, your father, ever the entrepreneur, was apparently not discouraged by the way things turned out in Fort Worth. When your family returned to Belton, Ben and his brother, Dub, immediately started talking about buying a fruit plantation to

87

supply their grocery store. Over the next couple of years, Ben and Dub made several trips down to Central America to set up the transaction. That was right after you were born, Emily, and it meant that your mother was often left alone here in Belton with three small children. Naturally, she began to spend more time with her mother, even though she knew Ben would object. He and your grandmother never got along, I'm sure you know."

Emily nodded sadly.

"Things came to a head when your father returned home from a trip and found out that your mother had not only spent most of her time with your grandmother and her followers, but had also hosted a prayer meeting in his house. He was furious and demanded that she leave his bedroom. I know she must have been torn between her love for her husband and family, and the insistent teachings of her mother encouraging her to leave her 'unsanctified' husband. It certainly didn't help that Ben was away so much."

"That wasn't very smart of him," Emily commented, as she began to see the deeper issues that had long been hidden. Her parents' relationship was much more complicated than she had been led to believe.

"No, it wasn't," Sarah agreed. "I think he underestimated how emotionally dependent Ada had become on her mother and the other women when he was gone, just as Tennie described to you from her own experience. Your father wasn't any different from most other men, Emily. They just don't understand things like that."

"His solution was to try to take us as far away as possible," Emily guessed as she began to see how this new information meshed with what she already knew.

Sarah nodded. "But your mother was not about to take an infant and two small children into the jungle of Nicaragua. As a result, your father traveled alone and y'all spent most of your time at your grandmother's house. You didn't actually move in with her until after the Dow brothers incident."

"Oh, yes, the Dows. I had almost forgotten about their story. Mama saved the *Belton Journal* articles about the trial. I saw them in here," Emily said as she removed the lid from the hatbox and retrieved a bundle of newspaper clippings. She studied the headline of the first article as she read, "Local News and Views, February 17, 1880."

Emily looked up at the two women. "It's another one of the many things that nobody ever talks about. It all happened when I was a baby, of course. I know it was something very ugly and that those nice men were beaten, but now everyone is all friendly with the Dows again. In fact, Brother Matthew is supposed to come up to Washington, D.C., to remodel the house we bought there. Exactly what did happen back then?" She put the clippings in her lap and looked at Sarah and Emma expectantly.

Sarah spoke first. "Well, this is how I remember it from the trial. About the time your father started spending so much time away from Belton, your grandmother got a letter from two brothers in Fort Worth. David and Matthew Dow were originally from Scotland, but had heard about your grandmother's church in Belton when they immigrated to Texas. Hoping that there was some similarity with the Sanctification Church they had attended in Scotland, the brothers wrote to your grandmother asking permission to come to Belton and meet her," she explained.

Emily nodded. "If I know Grandma, she was probably eager for them to visit, if only to find out if there were any men who would be willing to abide by her rules. You may know that she never absolutely forbade men from joining the church, but she did demand that everyone live up to her

89

requirements, married or not. That, of course, explains the small number of men in the church. Uncle Robert and Uncle Sam are the only ones left."

Sam McWhirter
Belton, February, 1880

Mama asked me and Robert to go to the stage stop and wait for the men comin from Fort Worth. I don't know about Robert, but it made me feel pretty grown up to be asked to bring visitors to the big house. No one ever comes to our house to visit, especially men. And when women come to visit, they usually end up stayin. That's why me and Robert had to move out of our room. Now we live in the log house that was on the property when our family first moved here from Salado, before I was born and they built the big stone house. When men do come over, they're usually lookin for their wives, and Mama yells at em and sends em away. Papa is the only man I know that she's friendly with, and that's not always.

The men asked us to call them Brother David and Brother Matthew. That Brother Matthew is the biggest man I've ever seen, with a red beard and red hair all over his body. They're both carpenters and each one had a heavy wooden tool chest. I was glad that Robert thought to bring the wagon instead of the buggy, cause there were a couple other trunks to take to the house, too. Robert is almost fifteen and a lot taller than me, but even though I'm two years younger, I'm stronger. I think Brother Matthew noticed my muscles when I picked up his toolbox. I've gotten so strong cause I help the Sisters chop firewood after school.

We took them to the log house and helped them put their things in the other bedroom. They had to change shirts and wash their faces and hands before we went to the big house for supper. You can get pretty dusty on the stage all the way from Fort Worth. When I handed Brother David a towel, he said 'Thank you,' but it sounded like 'Thankee.' There's a lot of words they must say very different in Scotland. I know they're speakin English, but when the Dow brothers talk, it sounds like a whole nother language.

When we got over to the house, Mama and Papa met us inside the front door near the main staircase and introduced the men to all the Sisters who had crowded into the front hall. Then Mama asked me, not Robert, to show 'our guests' the rest of the house.

First we went through the formal parlor. That's where the Sisters have their Bible studies and prayer meetins. No children allowed. Behind that room is the big dinin room which was already set for supper. I saw that my sister Ada put flowers on the table. She and her three little children, Hattie, George and Emily, come and stay upstairs in her old bedroom when her husband, Ben, is away.

There's a big pantry room behind the dinin room. That's where we keep the table linens, dishes, jars of preserves and the silver that Mama brought from Tennessee. That room opens into a sleepin porch that wraps around the side of the house. We walked through the porch, past the second staircase and came back inside in the south parlor where our classroom is. Tomorrow is geography day.

No one knows about the second staircase until you come inside the house. It goes down to the ground floor that's level with the back of the house where the property slopes down to the creek. At the bottom of the stairs is our indoor water well. Mama is so proud of havin a well right inside the house. It's close to the kitchen on the ground floor in the back of the house, and it's real handy for cookin. We hang the butter in the well where it's nice and cool. Papa sleeps in the downstairs bedroom where me and Robert were before we moved out to the log house.

Upstairs are two big bedrooms. One used to be Mama and Papa's and the other belonged to my sisters Emma, Ada and Nannie. Now they're both full of women and children. We didn't go up there. It must be awfully crowded. I'm glad that me and Robert are in the log house.

The men were very interested in the construction of the house, I guess, cause they're carpenters. Brother Matthew told me that they're also stonemasons. I told him that the limestone for the house came from a quarry right here in Belton.

Then we all went back to the dinin room and supper was on the table. The Sisters must have been excited about havin company, cause I haven't seen that much food since the Fourth of July picnic last summer. They fixed all my favorites: fried chicken, chicken and dumplins, cornbread, beans, creamed corn and sweet corn, stewed apples, apple pie and a pound cake. Made me wish we had company more often. I'm just thankful that I got to eat with the grown-ups this time. The other kids ate their supper earlier, and I know they didn't have what we had.

Actually, me and Robert didn't get to eat with the guests. We piled food on our plates and ate at the small table in the pantry room. That was all right with me. That way we didn't have to watch our manners. Papa is very strict with us at the table: Yes, Ma'am. Yes, Sir. Please. Thank you. No elbows on the table. Don't talk with your mouth full. I know it would have been even worse with visitors here. From the pantry, we weren't able to hear what the grown-ups talked about, but I could hear the funny accents of the men from Scotland.

I was surprised, but the very next day, Brother Matthew and Brother David started buildin a new frame house near the old log house. Mama must have told them about the problem we were startin to have with space. It seems like we have someone new over here almost every week.

It's fun to always have someone to play with, usually Carrie and Ella. They are exactly the same ages as me and Robert and have gone to school with us for years in the parlor classroom. They come over whenever their father has been drinkin. Their mother, Sister Henry, usually has a black eye or bloody nose or a big bruise where he hits her. It makes Mama mad that Mrs. Henry always goes home the next day.

A lot of women are workin here and their children go to school with us in the parlor classroom. I really don't know how many are stayin upstairs with Mama since me and Robert moved to the log house. I just know it's crowded.

Anyway, Brother Matthew and Brother David worked for months on the new house. Me and Robert started helpin them and then they let us do some of the carpentry by ourselves. They stayed in the log house with us and we all ate our meals at the big house. One night, when the new house was almost finished, we were all eatin supper in the dinin room when we heard some hollerin outside, then a gunshot. My teacher, Sister Rancier, thought one of the voices sounded like her husband, and she ran to the door.

I thought it was a dumb idea to open the front door to all that noise, especially after the gunshot. But when she did, masked men rushed in and grabbed Brother David and Brother Matthew and dragged them out the front door. Some other men were waitin outside to throw them in the back of a wagon that sped away.

All the women were screamin and cryin, and Papa hurried to get his rifle. By the time he got back to the front of the house, they were all gone. Mama sent Robert to run get the Sheriff.

When Robert got back with the Sheriff, Mama was really mad, and so was Papa. The Sheriff said it was too late and too dark, and he didn't have any evidence that a crime had been committed. He also wondered who we wanted him to arrest since they were all wearin masks. Then he said that if the Dow brothers were crazy enough to come back to town, they could come to his office in the mornin to press charges.

Mama pointed out the bullet hole in our front door (that I had showed her) and told the Sheriff that it should be evidence of a crime.

Just then, Brother Matthew and Brother David came staggerin up the street. I don't know how they could even walk, they were so beat up. Brother Matthew's face was a bloody mess and all covered with dirt and leaves. Brother David's shirt had been ripped off his back, and I could see that he had been horsewhipped. It hadn't taken the mob of men long to beat them up.

Papa helped them around to the back of the house and put them both in his own bed, while Mama and some of the other Sisters cleaned and bandaged them up. The Sheriff didn't really know what to do with them, so he decided to take them to jail.

Jail? Mama screamed at him. She told him that the brothers had done nothin wrong. The Sheriff said maybe she was right about that, but the men would be safer in the jail. So Papa put them in the wagon and they went with the Sheriff. Brother Matthew and Brother David stayed in the jail for a whole week.

CHAPTER 9

"It didn't take long after the Dow brothers got to Belton for them to realize that your grandmother's church was much different from what they expected to find," Sarah continued. "But they must have liked something about the town because they stayed and started working for the Sisters as carpenters. They moved into the old log house with Robert and Sam, and that's probably when the boys started learning carpentry. Your grandmother was anxious to get another house built for the women who had moved into the house on Pearl Street.

"After the new house was framed, many of the Sisters began to help the Dows during the day. They followed the brothers' instructions and sawed lumber, hammered nails and learned everything the Dow brothers could teach them about home building," Sarah added.

"I know that must have been something to see: women in dresses and aprons building a house," Emily said, smiling as she pictured the scene.

"You're right about that," Emma agreed. "The construction caused quite a stir in a little town where *sidewalk repair* is a news item in the *Journal*. In fact, talk of the project even got as far as where Mr. Pond and I were living in Salado. We heard all of the rumors flying about what the women were building. Was it a church for that *odd* religion? A *dormitory* or school for all of those *children*? A *brothel*, perhaps?" Emma asked with mock horror. "Every day, wagons and carriages drove slowly past the construction site just to watch the Sisters at work. They *really* created a spectacle, almost as good as the two-headed calf at the circus, and knowing Mother, she did *nothing* to discourage the attention. At some point, the husbands and other men of the town apparently decided to try to put an end to what the women were doing by taking it out on the Dows."

Ignoring Emma's remark about Martha, Emily looked down at the clippings in her lap. "Here's a curious headline. The story about the Dow brothers' beating is titled 'The Late Unpleasantness.' I'm sure that's not how the Dows thought of it."

"No, and it got worse," Sarah commented. "You can read it in the article for yourself, but the Sheriff put them in jail when they came back into town after the beating. He probably had no idea what to do with them, so they were charged with lunacy. Can you believe it? Those poor men sat in jail for a whole week. The Sisters visited them every day, bringing them food and clean bandages. The trial to determine their sanity was held the following Friday, exactly one week after the beating.

"I wasn't there, but it says in the newspaper that the courtroom was packed. You can imagine how curious everyone was to finally get their noses into what was going on in the house on Pearl Street. You see, that's really what the attack was in the first place, a way to get back at the women who had hurt and humiliated so many families by moving in with Mother. The men in that mob couldn't very well beat up the women, so they turned their anger against those poor brothers. The trial turned into a free show, an absolute circus."

David Dow
Belton, February 20, 1880

A fine welcome we had to the county of Bell. It was bad enough to be disappointed that the church we visited was not what we expected. It's glad we were, however, that we were able to help the Sisters start to build a house. We were having a difficult time thinking of how we were going to tell them that although our hearts are in line with theirs, the church would not suit us at all. Sister Martha is a fine woman, but a bit too hardheaded for our liking.

I'll have to say that the beating took us both by surprise. As large as me brother is, I do believe we could have taken on the lot of them had we seen them coming. Sister Martha was none too happy that we were taken out of her control, but I agree with the Sheriff that the jail was the best place for us. The Sisters took good care of us, but the distance from Sister Martha was most satisfactory

We were told that a 'writ of lunacy' had been brought against us and the trial was to serve as an investigation to determine our sanity, for our own protection and for the protection of the citizens of Bell County. At least that's how it was reported in the local newspaper. It's that murderous mob that the citizens of Bell County need to be protected from, if you ask me.

It appeared that the entire citizenry of Belton turned out for the trial. The large upstairs courtroom was packed, as were both stairways and the grounds surrounding the building in the center of the town square. People even sat in the windows of the room.

The first witness was a large old man, Major Hanna by name. We thought it interesting for him to be called as a witness, since neither me nor me brother had laid eyes on the man until he came to the jail the morning after our arrest. We even fell asleep while he was talking to us that early morn, since we had not yet recovered from being beaten half to death the night before. Came early that morning to advise us to quit the country for our own good, said he.

'How did the brothers receive your advice, Major Hanna?' he was asked by the prosecutor at the trial.

The old man pulled at this beard and spat a stream of tobacco juice. 'I don't think they understood me at first, being foreigners and all. They had no response to my helpful advice. So I told them again that THEY COULD BE KILLED if they stayed in Belton.' The old man smiled at us as if the shouting was our private joke. 'I thought that would help them understand me better.'

The folks in the courtroom laughed so much, the judge had to hit the desk with his gavel.

When the room quieted, the prosecutor asked if either of us had responded to his advice. Major Hanna quoted me brother's own words: 'Our religion is good enough to live by and good enough to die by.' That stirred so much talking in the room, the judge hit his desk with the gavel again.

The next witness was a Mr. Charles Pratt. He is the husband of one of the women in the Church. He had walked out on the poor woman when she was with child, leaving the young lass to raise the wee bairn on her own.

Mr. Pratt testified that he had asked to work for us when we were framing the house on Pearl Street. When we learned that he had deserted his wife in her delicate condition however, we declined to be associated with the scoundrel. What he told the court was that we would do no business with him because he was unsanctified, which was only partly true. The whole truth was that we dinna like the man.

98

Then was called Mr. J. C. Henry, the husband of wee Sister Margaret Henry. He told the court that his dear wife had been one of the first of Mrs. McWhirter's friends from the Methodist Church prayer group to join the Sisters. Mr. Henry testified that although his wife lived under the same roof with him, she acted and claimed to be simply a servant. He had built her a fine home on their family farm just north of town, he told the court, and could hire all the servants his wife could ever need. Only a woman of questionable sanity would behave in such a manner, said he.

Next, the physicians of Belton were called on to provide the jury with a medical definition of insanity. The five doctors impressed even me with their combined education and experience. It's pleased, I was, when our attorney's questions to the doctors revealed that not one had examined, questioned, or even met us, the accused.

'So while you are brilliantly qualified to provide us with a medical textbook definition of insanity and all the examples we could ever want to hear about the subject, you cannot accurately, or even ethically, diagnose the sanity of either Matthew or David Dow without actually meeting them, can you, doctor?' he asked one of the doctors. You can be sure that there were more than a few muffled laughs heard around the courtroom.

After lunch, Sister Josephine Rancier was called to the stand. The poor woman trembled as she sat on the witness stand and was asked if she was a member of the group that called itself 'the sanctified.'

'I am sanctified, sir,' the poor woman said, ' but we don't call ourselves "the sanctified," although I've heard other folks say it,' said the poor young woman. But the man continued to use the term, and then asked Sister Rancier what was her main duty as a member of the sanctified.

'To do as the Lord commands,' she responded. And when asked to explain just how the Lord communicated his commands, she told him, 'He speaks to me in prayer, through His Word, and by dreams and visions.'

The man laughed, pretending he was clearing his throat, but his disrespectful response started more noise in the room. 'Dreams and visions, eh, Mrs. Rancier?' he repeated when the room quieted. 'And what kinds of things has the Most High God commanded you to do?'

'He clearly commands in Scripture that we are to live apart from the unsanctified,' she replied with unmistakable confidence, despite her timid appearance.

Then he asked, 'Is that why you have left your husband, Mrs. Rancier?'

For a moment I thought the poor woman might cry, but she took a breath and replied, 'I do as the Lord commands.'

The prosecutor could barely contain his delight at the opportunity her response presented. 'And if the Lord commanded you to kill one of your children, . . .?' he asked without completing the question.

The noise in the room rose to such a level that the judge had to sound the gavel yet again to silence the crowd. But the brave lady took another deep breath and looked the prosecutor in the eye, 'I do as the Lord commands,' she said once more. At this, there was a strange silence. Very strange, indeed.

The last witness called was Sister Martha McWhirter, and it was obvious that she was the one the crowd had assembled to hear. As solid as a rock, she was. When asked about her relationship with us, she proudly told the court, 'I have been acquainted with Matthew and David Dow for almost one year. They have been visitors at my house frequently. I believe them both to be of sound mind, as sane as anybody in this courthouse.' I looked at me brother and we smiled at that statement. 'They have joined us when we assemble ourselves together in Christ's name, as the church of God,' she added.

Then, since it had been brought up as the reason for our alleged insanity, Sister McWhirter was asked about her involvement with 'the sanctified.'

She told them that she had been a member of the Methodist Church for twenty-five years. 'The Lord came and sanctified me twelve years ago. God never reveals to His people that they should turn back to their old modes of life, and therefore, there is no possibility of my being directed to go back into the Methodist Church and live as I did when I was a member of that body. There is but one Spirit in the world and this Spirit makes us new creatures. I know what we teach is right. As to sacrificing children - - that is, killing them - - God never gives such instructions.' Then she looked at the prosecutor as if he were insane.

This rattled the man just a bit, so he tried to change the subject and asked her about dreams and visions.

'I believe in dreams as I do in existence,' Sister McWhirter went on. 'Some dreams I pay no attention to. How they come cannot be explained, being the working of the Spirit.' When asked to explain on what she based her beliefs, she told him boldly, 'We find a foundation for everything we do in the Bible.'

Asked if her interpretation of sanctification came from the Bible, Sister McWhirter opened the one she had brought with her to the witness stand and began to read her answer right out of First Corinthians, chapter seven, beginning with verse twelve: 'But to the rest speak I, not the Lord: If any brother hath a wife that believeth not, and she be pleased to dwell with him, let him not put her away. And the woman which hath a husband that believeth not, and if he be pleased to dwell with her, let her not leave him. For the unbelieving husband is

101

sanctified by the wife and the unbelieving wife is sanctified by the husband; else were your children unclean. But now they are holy. But if the unbelieving depart, let him depart. A brother or sister is not under bond in such cases. But God has called us to peace.'

'We apply these commands to our lives,' Sister Martha explained. 'When a husband leaves a wife, she is free, and he must come back sanctified, or not at all. The woman has no right ever to marry again. If the law of God conflicts with the common law, the former is to prevail. I have advised wives to live with their husbands when they could, but there is no sense in obeying, for example, a drunken husband. If a husband should go to a wife and ask her, for his sake, for the sake of her children and the peace of society, to surrender her belief in sanctification as we teach it, I should say for her to do no such thing. For wouldn't that be giving up all our religion?'

Again, the courtroom was as quiet as a church. All eyes followed the good Sister as she went back to her seat. But alas, the opinion of the jury was that we were insane, and we found ourselves being sent to the Asylum for the Insane in Austin. I feel we need many prayers at this point.

CHAPTER 10

Emily sorted through the newspaper clippings in her lap. "The trial must have been awful for those two nice men. It says here that they were declared insane and sent to the asylum in Austin. What a terrible experience for them. How did they get out?"

Sarah took the newspaper articles that Emily passed to her, barely glancing at the familiar text. "It was all reported in the paper," she explained. "An unnamed someone, only identified as a 'concerned American,' wrote to the British consulate in Galveston and brought the brothers' plight to the attention of the authorities there. Then a letter went from the consulate to the Texas governor's office, and by the beginning of March, the Dows were returned to Belton. In order to ensure their travel safety, the brothers requested state troops to escort them from Austin to Belton."

Handing the clippings back to Emily, Sarah pointed to a line on the page at the bottom of the stack. "I think this was the Journal's idea of an apology. 'Our people sincerely deplore the occurrences that have placed this section in such an unenviable attitude, and it is now the prevailing opinion that mob law is forever at an end in Bell county,'" she quoted.

Shaking her head, Emma looked skeptical. "I'm sure the writer was familiar with the mob. I remember that there was an investigation into the incident, but no one was ever arrested for the assault of the brothers. Anyway, Matthew and David Dow came back to Belton and took rooms at a boarding house in town and, as you know, Emily, opened their own construction business. They kept their distance from the Sisters for many years, and no one has bothered them since, although I'm sure living in Belton was difficult at first. And despite their less than friendly welcome to town, the Dows have worked on some of Belton's biggest construction projects since that time. If I'm remembering correctly, they helped build the new courthouse, the Methodist Church and Luther Hall, the first building at Baylor College."

Emily nodded. "And the Central Hotel. Brother Matthew and his crew built this whole complex. When you think about it, it's amazing how time has changed so many things. The Dows are very well respected by the town today. Mama has one of their business advertisements in here," she said, reaching down to pull yet another scrap of yellowed newsprint out of the hatbox.

"And all of that excitement with the Dows happened just about the time of the railroad fiasco," Emma added. "Did Ada save anything about that slick deal?"

"Not unless it's in some of these same newspapers about the Dows," Emily said as she scanned the backs of the clippings in her hand. "I've always heard it said that the railroad was supposed to have come straight from Rogers to Belton, but went up to Temple instead. What else can you tell me, Aunt Emma?"

"What else can I tell you about the railroad? How about the truth!" Emma dramatically threw up her hands, remembering the suspicious manner the extension of the railroad into Central Texas had been handled. "First of all, honey, there wasn't even a Temple back then, as you know - - just acres of open farmland. The Gulf, Colorado, and Santa Fe had promised that Belton was going to be the terminus for Central Texas. In accordance with the contract the town had

104

signed with the railroad company, the land was surveyed, the right-of-way acquired, and the money donated. I was told that Mother even gave a substantial contribution out of the women's common fund. You just can't imagine the excitement that was building, as every week there was an item in the Journal reporting the progress of laying the railroad line. The town had even cleared a lot near the courthouse to be ready for construction of the depot. We just knew it would be in Belton by Christmas."

"So what happened?" Emily asked.

Emma shook her head slowly as she calmed down, her words becoming more deliberate. "No one really knows except perhaps Mr. Bernard M. Temple, the chief construction engineer for the railroad, but word leaked out that a large amount of land over by Bird Creek had changed hands. Suddenly the rail line made an eight-mile detour off the survey, straight to the land that the railroad had purchased, and by February, the town of Temple was born. There, the railroad built all of its company repair shops, and Temple became the 'boss town' of the Santa Fe railroad instead of Belton. Somewhere along the line, someone made more money than King Solomon. That's what it always comes down to. Money."

"So that's how the Temple-Belton rivalry started. No wonder there's still friction between the two towns," Emily observed.

"It was still another year before Belton got a dead-end spur and a little bitty depot on the north edge of town. Now, of course, the line continues straight out past Lampasas, and we have a Katy depot right in town. But I think the whole thing was handled very poorly," Emma said, her resentment evident. "After all, Belton is the county seat."

While Sarah, too, had been disappointed by Belton's apparent mistreatment by the railroad company, she preferred to look on the positive side. "Actually, Belton is better off than some towns. My husband is an inspector for the Katy Railroad, you know, and he tells me that the places that don't have any connection with the railroad will be absolute ghost towns within ten years. Just look at what's already happened to Salado. And you know this hotel wouldn't be here if it weren't for the amount of railroad traffic that does come through town. Despite the broken promises made to Belton and our disappointment with the Santa Fe depot, our town began to change for the better with the arrival of the first train. Right from the start, the railroad brought in visitors, traveling salesmen, even circus people."

"Circus people?" Emily laughed out loud, then clapped her hand over her mouth as she looked through the open bedroom door to see if she had disturbed her mother.

Sarah smiled at Emily's sudden change in demeanor. "Yes, the circus people used to stay at the Central Hotel every year. If anyone could handle circus folks, it was your grandmother. But more importantly, the connection to the railroad network helped your father and his brother decide to go ahead and buy the plantation in Nicaragua. By importing fruit and other produce from their own plantation and shipping by rail, they could make a larger profit in the grocery business. At least that's how they figured it. Dub was so confident, he even expanded the Belton store and opened a second one in Waco."

"Sounds like a good business idea to me," Emily said brightly as she took note of another of her father's positive attributes.

Sarah nodded. "Good idea, yes, but bad timing. I don't know if your mother ever knew, but your father was trying to talk his brother into moving down to Nicaragua so he could

106

stay here with y'all in Belton, when Dub suddenly died. Apparently your Uncle Dub picked up a very deadly strain of malaria on one of his trips to Central America. Your father was pretty shaken by his brother's death, but he decided he had no choice but to work the plantation himself, with or without the family."

"That's when we moved in with Grandma?"

Ada McWhirter Haymond
Belton, January, 1881

I have always loathed the weather in January. Sometimes I can't even remember what warm feels like. It's as though I've always been cold and I'll never be warm again. Now it seems that even my bones are chilled.

Ever since he started traveling to Central America, I had a feeling that Ben would eventually leave us and not come back. Every time he was away, I would tell myself that it was good preparation for when he finally moved out. So I thought I was ready.

But when I woke up this morning to find he had taken all of his things, I discovered that I wasn't as prepared as I thought I'd be. That's when the cold crept into my bones. I feel numb now. After our fight last night, I should feel relieved, even glad that the fighting is over and the children and I are free of his hurtful words.

But what I really wish is that it could all be the same as it was in the beginning, back when the most important thing in our lives was our love for each other. It's hard to admit it, but I still love Ben. I love his energy and enthusiasm. I love him for wanting to take us away from this madness that Mama has created. But he is not being realistic. Surely he can't think that I would take my babies to live in the jungle. I know he thinks he's doing what's best for our family, but we can't go there with him. Right now, Mama's the only one I can turn to for help. Ben hasn't been thinking clearly since his brother died. Maybe someday he'll see that and come back to us.

Last night was the worst fight we've ever had. Ben had just come home from his latest trip to the plantation. He's been in a very strange mood since Dub died. Instead of being excited about his new project, the business venture has become more like a mission, as though going to the plantation they bought together will bring his brother back. Ben's sense of duty has clouded his judgment. At supper, he demanded that the children and I go back with him next week.

As much as I want our family to stay together, I can't leave Belton again. When we first moved back here from Fort Worth three years ago, I sensed a silent hostility toward the women who had become involved with Mama. Even though I had not yet chosen to place myself among them, I soon realized that as the daughter of Martha McWhirter, that decision had already been made for me. After our arrival in Belton, none of my friends came to call on me as I expected. Not even Sarah. When I went shopping in town, the store clerks practically ignored me, even the ones I had worked beside and traded with for years. Folks I recognized crossed the street to avoid talking to me. Then after the Dow trial last year, there was no mistaking the division that had occurred in the town, and I realized that I had absolutely no one to talk to outside of Mama's prayer group.

I explained to Ben once again how I couldn't take the children to live in a jungle or leave the women at Mama's church. 'They're my only friends,' I told Ben. It was the wrong thing to say.

Right away, he began to get angry. It was as if I had struck a match and was watching water boil. First, his voice got a little louder. 'Are you blind, Ada? That church of yours is tearing up our family like it has all the others involved with your mother. Just take a look around, Ada. People are hurting like hell. Don't you see that it's because of your damned church, and now it's destroying us, too?'

I asked him to not talk like that around the children.

'The children! What do you care about the children? They've already been poisoned, Ada. Ruined! They never even listen to me. Why don't they go to a normal school? Someday I'll send them away to a real school.' Then his anger grew hotter and his voice got louder. 'Their lives are being wasted with those women. Don't you see that I have to get y'all away from them? Those women are just a bunch of damned fanatics and prostitutes!'

I was horrified that he would use that language around the children and quickly sent them to their room. Seething with rage, Ben continued to say hateful things about my mother and my friends. When I tried to defend them, it only fueled his fury and he shouted louder. At one point, he drew back his hand as if to strike me. I held up my arms to shield myself, and he grabbed my wrists so tightly I expected to hear my bones crack. Then his anger exploded and pulling me close, he shouted right in my face: 'You are my wife! You will do as I say! Listen to me! Stay away from your GODDAMN MOTHER!'

I could see the children huddled in the doorway of their room. George was holding onto Emily and they were both crying. Hattie was trying her best to be the brave big sister, even though she's only six years old. I called for her to run get her grandfather, but by the time she was out the front door, Ben had let go of my wrists, so I called for her to come back.

SET APART

Ben shoved me aside roughly and strode through the open door, cursing and shouting threats as he went. I sank to the floor and drew my poor, frightened children into my arms. Once again, we spent the night together in the room we have all shared since shortly after Emily's birth. When I woke up this morning, Ben was gone. All of his things were gone, too. It was when I was staring at the empty space where his clothes had been that I felt the cold begin to seep into my bones. I want to get back into bed with every quilt in the house, but I have three little children who will be awake soon. How am I going to . . .? No. I won't think about that now. I know I can get warm in Mama's kitchen.

CHAPTER 11

"You must have been about two years old when your father moved to the plantation in Bluefields, Nicaragua, and y'all moved into the house on Pearl Street to share a room with Mrs. Agatha Pratt and her daughter, Anna," Sarah replied.

"Two mothers and four children in one room of the stone house? I'm sure that was an exciting time," Emily said, trying to recall the confusion. She shook her head. "I guess I was too little. I don't remember that at all."

"It worked out well, from what I understand, because that was when Mrs. Pratt was first studying dentistry. Your mother watched Anna while her mother trained with Dr. Lasater in town. Hattie and George were probably in the classroom much of the day," Sarah explained, "leaving her with just you two little girls to supervise."

"It's always seemed so natural for us to have our own dentist that I never thought about it being unusual until we got to Washington, D.C. The newspaper wrote a big story about us when we first moved there and made it sound remarkable that we were so self-sufficient. Of course we all sew, cook, make preserves, weave rugs, milk cows, and churn our own butter, but so do a lot of women in Texas. I suppose part of their fascination is that we've operated a successful business for so many years without help from any men. The woman dentist from Texas made the biggest headlines, though. And to think that my mother made it possible for Sister Pratt to be trained," Emily said proudly.

Agatha Pratt
Belton, March, 1881

When Ada and her children moved into the house on Pearl Street, it was the answer to my prayer. She and I are close to the same age, and her youngest daughter, Emily and my little Anna are just months apart. Even in this intimate group of women, I have yearned for a close friend. I'm not glad that her husband has left her, but at least we have that in common as well.

Just recently, Ada and the children and I moved into one of the new frame houses built on the McWhirter property. I know that Sister Mac and Major McWhirter have to be thankful that our four lively children are out of the big house.

One morning last week, I went to Dr. Lasater's office to return a book I had borrowed from him. After she and Emily and Anna walked Hattie and George to the classroom, Ada went out to work in the flower garden she's been talking about. Although it's still quite cold, the weather is finally pleasant enough for her to get the hotbeds behind the big house started, so the seedlings will be ready for spring planting. I'm glad that she's taking an interest in gardening again. It's the first time since Ben left in January that she's shown interest in anything.

When I returned, Emily and Anna were busily playing in a small pile of rocks that Ada had removed from the soil. Ready for a break, Ada shed her garden gloves as the four of us walked to the back door of the big house, opening it to the aroma of the morning's baking.

Inside, the kitchen was cozy and inviting and felt just like home, as it has since I first walked into Sister Mac's house the day after my husband left me. I was expecting Anna at the time, and I knew that Mrs. McWhirter would help me in my desperate situation. I've always felt welcomed in this home.

Major McWhirter was seated at the table in the kitchen, staring at half a dozen oil lamps. A look of relief passed over his face when he saw us enter the room.

'Morning, Papa,' Ada greeted her father as she hugged his neck. The little girls shrieked with delight and ran to his side. 'Where's Mama? She was just starting on the baking when I went out to the garden.'

I could hear the concern in his voice as Major McWhirter explained that his wife was having terrible pain with the facial neuralgia that has plagued her for several years. "She cooked breakfast, got the others off to their work, turned out the loaves, and then she went to her room,' he responded as he absently gestured to the cooling bread. He reached out and patted the little heads at his knee. 'It always acts up on her like this when it's cold outside. It's not hog-killing weather, but it's nippy this morning.'

We had taken off our coats and were starting to unwrap Anna and Emily when Major McWhirter stopped us. 'I'm fixing to walk out to the barn. Why don't you let me take my favorite little chicks along? Those roosters are hungry as horses and I'm sure they'll find these two mighty tasty.' He pecked at the toddlers with his fingers to make them giggle. Then he stood up, put on his jacket, scooped up a child in each arm and lumbered through the back door.

The kitchen was suddenly quiet. 'Poor Papa,' Ada spoke aloud. 'He loves Mama so much, and she still shuts him out.'

113

SET APART

Although I have the greatest respect for Major McWhirter, I have never been able to understand his relationship with his wife. I didn't know how to respond to Ada's comment. 'I thought your mother went to see Dr. Ghent about her neuralgia. Wasn't he able to help her?' I asked her.

Ada told me the doctor had prescribed laudanum for her mother, but that it didn't seem to do much good. 'Whenever she has trouble sleeping at night, she just heats up some wine to drink,' Ada reported. 'But she'd like to find something that will help her during the day.'

'Yes,' I agreed. We sat down at the table and began to fill the lamps with oil from a big metal can. While I trimmed the lamp wicks with scissors, Ada carried the sooty glass chimneys to the sink and began washing them.

As we worked in companionable silence, I thought about how much I admired Ada's amazing mother. I have met many godly women in my life, but none with the spiritual devotion that I see in Sister Mac. In the two years that I've been involved with the Sisters, I have seen her endure the estrangement of friends and family in order to follow what she believes is the Lord's will for her life and the lives of those she feels she has been chosen to lead. Whenever there seems to be a closed door in our path, Sister Mac is able to find the open window. There is a sweet fellowship within our community, and I feel fortunate to be able to play a part in this ministry of God's people to each other. I also appreciate the unique opportunity I have to be able to raise my daughter in this family of friends. I truly do not know how I could have supported the two of us on my own.

I picked up a cup towel and started to dry the glass chimneys that Ada had put on the drainboad by the sink. 'The pain must have kept her up,' I said as I set a clean chimney on the table.

'I've come to think that she doesn't ever get much sleep,' Ada replied. 'If it's not the pain, she's up recording a dream in her diary, or else she's praying. She once told me that sometimes she's up all night. Started years ago when she first heard the voice.'

Ada was quiet again, and as she concentrated on her washing, I looked at her face to see if I could tell what she was thinking, as I could detect neither admiration nor condemnation in her voice as she spoke of her mother. I'm still not sure if she's living here because she follows her mother's teaching or simply because working in the church offers her a way to support her family since Ben left. Only the Lord knows a person's heart. I've discovered sharing feelings to be one of the most difficult aspects of any relationship. Especially marriage. And as I learned from my own experience of being in a hurtful marriage, it becomes a habit to hide your true feelings. Ada's gotten very good at it.

As if she could read my thoughts, Ada abruptly changed the subject. 'Has Mama told you about our new opportunity for income?' she asked with a touch of humor in her voice.

'It's not more laundry, is it?' I groaned.

Ada smiled and I realized that it had been a long time since I had seen her happy. 'No, it's not, fortunately. A woman stopped Mama when she was in town the other day and asked about hiring one of us to do some cooking and cleaning. How would you feel about that, Agatha?' Before I could respond, she continued. 'You understand that in this small town, it's likely that we'd be working for folks we know. Mama said that it could be an opportunity to practice real humility.'

I thought about it for a moment. Humility was the right word, as we could very well be dusting some of the rooms into which we used to be invited for tea. I have to admit that the whole idea took me by surprise. Ever since the Dow brothers' trial last year, folks have gone out of their way to avoid speaking to any of us. How ironic for them to be asking for our help now.

'Perhaps it's the Lord's way of teaching us how to be servants in the world. A way to learn true humility and service. Your mother will tell us what He wants us to do. She always does,' I assured her.

This week, Ada went out on the first housekeeping job. I watch the children whenever she's gone, and she keeps them when I go to Dr. Lasater's office to study dentistry. I'm learning about a technique to remove the diseased portion of a tooth and replace it with a type of filling material, as well as how to do extractions and make dentures. Every time I go to the dentist's office, I come home with a new book to study. I know I couldn't spend as much time studying and learning from Dr. Lasater if it weren't for Ada's help with Anna.

Between taking care of the children, her gardening, and the new housekeeping job, Ada has been too busy to think much about Ben. If she misses him, she hasn't mentioned it to me. She is very close to all three of her children and gives them all the time she can spare from her busy work schedule. She is a devoted mother and a respectful daughter, but I've always had the feeling that if Ben returned and asked her to move with him to some other town in Texas, she would leave with the children and not look back.

CHAPTER 12

Emily smiled broadly as she thought of her best friend. "It's been so nice to have Anna with me in Washington. After we helped set up a room for her mother's dental office, we started exploring the city. We've been to the White House and all over town. I never would have imagined that government buildings could be so interesting. You should see the new styles in the city. Anna and I want to learn to ride bicycles and then buy some bloomers!'

In Emily's appealing smile, Emma saw the adventurous Ada she had known as a child and wondered how her sister had come to conform to the rigid rules of the sect. "Bloomers! Well, then. If y'all can get away with that, it sounds as if a lot has changed since the early days. In the beginning, I know your grandma had strict limits on both activities and clothing. The Sisters did not mix with the world socially or 'partake of its ways,' as she would say. They all dressed as plain as could be. No stylish fashions, no lace, no jewelry. I see that you're wearing a new waist with your skirt. It's very becoming on you."

Emily smiled her acceptance of the compliment. "There aren't quite as many rules these days, but I remember when there were. Anna and I delivered the eggs and butter to Mr. Hefley's store when we were small, and the children in town used to make fun of our 'sanctified clothes.' Grandma always told us that fancy dresses would only make us proud, but oh, how I wanted some pretty hair ribbons. It was hard to take the eggs all the way to Mrs. Hefley in the back of the store and not stop to look at all the nice things in the cases along the way. Anna and I used to dream about all the pretty dresses we could make with the lovely fabrics and trims we saw there. I don't know what happened to change Grandma's mind, but it's not quite as confining now for the younger girls. Anna and I like it ever so much better. We might even get jobs outside the church."

"I know you two enjoyed growing up together. When you were little, y'all stayed with Anna's mother for a whole week while your mother was with me," Sarah said.

"Really? I thought you said that once Mama moved in with the Sisters, you didn't see her anymore," Emily recalled.

"Yes, but this was on . . . business," Sarah replied hesitantly.

"Business?"

"It was about the time that the Sisters started to expand their business by going out into the town on nursing and cleaning jobs. Your grandmother thought it was a good way to get rid of any false pride the women may have had," Sarah explained.

"I've often thought about how awkward that must have been for the Sisters to clean in homes where they used to be received socially," commented Emma.

Sarah nodded. "That describes Ada's week with me. Awkward. Strange, isn't it, since we had grown up together." She paused for a moment, reflecting. "Jacob, my second child, was born a little earlier than we expected him. Mr. Miller was travelling with his job at the time, and Tennie and Papa were out of town for the week. First, I sent for the midwife, but when I heard that the Sisters were beginning to go out on private nursing jobs, I wondered whether Ada would help me until Tennie got home. I was so pleased when she agreed to come.

"When she first got to my house, though, I realized how unprepared I was to actually see her. It had been almost six years since we had last spoken, and the first few moments were very uncomfortable." Sarah hesitated, aware that it was time to clarify her relationship with the young woman's mother.

"I've been talking to you like I've always been one of your mother's best friends, Emily, but I'm ashamed to say that I was one of those who shunned her when she came back from Fort Worth. I'm afraid I wasn't a very good friend at all. To this day, I regret not calling on her the minute she returned. Nearly everyone was avoiding the Sisters."

Sarah looked away from Emily and glanced through the bedroom door at Ada's still form before continuing. "That was when Tennie was over at the house on Pearl Street so much. I blamed your grandmother and the other women when I thought we were losing her. The same thing had happened to so many other families. Then when Tennie came back to Papa, I didn't have the courage to make contact with Ada. When I suddenly needed her help, I had to swallow my pride. But I saw it as a good excuse to get to see her again."

Overcome with sadness at the memories that returned so vividly and the guilt of having rejected her childhood friend, Sarah stood abruptly and, with Emily close behind, walked into the bedroom. Ada lay sleeping in the eerie glow of the lamplight, her skin as pale and translucent as wax. Stripping off her gloves, Sarah sat and tended her friend of many years, cooling her hands and wrists with the dampened washrag.

"But she did come to help you," Emily prompted gently as she stood at the foot of the bed.

Sarah looked at Emily and smiled as she recalled the days following the birth of her son. "Yes, she did. Since the baby was born early, I was nervous about being alone with him. My daughter, Abbie, was there, of course, but she was only three years old, and I felt I needed an adult with me. Your mother arrived early the next morning, just as the midwife was leaving.

"When Ada came into my room, the baby was asleep. As she stood quietly beside my bed in her simple dress and apron, I studied her solemn face, hoping to see the girl I used to know. It was good to be with her again, but my heart was heavy as I realized what had been lost. Years before, our lives had been so similar. After all, we had grown up in the same household. She and Emma and I did everything together and had always thought of ourselves as real sisters. You could have read any of our journals from that time and not know whose it was. Looking up at her that day in my bedroom, I was filled with hope that we could at least still be friends, and I told her so.

"All she said to me was, 'I'm here on a job.' Her voice sounded so cold I actually felt a chill, and in that moment I realized that I no longer knew her. It was almost like she was a stranger." Sarah brushed away a tear with the back of her hand as she reached out to stroke the arm of her sick friend. "She changed Jacob's diaper in silence, and to fill the uncomfortable quiet, I chattered on and on like I do whenever I'm nervous. I knew that eventually she would have to say something. And she finally did. For a while, we made small talk. We talked about the weather, the railroad. I asked about the children and Ben, and she asked how Tennie was doing. That's when I thought for sure I'd ruined everything. I just knew she was going to walk out of my house and I'd never see her again."

"Why? What happened?"

Turning her head away from Emily, Sarah replaced the rag on Ada's forehead before answering in a hushed tone. "Well, when she asked about Tennie, I blurted out that she had never been happier since she quit the Sancties."

Emily gasped at the use of the hurtful slur. "No! You didn't! Did Mama leave? I would have turned around and walked right out of the house!"

Sarah bowed her head, remembering the day with shame. "No, she just closed her eyes and turned her face away from me. I apologized again and again. I couldn't believe I had used that term. She finished diapering Jacob, kissed his head, and handed him to me without saying a word. Then she turned around and left the room. I just lay there on the bed and wept as I nursed my baby. I was convinced she'd never speak to me again."

"And she stayed the rest of the week?" Emily asked, still bristling from hearing the familiar taunt.

Sarah turned her attention from Ada to meet Emily's hostile gaze. "Yes, but it really got better after that," she assured the girl. "We both knew that, while we were still linked together by our past, we would never be as close as we once were. It's strange, but it was as though my speaking that terrible word allowed us to acknowledge the differences that had come between us. We didn't have to pretend they weren't there. I'll always consider her my sister, though, and I hope she feels the same about me." Sarah looked expectantly at the sleeping woman as if she might respond.

"It was nice to be able to spend the week together, and I was hoping she might consider it more than just a job. She did comment once, though, that there wasn't much for her to do, since Sadie was really doing most of the work. Every day, Sadie washed the baby's diapers and did some of the cooking before she left to work here at the hotel," Sarah explained. "Mostly, Ada just kept me company."

Emily's eyes brightened as she made the connection. "That's right! Sadie, our colored woman here at the hotel works for you, too. Well, no wonder you knew everything that was going on with Mama. I was getting confused when you mentioned that you had lost contact with her for so long. You meant direct contact, didn't you? You were still keeping up with everything that happened to Mama through Sadie. That nosey old darkie."

"Oh, now, don't go getting Sadie in trouble, Emily. She only answers my questions. I've been concerned about your mother. I love her. You know that. Now it's my turn to help her, and I don't know what I can do." Her gaze fixed on the ashen face of her friend, Sarah pulled the sheet up to Ada's chin. After tenderly replacing the washrag on the warm forehead, Sarah silently walked toward the sitting room.

Sadie
Belton, May, 1881

I been workin fo the Mac-Whirter fambly since they move to Belton. They was six chilrens back then, includin them lil twin boys, Robert and Willie. The leastun, Willie, was mighty sickly and the Mistus, she need extry help with him and that's why I start up workin over there. Mistus Mac, she like to do her own cookin, but I done the laundry and housecleanin and I carry that lil child everwheres I go. I fed him ever time he opened that tiny bird mouf, but he still wouldn't grow hardly at all. Doctor couldn't find what was the matter. When all the chilrens took sick the next spring, the leastun, Willie, he turn blue as a berry, and one mornin he gone to be with Jesus. Mistus Mac, she don't come out her room fo days and days, she miss that lil boy so bad. She be prayin and readin her Good Book and not eatin nothin. Massa Mac, he glad I were there to help with the other sick chilrens while his wife be in mournin for that baby boy.

I likes being a house nigger. Befo the War, I work in the fields with my Mammy and Pappy. I members the day old Massa buy we'uns at the slave auction. First, he look my Pappy in the mouf and pinch he skin to see he be healthy, and then he buy my Pappy. Pappy beg Massa: Please Massa, I gots a wife and child! Massa, he see Mammy be strong and healthy and she get bought, too. Don't need no mo nigger chilrens, he say. Mammy and me, we cry and cry and ever nigger get sold but me. Then I hear: Goin once, goin twice, sold fo five hundred dollar! And the Massa, he have mercy on we'uns and he buy me too.

We work in the fields, but when I be sixteen, Massa move me to a cabin with Big Joe. Joe live by hisself in a cabin with a big fireplace on one end fo heatin and cookin, and I be thinkin: Massa want me to cook and clean fo that big old field nigger. But Massa tell Joe: You portly man. Sadie portly girl. You uns make me some strong nigger chilren. But the first night Joe try to crawl in my bed, I hit him with the fireplace poker and tole him: Git way from me nigger fo I busts yo brains out and stomps on em! Ever night, I keep that man offa me with the poker. Course, Joe, he take my poker so's I get myself a big pointy stick to hide under my bed. I cooks and cleans and works in the fields, but fo years, I make that man sleep on the dirt flo. Sometime Joe get so mad at me when Massa axe him why we'uns ain't made him no nigger chilren, but I gots the stick and I still keeps him on the flo. Then come the War and Joe get sold to a gentleman army officer. When

123

Freedom come, Pappy and Mammy and me works fo the Massa til we buys a farm. When the Mac-Whirter fambly move to Belton, I go to work fo them.

Mistus Mac, she have another boy child after lil Willie pass. This one name Sam. One night, she come home from a church meetin, sayin she be hearin the Voice of the Lord God A'mighty. Then she start all over again with the prayin and the Good Book readin and stayin in her room. I have to carry that Sambaby around and feed him, too, so's he won't die neither. He just cry and cry fo he mammy, but she won't see that baby or any other of them chilren. And poor Massa Mac, he beg and beg her to let him please, please come in the bedroom. The Mistus, she couldn't hurt that poor man worse if'n she beat him with a pointy stick. That man love, love that woman, but she won't have a thing to do with him after that night she hear the Voice of the Lord God A'mighty.

In a coupla years, Miz Emma and Miz Ada both gets married and moves away. Massa John and Miz Nannie gone, too. Just them two lil boys left. Robert and Sam. Massa Mac still waitin fo to move back into his own room with the Mistus. He sure do love that woman. But the only thing Mistus Mac care about is her lady friends what comes over to pray. Then some of them ladies move into the big house with they chilrens. Even Miz Ada move back into the house with her lil ones. They don't even tell me nothin, just speckt me to take care of more chilrens when they not in that classroom in what used to be a real nice, fancy parlor. They husbands always comin around the house. They begs they womans to please, please forget this foolishness and come home, or sometime they be havin a screamin fit at Mistus Mac. She always be runnin them off.

Not too far back, them ladies got a thought to start washin other folkses clothes. Now, this were a laugh to me cuz most of them ladies never even done they own laundry. Most all have nigger women over at they big houses washin they fancy clothes, just like Mistus Mac have me to do. When they start to washin in Mistus Mac yard, she have me show them women how to do it right. I learn them how to wash and rinse and rinse again. I learn them about bluin and how to cook starch and iron everthin just so. Like my mammy learn me. Can't hardly get over seein white women doin nigger work. Now they even cuttin firewood and cleanin other folkses homes. Maybe it were the War, but somethin strange done happen to these women.

They be doin so much of my work, I tell Moses, the driver what works for Mistus Sarah Miller, when I be in town one day. Moses tell me Miz Sarah, she done had her first baby at that time and need some house help. I axe Mistus Mac can I work there, too, and she tell me I have Freedom and I can work where I please, long as I gets her work done. Now Miz Sarah and Massa Miller gots two chilrens and I be raisin the both of them.

One time Miz Sarah axe me howcome I never jump the broom and had me some chilrens of my own. I tole her Miz Sarah, Honey, I already had me a talk with the Lord God A'mighty years ago bout that very thing. I tole Him: Ise sorry, Lord, but You just gotta find somebody else fo to plenish the earth. After Big Joe, I decided I had plumb enough of men fo one lifetime. And I figure Ise doin my share of raisin chilrens, even if they not my own.

In the evenins when I finish my work fo Miz Sarah, she be learnin me how to read and write, so's I can learn out the Good Book. I don't know if'n Ise ever gonna be able to read it front to back, but what I learn so far seem to be about a different A'mighty from the One what told Mistus Mac to turn her back on her precious fambly like she done. I been reading about a Heavenly Father what love, love he chilrens. We just posed to bleeve in Him and He begotten son, Jesus, love him back, and do what he say, like all good chilrens behave when they love they Pappy. Or maybe she been readin a different Book.

CHAPTER 13

Emily followed Sarah from the bedroom to the sitting room. "Don't worry, Mrs. Miller, I won't get old Sadie in trouble. I know she's a servant, but she's been around so long, she's really more like family. Of course, that also explains how she knows everything that goes on around here."

As she was putting a handful of photos back into the hatbox, Emma picked up on the conversation between Emily and Sarah. "I know just what you're talking about. You get so used to having the darkies around to help that sometimes you forget they're always there, listening to every word. I know you all trust Sadie, but it seems to me that whenever you can't figure out how a story gets all around town before you even finish telling it, you can usually trace it back to one of the servants."

"I'm sure that happens. But as far as I know, Mrs. Miller is the only person Sadie talks to who truly cares about the truth. That's obvious. The rest of the folks in town have always been content to simply make up their own stories," Emily replied, irritated by the thought of the many legends and vicious rumors surrounding her unconventional upbringing.

"But I've never believed any of those stories," Sarah insisted, "because I do know what really happens. And even though Sadie just talks and talks when she's at my house, I know she's truthful. She's really very bright, you know. When she first learned how to read the Bible, she went on and on, comparing the Emancipation to the Hebrews being freed from slavery in Egypt. She said that after the excitement about freedom had worn off, her family and friends began to grumble in the same way the Hebrews had when they faced their trials in the wilderness, where the free life was harder than they had anticipated. She said she wandered around in her own wilderness until she learned about God's promises in the Bible. While it didn't make life any easier, she was glad to be able to make the Lord her new Master. I've never seen anyone take to studying the Bible like Sadie does. I'll tell you that she has preached me many a sermon as she ironed my clothes!"

Emily contemplated this new information about the pleasant Negro woman who had always been an active presence in her life, but about whom she knew almost nothing of a personal nature. "Well, I don't know about her preaching, but Mama insists that Sadie is absolutely the best washerwoman there ever was. She was the one who helped the Sisters when they decided to start doing other folks' laundry. Even though we've used the steam laundry for years now, we still put what we call a 'Sadie finish' on the hand-washed items, and we also use her Mammy's recipes for starch and for getting out stains."

Emma looked up from a newspaper clipping she had picked out of the box. "Speaking of laundry, do you remember the washday arrest, Sarah?"

Suddenly mindful of the wrinkles in her new dress, Sarah primly arranged the folds of her skirt before answering. "Oh, goodness. Who could forget the washday arrest? I didn't need Sadie to tell me that story. It was well covered in the Journal. I see you found the article."

"What happened? Who got arrested?" Emily asked impatiently, aware once again that so much of her family history had been hidden.

"You really must get your mother to tell you these stories, Emily. She's had a very interesting life," Sarah said, emphasizing the words dramatically. "Or just ask Carrie or Ella Henry. They were both there. It happened right in their yard"

"Please. One of you must tell me who got arrested. You can't just leave the story like that," the girl insisted.

Ella Henry
Belton, June, 1882

This has to be the hottest, most miserable summer of my entire life. My usual job is to help Sister Rancier with the younger children in the classroom, since I'm fifteen and finished with primary school. On hot days like these, we usually teach the class outside under one of the big, old oak trees. Sometimes we even take a break and let the children wade in the creek behind the house. But on the days that the laundry rotation comes to our house, Mama expects me and Carrie to be out here in the yard with her.

Our lives are so mixed up. When Papa's not drinking, we live at home in our big house on Main Street. A cook fixes our meals and another colored girl cleans the house. Mama, Carrie and I spend our days working at the house on Pearl Street and come home in the evening to have supper with Papa before he goes to work at the saloon. On the nights Papa comes home drunk, though, he and Mama wake us up with their arguing. Then if he starts hitting her, we go straight to Sister Mac's house and spend the rest of the night. Sometimes we stay longer. This has been going on for more than ten years now. As long as I can remember, anyway.

SET APART

I wish we could just stay at the McWhirter's. Papa Mac is so kind, and Robert and Sam are just like brothers to us. Mama has to be tired of the way Papa treats her. Today was the worst yet.

Mama got up at dawn to start the fire under the black iron washpot in our yard. Soon four other Sisters arrived from the Pearl Street house with sacks and sacks of dirty laundry, already sorted. In another handcart were small washtubs, rub boards, soap and a bottle of Mrs. Stewart's bluing. Since the railroad came to town, the laundry business has just about doubled, and now we wash every day for several neighbors and for whole boarding houses.

Before the big pot of water was warm enough to start the wash, even before the sun was all the way up, the perspiration was dripping down our faces. Our long dresses were soaking wet by the time the first load of laundry was in the pot. We had our hot sunbonnets on by seven o'clock to keep our faces from blistering.

No one said a word. The only sounds to be heard were the rubbing and bubbling noises of the laundry. Sometimes a groan accompanied the lifting of a heavy paddle of wet fabric from a tub of rinse water. Otherwise, we worked in silence. It was too hot to even visit like we usually do to make the work go faster.

Just when we were going to take a break, I could hear that Papa was awake inside the house. 'Margaret! Where's my coffee?' he shouted loud enough to be heard outside. Mama stood at the bottom of the back porch steps and called back, 'On the stove, John, as always.'

I hoped he would drink his coffee and stay in the house, but Papa came to the back door. I could see him through the screen, squinting at the harsh sunlight.

'What the devil is going on here, Margaret? I told you yesterday to keep these witches out of my yard. My brother will be here from Georgia today and I want this rubbish off my property immediately!'

'Let me fix you some breakfast, John. I'm coming inside,' Mama said sweetly as she tried to soothe him. She took off her bonnet and started up the porch steps. But Papa banged open the screen door and stomped down the back steps toward the Sisters, fire in his eyes. He snatched the clean, wet laundry off of the lines and threw it on the dusty ground. He stormed over to the long bench that held the tubs of rinse water and turned it over. Washtubs, water and rub boards went flying in all directions. As we scrambled to collect the laundry and supplies, I was horrified to look up and see Papa as he scooped up handfuls of rocks from the yard and began to throw them at us. Meanwhile, Mama ran over to stop him and to try to salvage all the hard work we had done.

'NO, John!' She screamed at Papa and grabbed his arm.

He roared like a wild animal and threw Mama off. She was lifted into the air and landed hard against the wheel of one of the handcarts. Carrie and Sister Ada rushed to her side and used a clean towel to stop the bleeding on her head. 'Run and fetch my mother,' Ada told me. As I ran toward Pearl Street I saw Papa rush off in the other direction.

By the time I got back with Sister Mac, Carrie had Mama's head bandaged up. All of the laundry and supplies had been loaded back into the handcarts, and they were starting to put Mama on top of one of them. She was so weak and upset that she didn't think she could walk the short distance to Sister Mac's house.

We were about to leave when Papa returned with Sheriff Blanton. 'I'm glad you're here, Sheriff. These women have just been assaulted,' Sister Mac told him in an angry voice.

131

'These women, Mrs. McWhirter, are being charged with trespassing. I'm afraid I have to arrest them,' the Sheriff responded.

When Papa saw Mama all bandaged up and sitting in the handcart like that, I could tell he felt sorry that she was hurt. He started to walk toward her.

'Don't you get near her, John Henry!' Sister Mac yelled at him. 'Don't you think you've finally hurt her enough? For years, we've patched her up and calmed her down, and she's always gone back to you, but this time you've gone too far. Take a good look. This may be the last time you see her. Think about that.'

I have a feeling Papa won't be hitting Mama again.

CHAPTER 14

"This article will tell you how the Sisters got arrested for illegal laundering," Emma said as she scanned the clipping in her hand. "As I recall, four of them were involved in the laundry incident, including your mother."

"Mama arrested?" Emily questioned in pious disbelief. "Surely not!"

"Oh, yes. I'm afraid so. Mr. Henry didn't approve of the Sisters doing the laundry in his yard, and he had them arrested," Sarah explained simply.

"I can't imagine anyone being arrested for doing laundry," Emily said emphatically, convinced that Emma and Sarah were merely teasing her. She studied the two women's faces and was astonished to find no trace of a smile on either one. "Arrested! Well, then, I'm sure it's an interesting story, but I'm not surprised that I've never heard this one. Evidently, it's not something Mama cares to repeat, and even though all of the Sisters are as close as a family, there are still some things Carrie Henry is very private about. She hardly ever talks about herself. I'll be sure to read that article later."

Sensitive to Emily's feelings, yet anxious to provide her a more complete picture than what she would find in the newspaper, Sarah went on. "That was also the day that Mrs. Henry finally left her husband, taking Carrie and Ella and moving in with the Sisters permanently. At that time, Carrie and your mother were going to Temple every morning where they worked as day chambermaids in a boarding house. You probably remember that Ella Henry assisted Mrs. Rancier in the classroom and helped look after some of the little children during the evening prayer meetings."

Emily smiled. "I was one of those little children. I remember spending a lot of time with Ella when Mama was working in Temple and Sister Pratt was busy with dentistry. She was always so much fun. Just like Carrie. As I recall, she watched over me and Anna Pratt and Maggie and Mollie Johnson."

Sarah nodded her head. "Oh yes, Mrs. Johnson's daughters. I'm sure you were too young to remember when their mother was taken away. That's probably one more clipping your mother put in the box. I know I read about the trial in the Journal."

"I don't remember anything about Sister Mary Johnson being 'taken away.' Where did she go? What happened? Who's going to tell me?" Emily asked impatiently as she steeled herself for confrontation with yet another dramatic episode from the past.

Emma and Sarah looked at each other, still finding it difficult to grasp the full extent to which Emily had been shielded from the events that shaped the unique lifestyle she had inherited.

"Your turn, Emma," Sarah announced.

The older woman smiled uneasily. "At least this story has a relatively happy ending. I don't know how long Mrs. Mary Johnson had belonged to Mother's church when it happened, but she was living in one of the houses built by the Dow brothers, with little Maggie and Mollie, the youngest of her seven children. The girls were real little, perhaps two and four years old at the time, I believe, when Mr. Johnson died, leaving his wife a two-thousand-dollar benefit and expense policy from the Knights of Honor. Mrs. Johnson surprised everyone when she refused to accept the money from the insurance company, saying that insurance was a form of *gambling*. She insisted that she wouldn't have taken money from her unsanctified husband, anyway." Emma's dramatic hand movements underscored each vocal emphasis as she related the strange tale. "Mrs. Johnson's brother thought that was ridiculous, and when he couldn't get her to change her mind, he had her *arrested* and charged with *lunacy*. He maintained that a woman with seven children who declined that much money must be insane. So there was yet another lunacy trial here in Belton, and Mrs. Johnson spent over a year in the insane asylum in Austin."

"Oh, my goodness! No wonder I never heard that story," Emily said, her eyes wide. "So how did Sister Johnson get out of the asylum?"

Emma looked at Sarah and shrugged her shoulders. "I really don't know."

"I know," Sarah admitted hesitantly as she recalled the source of her information. "It was Sadie who told me that the way to get Mrs. Johnson out of the asylum came to one of the Sisters in a dream. A dream about Ireland, where Mrs. Johnson was in a castle and couldn't get out. When your grandmother made her interpretation, she said it was simply a sign that they should appeal to the governor of Texas, Governor Ireland, to release Mrs. Johnson from the asylum. And that's what happened."

Emily's mouth opened wide in disbelief. "Oh, my! I've never heard anything about that. You know, it's odd that no one has ever mentioned any of this. I can see that none of it was pleasant, but everything you've told me about the church is a part of my life. I should know these things." Emily's hands lay in her lap, clenched into tight fists. When she became aware of the tension, she extended her fingers, then discretely laced them together in a semblance of self-control. If she had learned anything from her mother, it was the importance of concealing one's emotions. "Don't wear your feelings on your sleeve," Ada always told her. "That's a sure way to get hurt."

Emma and Sarah pretended not to notice Emily's agitation. There was an uneasy silence in the room until, finally, Sarah spoke. "Emily, dear, perhaps that's the reason your mother has saved this box for so many years," she suggested. "It may be for you. She knew that someday you would be faced with the responsibility of making decisions about your own life, just as she had to do when she was your age. You're a young woman now, Emily, and big changes are coming. The opportunity to move to Washington. A new job, perhaps. It may be that your mother has preserved all of this information for your benefit."

Emily sat quietly for a moment, considering Sarah's suggestion, then suddenly rose to her feet. "Is anyone hungry? I think I'll go down to the kitchen and bring up a tray for Mama. She should be awake soon, and I know she'll be starving. I'll get a plate of leftovers from the club meeting for us." Without waiting for a response, she hurried from the room.

"Did I say something wrong?" Sarah asked after the door closed.

Emma put the collection of clippings back into the hatbox and replaced the lid, then folded her arms across her ample stomach as she leaned back in her chair. "No, Sarah. I think Emily's more than a little overwhelmed at the moment. She may have a lot of questions, but that doesn't mean she's prepared for some of our answers. This is a lot of information to get at one time. Especially when it's information that her own mother can't, or won't, talk about. You have to remember that even if Ada wanted to be objective about some of the things that have happened, she's still very much under Mother's influence. Always has been. And Emily's very close to her grandmother as well. I haven't been around Mother for years, but I can only imagine that after twenty years of controlling so many lives, she has only gotten better at it. And apparently, these women are happy to give her that responsibility. I'm sure you feel the same way I do about Emily, though, Sarah, that she should be able to make her own decision about whether or not to continue to be involved with this 'church'. Although my sister and her family have been sacrificed for the sake of what you and I know is a tragically misguided movement, I still don't know if Ada sees it that way. And, of course, Emily doesn't know any other way. In fact, she has less information than I expected."

"Well, I hope it's all right that we've answered Emily's questions so bluntly," Sarah said, her brow furrowed with concern. "I've just gotten to know Ada again, and I don't want to damage our renewed friendship. Somehow, though, I feel like we're doing the right thing. Then again, we know there are some issues we're not prepared to address at all."

"You're right. I've thought about that, too. But it seems to me that, as long as we're respectful of Emily's loyalties, we shouldn't pass up this opportunity to talk to her, Sarah. She'll be leaving tomorrow, and then we may never see her again. Once all the women of the church are together up in Washington, they may never return to Belton. And if they do anymore traveling, Lord knows Mother won't be coming here to visit me! I do think you were correct in suggesting that Ada meant for Emily to have the hatbox. If she hadn't wanted Emily to know what was in there, she would have destroyed it long ago. And Emily's right. She should know more about these things. After all, it's the church that has shaped her life."

"Shaped or warped? I had no idea your mother's church had strayed so far from the truth, Emma. I didn't know what to say when Emily told us that there were no more gatherings for Bible study or prayer. She herself described the church as nothing but a business. How can she make a decision for her own life based on that kind of foundation?"

"Shifting sand," Emma agreed. "You'll remember that in the beginning Mother was as well grounded as any preacher. I don't know what happened that day she had her vision, but I've always suspected that - if she didn't make the whole thing up - it had to have been the devil appearing as an angel of light. Papa always called it her 'delusion,' but I say it was deception. Although she continued to teach the Bible and preach a certain amount of truth, the trap of deception grew as she taught from those 'personal revelations' that contradicted Scripture. And now the whole group seems to have abandoned even that false gospel to follow the god of commerce. Like I said, purely shifting sand."

Sarah sighed and shook her head. "Poor Emily. What a legacy to inherit. We may have to keep some of this information for another time, though. She already seems overwhelmed by what we've shared so far, and it's getting late. There's so much more we could tell her. What time do the hacks quit running from the livery stable?"

"Oh, Sarah. Don't you worry about that. My buggy's over in the wagon yard, so I can take you home. It's on my way. But as long as we've stayed this late, you don't want to leave now. Surely Ada will be up soon."

Sarah smiled at her friend and reached over to pat the back of her hand. "Yes, and thank you for the ride. That will give us even more time to visit. It really is good to see you again,

Emma. It's been too long since we last spent any time together."

"Yes, this has been an unexpected reunion, although I do wish Ada were sitting in here with us. We did have some good times. Do you remember how she used to come running back into the bedroom after a midnight trip to the outhouse and take a flying leap onto the bed while we were all asleep?"

Sarah laughed. "Until the night we pulled the bed to the other side of the room while she was gone! We were lucky she didn't hurt herself when she fell on the floor. I can still remember the sound of her landing in a heap like a sack of potatoes. Who thought of that trick? Was it you?"

"Me?" Emma asked, feigning innocence. "Surely not. We can say it was Nannie, since she's not here."

"Do you hear from Nannie? Is she still in Breckenridge?"

"Yes, Mr. Davenport runs the newspaper there, and Nannie still writes from time to time. She has a daughter, Merlin, a son, Roger and little Gene is just four years old. They have a subscription to the Belton Journal mailed to them, so they get all the latest headlines. I try to keep Nannie up to date on anything else I find out about Mother. I really doubt whether we'll ever all be together again."

"I know you miss seeing her, Emma. I didn't realize she had a daughter named Merlin. How old is your Merlin now?"

"Oh, that boy's gone and made me a grandma! Named her Emma, of course. Birdie's married and Joe is off at The University in Austin. Only my little Nan and Doug are still at home. And yours?"

"Well, Abby's married and living in Fort Worth, and Jacob is down at Southwestern University. Daniel and Timothy went with their father on a rail inspection trip. They should be home by tomorrow evening."

Unable to keep her sister's scattered family out of her mind, Emma nodded vacantly. "And Emily will be long gone by then, I expect." Before she had a moment to dwell on that sad thought, though, the sound of Emily's footsteps on the outside stairs distracted her. "That must be our scavenged supper," she said with a laugh as she opened the door and took the heavy tray of food from the girl.

"Thank you, Aunt Emma. I dished up a little of everything that was left. I'm so hungry, it all looked good. I'll just go ahead and bring this chicken broth in to Mama. I want her to eat something if she's awake." Emily removed a covered bowl from the tray and disappeared into the bedroom, closing the door behind her.

As Emma placed the tray on the lamp table beside the settee, Sarah took note of the variety of food on the tray. "Oh, she brought up some of the Central Hotel's famous oyster stew! And do try this, Emma. I had it at last week's meeting. It's made with herbs from Ada's garden," she said as she placed a dollop of a flavored spread on a soda cracker. She and Emma filled their plates with leftover refreshments.

"Sarah, do you find it strange that the Wednesday Club chose to hold its meetings at the Central Hotel?" Emma asked as she poured two cups of tea.

"I've wondered about that myself. Actually, everyone knows there's really no better place in Belton, and you can be sure that the women of the club want only the best," Sarah replied, mocking herself good-naturedly. "Perhaps by showing up here each week, the club ladies are sending a not-so-subtle reminder to the women at the hotel of what they've given up, not only for themselves, but for their families, as well. Just think of it: If Ben and Ada had made some different decisions years ago, he would still be a successful downtown merchant, and she and Emily would not only be members of the Wednesday Club today, but of an authentic church, as well."

"Yes," Emma agreed. "I can see how that could be. And at the same time, by being gracious hostesses, or humble servants, the Sisters at the hotel send a return message that they're fulfilling what they believe is their God-defined role, to be set apart from the 'unsanctified.' I'm just glad that things have calmed down a bit. I'm sure there will always be bad feelings about the damage that's been done to so many families, but at least for now, the dust seems to have settled."

Sarah stirred sugar into her tea with a silver spoon. "I think 'seems' is the right word, Emma. If everything was really all right, I don't think your mother would be moving the church to Washington, D.C. I'm sure there's still some underlying hostility that we're not fully aware of."

"That may be, but I think we both know that Mother doesn't always need a good reason to do the things she does. Perhaps we'll never know what prompted this move. All I know it means is that I'll probably never see my sister again once she gets on the train to Washington."

Emily emerged from the bedroom and closed the door behind her. With a look of concern, she announced that Ada was still asleep. "Do you think I should wake her so she can eat something? That chicken broth is nice and warm right now, and she hasn't eaten anything since supper last night."

"I know that when I'm sick, I don't want to do anything but sleep. Your mother's resting comfortably and the doctor will be here real soon. You just sit down right here with us and fix yourself a plate. I know you're hungry." Emma fussed, filling Emily's teacup. "Sugar?"

Emily sighed. "Yes, please. You're right, of course. I'll stop fretting over her." Accepting the cup from Emma and leaning back on the settee, she tried to look more confident than she felt. "While I was downstairs, I saw Carrie at the front desk. She said she was glad to get a short break from Waco. She sure does have her hands full, managing both of those hotels at once."

"Two hotels? I don't know how she does it," Sarah commented.

Emily leaned forward to offer an explanation. "Well, if you really want to know, the Palmo and Royal are right around the corner from one another, and there's a back alley between them to make it a little more convenient for her and the other Sisters working up there. They're both outstanding hotels. The Royal has the nicest sample rooms I've ever seen. A salesman can display almost a whole train car full of merchandise at once. Both hotels have electric fans and message bells in the rooms. In Mama's hatbox, I saw the advertisements from the Waco City Directory for both hotels. They listed 'Mrs. Martha McWhirter, proprietress, and Miss Carrie Henry, manager.'" Emily smiled at the formal-sounding titles and put down the teacup in order to fix herself a plate. "Carrie's very capable. It's a good thing she enjoys staying busy because the Waco hotels are always full."

"Both Carrie and her sister Ella grew up in the church," Sarah stated as she thought about the number of children who had been influenced in much the same way Emily had. "Even before the washday incident. Isn't that true?"

Emma nodded her head, quickly wiping her mouth with her linen napkin so she could answer. "Yes, that's right. Mrs. Henry's been involved pretty much from the beginning. She and Mother have been close friends since the early days when we first moved to Belton. And we all have Mr. Henry to thank for the Central Hotel," she said with a smile as she lifted her delicate china cup in a mock toast.

"I had forgotten about that," Sarah admitted, laughing at the irony. "Despite the fact that Mrs. Henry and the girls moved out after the laundry incident, John Henry left the house to her in his will. When he died the next year, the house became hers. And a short time later, the Henry house became the original Central Hotel."

Margaret Henry
Belton, June, 1883

After John died, the girls and I went back to walk through the house. Even though it had only been a year since we moved out, the house looked long neglected.

Every time I went to town over the last year, I had to walk past my house, so I knew that John had done nothing to take care of it after we left. Weeds and wildflowers were so high that you couldn't see the front walk. Although I never was much of a gardener, I was proud of the hollyhocks Ada gave me to put at the front porch. Now even those are gone.

It made me sad to see the house in such bad shape. John and I were so excited to build it when he first came back from the War Between the States. I remember how eager he was to get home to me and our five children. He was full of energy and plans for starting his life again. The first thing he decided was that the family needed a bigger house, and we drew up plans to build the home of our dreams. We were proud of the two-story brick house roofed with gleaming metal. It was completed soon after Carrie was born. Then Ella came along, before her sister was out of diapers, to become the ninth member of the Henry family.

SET APART

When we came to Belton years ago, John started the first saloon in town with nothing more than a barrel of whiskey and a tin cup under a tree. There wasn't much here to brag about back then, just a small settlement they called Nolanville. A few years later, in 1850, Bell County was formed and the name of the town was changed to Belton. By the time John left for the War, the saloon was a thriving enterprise in a wooden building on the Courthouse Square, and John was a respected member of the merchant community. During the War, the children and I managed to keep it open, although it really turned into as much a restaurant as a saloon. Most folks paid by trading, but that was just fine with me. I was able to keep the family well fed.

When John first came back from the War, he was thrilled that he had a business and customers to come home to. Between building our new house and working at the saloon, he was busy from sunup to sundown. Although there were hundreds of Yankee soldiers camped in the grove on the south side of Nolan Creek, new folks poured into Bell County like rain off the roof. As it was before the War, John Henry's saloon was the place to go for a drink and a good meal after a hard day's work. Much of Bell County's early business and land deals were decided at our place. John was a good businessman himself and was known to never touch a drop of his own product. Everyone was glad to see good old J.C. Henry back behind the bar.

I remember how busy we were those first couple of years after the War. Even though we had seven children, the activity made us feel young again. I even convinced John to start coming to church with us. Every Sunday, the Henry family filled an entire pew at the Union Church. I was just about as happy as I thought I could be, so I didn't even notice when it was that John started drinking. I do remember that not long

144

after Ella was born, business started to slow down a little as more saloons opened downtown. They were all anxious to duplicate John Henry's success.

Some nights, John's friends had to close the saloon for him and carry him home. They told me that the drinking started when someone first got John to talking about the War. At home, he never mentioned the War. He also never explained the horrible scar I once saw under his shirt, and I never asked.

The man who came home drunk was a different man from the husband and father who had left for work in the afternoon. When he began to hit me, I was confused. I had never seen that side of my husband before. I tried being a better wife. I instructed the help to fix only his favorite meals and to clean the house better. I made sure I kept the children quieter. But he still hit me whenever he drank.

Then my friend Martha started a new prayer circle. I prayed for an experience like the one she shared with our group. If I were sanctified, I would have an excuse to leave John, like Martha encouraged me to. I suppose I was never fully convinced of my sanctification, or maybe my loyalty to John and our marriage vows was stronger, but I never did leave him. Not until last summer. And now he's gone and left me.

But he also left me the house in his will. The girls and I had been living in one of the houses on the McWhirter property, so when I first learned that John had left me in charge of the estate, I had no idea what to do with the big brick home. For a while I rented it out, putting the money into our prayer group's common fund.

Then Martha had a dream, and she decided that the Lord wanted the church to purchase the house from the estate and run it as a hotel and boarding house. Ever since the railroad came to Belton a few years ago, there has been a demand for

145

rooms to rent. With its location on Main Street, across from the livery stable, a hotel should do well. Martha's daughter Ada and my Carrie have been working as chambermaids in one of the new hotels in Temple, so they will be able to teach us what we need to know. I'm confident Martha will have the estate settled with my older children and the new hotel business organized in no time. She assures us that it's the Lord's will.

CHAPTER 15

"I never knew Mr. Henry, but we're all grateful to him," Emily said. "I think it was about three years after he died that Grandma and the other Sisters turned the Henry house into the first Central Hotel. That's really where most of my earliest memories are."

"Well, a lot happened before the hotel opened," Sarah responded. "The Sisters worked hard to expand the business. Sadie once told me that the church made five to six dollars a day on the sale of eggs and dairy, eight to ten a day on the firewood, and at least two hundred dollars a month from the washing, not to mention a dollar a day from each outside housekeeping and nursing job."

"That seems like quite a bit of money," Emma commented. "Back then, a farm family could live for a year on less than one hundred dollars cash. If business was that good, it may be that those articles in the Belton Journal worked to their advantage. Remember that the paper had faithfully covered all of the trials concerning the church. I don't know that Mother ever worried about what others would call 'adverse publicity,'" Emma said, shaking her head from side to side in amazement.

"Other newspapers must have circulated the stories around the country," Sarah suggested, "because your grandmother started getting a lot of mail from outside Texas. Do you remember reading the article in the *Texian*?"

Emma couldn't help but laugh "That reporter asked Mother some very interesting questions. I wonder if he had any idea what he was getting into. I know that I wouldn't want to try to keep control of an interview with Mother."

"Would that reporter be Neal Ramey? Here's something from the *Texian* dated August 22, 1883." Emily said as she read from a neatly clipped article she had taken from the hatbox.

Neal Ramey,
Editor And Proprietor, The Texian
Austin, Texas, July, 1883

When I heard about the women's community in operation right up the road in Belton, I was anxious to contact Mrs. Martha McWhirter, the noted founder and evangelist of the church at Belton known as the Sanctificationists, and find out more about this newsworthy experiment. When she finally responded to one of my telegrams, I left on the next train.

The McWhirters live in a large stone house on a quiet street just north of the business center of Belton. I understand that Mr. McWhirter is a retired merchant and investor. When she came to the door, I saw that Mrs. McWhirter was a much smaller woman than I had imagined. I assumed that the leader of such a well-known band would be a more formidable presence. She has dark red hair with no signs of gray, though she is fifty-four years old, as I found out later in the interview.

A very gracious hostess, Mrs. McWhirter kept me well supplied with cool water throughout our meeting. The summer has been extremely hot and dry this year, and for some reason,

I was more nervous during this interview than I have been in many years. It was clear from the moment we began that Mrs. McWhirter was in charge of the meeting.

I began by asking about her personal history and she was more than happy to provide me with details of her life. She was born Martha White in Jackson County, Tennessee, in 1829. In 1845, she married George Merlin McWhirter and moved with him to Bell County, Texas, in 1855. Of their twelve children, six are living. She told me that she joined the Methodist Church at age sixteen, but it had been a spiritual experience at a local creek sixteen years ago that put her in touch with God.

'How did that experience change things for you, Mrs. McWhirter?' I asked, knowing full well that it was the question she had set me up to ask.

'Well, that's when the Lord first started teaching me what is was to be sanctified, or set apart for Him,' she said. 'I realized that it was the first time I could say that with the teaching by His Spirit, I really started to know God. Just because we are raised in a country that acknowledges God does not mean that we all know Him. And, of course, we must know Him before we can obey Him. He can communicate with His people in dreams, much like He inspired the writers of the Scriptures. Today, He also gives us revelations and interpretations of the Scriptures in dreams.' She paused for a moment, expecting me to ask about the dream interpretation that has come to be associated with the women in Belton. When I let the comment pass, she continued.

'We can know God through reading the Scriptures, but not until we accept that they are written in figures or symbols. Jesus told the disciples it was written that way so they would understand, but the world that did not seek Him would be blinded to Him. Egypt was a symbol. John tells us in the book of Revelation that it represents the world. The wilderness that Moses wandered through with the Israelites symbolized their unbelief and unwillingness to surrender to God. Mount Sinai, the setting for the story where Moses received the law, represents the bondage of the Jews, while Moses at the summit shows us that living in a close relationship with God reveals His grace.'

She shook her head slowly and her face took on a scornful look. 'When I read in the newspapers that some men think they have found the place where Abraham, Isaac, Jacob, or some of the old patriarchs lived, I feel that God pities them for their ignorance. Words are symbols, Mr. Ramey. That's why the Scriptures are called the Word of God. We can't understand these symbols in the Scriptures except through the Spirit of God. We can't find evidence of symbols. We may study Scripture with our natural minds forever, and no two persons would interpret them the same. But by viewing the scriptures spiritually, all people will see alike. There is but one Spirit. There can't be any division in the body or in the true church of Christ.'

She looked at me to see if she could tell whether or not I had understood her. But I wasn't there to understand or believe. I was there to conduct an interview and write a news story. I kept my attention on my notebook as I recorded her words, trying to mask my feelings about what she was saying.

'Is that what you call your church, Mrs. McWhirter, the True Church of Christ?' I asked her.

She frowned at my impersonal attitude. 'We don't claim any particular name, but we do consider ourselves to be Christians. We address each other as "Sister" or "Brother," but in the town, we are called "Sanctificationists" or "the Sanctified." At present, we have forty-two members, including the children.'

'Is your church united with believers in other churches?' I asked carefully, expecting a forceful response.

To my surprise, Mrs. McWhirter chuckled. 'Mr. Ramey, you know the answer to that or you wouldn't be here. We're always happy to welcome folks who have surrendered to God's sanctifying power and choose to live according to His Spirit, but we can't unite with established churches in general.

'We believe them to be the Babylon spoken of in the eighth chapter of Revelation. We don't believe in or practice Baptism in water, but in Baptism by the Spirit that creates us. The water is another one of the symbols used in the Scriptures. It is a figure of cleansing and purifying. We don't take the Lord's Supper either. We can't possibly take it literally that, since Christ said that the bread and wine were his flesh and blood, we should eat it. This is a spiritual lesson, Mr. Ramey. Christ was telling his disciples "put me within yourselves" and that, of course, was His Spirit, the new covenant, which they were to look for after His death. No, Mr. Ramey, we aren't united with other churches. They have all lost sight of the spiritual and run off with the literal.' She paused for a moment, reflecting on her own words.

Her voice suddenly took on a harsh quality. 'In fact, we have been held up in the town for years as breakers of the peace and destroyers of the happiness of families, but we could not be the Christians that the Bible speaks of otherwise. They had to leave their homes. They were stoned, sawn asunder, slain with the sword and put to death in a thousand cruel ways. And why? Because their lives were different from their neighbors and families. It brings to pass the words of Christ that all men would hate us, our own children would rise up against us, and those in our own house would be our enemies. His words are being fulfilled here and now and wherever the life of Christ has been lived. We realize that we are strangers and that the world cannot know us because it is the enemy of God. In hating us, they are hating Christ.'

As she finished this speech, I was almost afraid to look up from my notebook, she sounded so stern. In that instant, I understood the power and control she held over the others. I have no intention of recording this impression for the newspaper, but it was the reason I had come to Belton myself, instead of sending one of the reporters. I had to know what kind of woman was behind such a successful movement, one that so moved its members that they would separate themselves from their own families. And although I had a thousand questions of my own about the things she said, I suspected that the content of her teaching really has little to do with her ability to lead her flock. Her self-confidence and strength of personality are absolutely extraordinary.

When I thanked Mrs. McWhirter for granting me the interview, she told me that she believed I had been sent by the Lord to let people know that what she teaches is the truth. I decided right then that I would print the interview just as I had recorded it and let folks decide the truth for themselves.

As I was gathering my things to leave, Mr. McWhirter entered the room. When he realized that I was a reporter, he got angry and threatened to charge me with trespassing.

Mrs. McWhirter calmly assured him that I was there at her request, whereupon her husband turned into a perfect gentleman. He apologized and explained to me that his wife had been often maligned and misunderstood by the local press. As a result, he felt a responsibility to protect her and the other women of the group from being mistreated. In that regard, I feel he has taken on a big responsibility. I was not surprised to hear that not long after the interview was published in the August issue of the *Texian*, he moved out of his house.

CHAPTER 16

"After that article was published, Papa moved out of the house," Emma said sadly. "Maybe after he read what Mother told the reporter, he realized that she wasn't likely to abandon her 'delusion,' as he used to call it."

"Or maybe it just got too crowded in the stone house," Emily offered. "Before we moved to the Henry house and opened the hotel, there were almost fifty women and children in the church. Some still lived in their own homes, but many had moved into the house on Pearl Street and those houses the Dows built nearby."

Emma shrugged. "Well, for whatever reason, Mother fixed up a room for Papa in the second floor storage area of the mercantile. She sent meals over to him every day and did his laundry regularly, but she never once went to see him after he moved out. That worked out just fine for me, though, because it made it possible to have nice, long visits with Papa. Until then, whenever I used to come over on the stage from Salado to see him, we always had to go and sit out by the creek to talk since Mother refused to let me come into the house, like I had some terrible disease. So believe me, I took advantage of him having that room over the store. He never came right out and said that he missed Mother, but he talked a lot about the old days.

"The old quilt on his bed brought back memories, at least to me, of how Ada and I had worked on it together one summer when we were girls. Papa had suspended a quilting frame from the rafters of the log house in Salado with ropes and pulleys so that we could pull it down to stitch and raise it up to get it out of the way. Ada always used to fuss at me as we quilted together because I was such a bad seamstress. Still am." Emma's expression brightened as her thoughts returned to the peaceful time before her mother's peculiar beliefs took shape. Her pensive gaze drifting upward, she looked as though she almost expected to see a half-finished quilt hanging from the ceiling of the hotel sitting room.

"Papa seemed happy to be surrounded by so many familiar things," she continued. "There were several photographs around the room, including one he had taken of the big house. He was so proud of that stone house, so happy to be able to build it for Mother. See if any of those photos are in the hatbox, Emily."

Once again, Emily explored the contents of the box. "Here's the one I think you're talking about, Aunt Emma. Grandma's up on the front porch, and Grandpa's standing just outside the fence. It must have been taken before he moved out of the house. Goodness! That little boy on the fence looks like my brother George," she said with a pleased smile as she handed the photo to Emma.

Emma nodded. "It sure does. Let's see. George would have been about six years old when Papa moved out. It looks just like him." Emma passed the picture to Sarah. "That photo tells the story, doesn't it? Mother and Papa on opposite sides of the fence. When I visited him, I got the impression Papa rather liked being by himself. At least the old wooden store had been replaced with a nice stone building by the time he moved over there."

"I seem to remember a lot of new construction in Belton about that same time," Sarah commented. "The streets were all torn up when they laid the new plumbing lines, and the old courthouse was replaced with that absolutely beautiful limestone structure. Of course, that was after Temple raised a fuss about wanting the county seat moved so the new courthouse could be built over there." Sarah made a face and shook her head as she thought about the ongoing competition between Belton and Temple.

"Both the Methodists and the Baptists built new church buildings, too," she continued. "Matthew Dow bought the old Methodist church building on Pearl Street and borrowed money from the Sisters to start a steam laundry business there. By that time, the women had accumulated plenty of money and considered the loan to be a good investment. For one thing, it meant they could stop doing the laundry by hand and take advantage of Mr. Dow's new washing and ironing machines. And then a short time later, when the laundry business failed, they acquired all of his equipment, plus the old church building."

Emma could not suppress her laughter. "How ironic! Mother and the other women ended up owning the church building they had been locked out of years earlier! I've never thought about it that way before. Like the chickens buying the farm. I'm sure they saw some sort of justice in that."

"Well, it was never a church again. Or a laundry business, for that matter," Emily explained defensively, failing to see the humor. "In fact, we stopped taking in other folks' laundry when we opened the hotel that summer and just used the facility for doing the hotel laundry. Although I do remember doing the washing for the college when it first moved to Belton."

"I didn't know that," Emma said. "But I did know that the Sisters donated money to help Baylor Female College get relocated here. Another Belton-Temple rivalry," she grumbled

155

with a look of distaste. "Y'all might remember that after the railroad bypassed Baylor University's original hometown of Independence, that community was all but dead by 1885. Since the Female Department had split from the men of the university, the search began for a new home for both institutions. Baylor University was soon relocated to Waco, while the Female College was looking to move to either Temple or Belton."

"Yes, here's the article," Emily interjected. "It says that Belton pledged to donate $11,000 toward the move - - one thousand dollars more than Temple's offer. So that's how Belton came to be a college town. By one thousand dollars. I know Temple can hardly stand losing that one."

Emily rummaged through the hatbox again and pulled out another news clipping. "Here's something else about the college, and judging from the date, it was just about the time we moved into the Henry house and opened the old Central Hotel. It's an article about the parade and celebration the day they laid the cornerstone of the first college building, Luther Hall." Emily's eyes brightened as she scanned the story about the festive occasion. "Why, I remember this. All of us children rode up there in the old wagon. Hattie, George, me and Anna, Mollie and Maggie, and a bunch of others. I was seven years old. It seemed so far away when we were small, but as you know, it's really less than a mile up Main Street. I've still never seen so many people in one place, not even on the Fourth of July. Were y'all there?"

Anna Pratt
Belton, April, 1886

I like living in the Henry house. Mama and I have a real nice room on the second floor. We have a new bed, the kind with metal springs under the mattress. It squeaks when you turn over. Mama made a new coverlet. She has another room set up downstairs with her dental equipment. There's a treadle drill, a lamp, and some other machines. I like the cabinet with all those tiny drawers for her dental tools. If I had a cabinet like that one, I'd put my feather collection in it. Mama is busy almost every day, working on real teeth or fixing false teeth. We helped Sister Rancier move our classroom over here, too. I like the new classroom. I get to sit next to Emily. She's my best friend.

Emily has a bedroom on the second floor, too, where she stays with her Mama and Hattie and George. Me and Emily got in trouble the first week after we moved in 'cause after we went to bed, we started tapping messages to each other on the wall between our rooms. It's a game we made up where we play like we've been stolen by the Indians and we can only talk to each other across the Indian camp at night by tapping rocks together in our secret alphabet we made up. Only, we had to tap on the wall. Mama moved our bed to the other side of our room.

Mama says the Henry house is a hotel now, the Central Hotel, even though no one has stayed here yet. She told me that railroad travelers will be needing rooms, and once the college opens this fall, other folks will come to stay here. I can't imagine what it will be like for strangers to be staying in our home that's also a hotel. Mama tells me that all of us children will eat in the kitchen, and the boarders and hotel guests will eat in the big dining room. We're supposed to stay out of the way at all times, except when we're doing our chores. After our class with Sister Rancier in the morning, we have chores to do all afternoon. There's a chart in the classroom to remind us. This week, me and Emily are working in the kitchen, washing and drying dishes. So far, we've only broken one glass and chipped a saucer, but we hid the saucer on the bottom of the stack. We're trying to be more careful, but drying saucers makes us start to giggle.

The new college that's being built up the road is just for young ladies. Me and Emily have talked about going there when we grow up, but we haven't told anyone. That will have to be our secret because I don't think it's a sanctified school, and we don't get to do much that's not sanctified.

That's why I was surprised when Emily's grandma, Sister Mac, told us we could go to the parade and celebration at the new college today. We were all up early this morning and dressed in our best clothes. We went out on the front porch of the house - - I mean hotel - - to watch the parade going right up Main Street. First was the Belton Brass Band in their fancy uniforms. Next were all of the firemen from Temple and Belton. Then came the school children from the Academy in their school uniforms, then all the rest of the people from Temple and Belton. Some walked and some went in buggies or wagons.

All of us sanctified children got in the old wagon, and Sister Mac's son Robert drove us up to the college road. I sat next to Emily. By the time we got there, the crowd was almost all the way out to the train depot on Main Street, but Robert pulled the wagon up as close as he could. We had walked up Main Street many times before to watch the men working on the big college building, so we knew that the dirt road to the college ended in a circle in front of the steps of the new building.

When we stood up in the wagon bed, we could see that they had built a platform over the steps for all the men who were going to give speeches. That's when we all got bored and jumped off the wagon to play in the bluebonnets. Me and Emily picked some flowers to put in our hair so we could play like we had hair ribbons. Maggie and Mollie copied us like they always do. Mollie cried 'cause she's afraid of the bees. She's afraid of all bugs and won't even touch a snail. When a fly gets on her food she screams her head off. I picked a bunch of wildflowers to give to Mama and found two new feathers for my collection. Blue jay. When the band started playing again we all got back on the wagon and went home. Tonight, the Belton baseball team plays a match game against the team from Moffatt, but I know baseball's not sanctified, so I don't think we'll be allowed to go watch.

CHAPTER 17

"Yes, I was there that day. What a proud occasion for Belton." Sarah smiled and nodded her head. "It reminded me of the Salado College picnic we talked about earlier, the one your mother went to when she was a little girl. Funny how history repeats itself."

"Funny? I hope I won't repeat much more of her history," Emily said quickly, thinking of the heartache and humiliation her mother had endured.

"Have you made some plans of your own?" Emma asked hopefully.

"Well, not exactly, but as I said before, Anna and I have talked about getting jobs in Washington, D.C. When you get a government job you can keep it forever, as long as you're honest. I hope you'll come to visit us there. I think you'd be surprised at how nice it is. On our street, it's so quiet, you don't feel like you're in a big city at all. We have a house with a large lawn, fruit trees, a chicken house and tomato gardens. There's a nice sunny spot near the carriage house for Mama's flower garden. I know she's already drawn a design for how she'll plant it. Just yesterday, she was out digging up bulbs and making cuttings of some of the plants she wants to take with her. I can't wait to show her the city."

Emma and Sarah sat quietly as Emily babbled on about Washington. Hoping that she wouldn't interrupt her niece's happy discourse, Emma gave her an encouraging nod as she reached over to turn up the wick on the lamp.

"Every Wednesday the Marine band plays a concert at the Capitol, and every Saturday they on the grounds of the White House. It's such an exciting city! We can hardly wait for the rest of the church - - or the Commonwealth, as Grandma calls it now - - to join us up there."

Sarah wondered whether Emily saw the move as a way to change the direction of her life or simply as an exciting change in her environment. "It sounds like things really might be different for you in Washington," she prompted, "as though you'll live in a whole different world. But, of course, as an adult, you will have new possibilities wherever you live. Opportunities for women are changing quickly, as you well know. There haven't always been many choices that women could make about their own lives, although your grandmother certainly challenged that notion in Belton."

Sarah leaned toward Emily and patted the girl's arm. "I'm sure you realize that you'll be faced with making some decisions of your own that could affect the rest of your life. Now, I'm not here to give you advice on that subject, of course, but just remember that whenever you don't make your own choice, you'll be the victim of someone else's." Leaning back in her chair, Sarah paused to let the meaning of her words sink in before steering the conversation toward a lighter subject. "It sounds like you'll enjoy living in Washington, and I think your mother will, too. She's told me how much she's looked forward to receiving your letters."

"After seeing some of the things she's tucked into this hatbox, you won't be surprised that she keeps my letters in here, too," Emily exclaimed as she withdrew one from a ribbon-tied bundle. "Oh, but this one's not from me," she said as she noted the unfamiliar handwriting. "Hmmm. It's from

Uncle Robert. Judging from the date on the postmark, he must have written it right after he moved to New York City."

"I'm glad to know that Ada keeps up with Robert. I'm sure Mother instructed him to stay away from me," Emma said, a frown creasing her forehead. "I haven't seen or heard from my brother in years."

"Well, we don't see much of him or Uncle Sam either," Emily admitted. "When I was growing up, they didn't live with us. They were living and working with the Dow brothers, and we only saw them on Sundays when they came over for dinner. Then not long after we moved into the Henry house, Grandma sent Uncle Sam to Nicaragua to work on my father's plantation, and she sent Uncle Robert to New York City to sell pianos. A while back, the church bought a boarding house up there, and now he's the manager."

Emma's frown changed to a look of genuine concern for her brother. "I felt so sorry for Robert when I learned that he had been sent to New York. At least Sam was going off to work with Ben. Except for the piano salesmen he knew from their sales trips to Belton, Robert was totally alone in New York City at the age of twenty-one. I know he must have been miserable."

Carrie Henry
Belton, May, 1886

Ada and I have been making the trip to Temple every day but Sunday for almost three years now. We leave in the buggy before sunrise and don't get home until after dark. Our work as chambermaids there has taught us much about service and even more about business. Sister Mac has decided that since

162

we have opened our old Henry family home as a hotel, Ada and I will soon stop going to Temple so we can work in Belton at what we're calling the Central Hotel. I can't say I'll miss the long buggy ride.

Last night when we got home, Ada and I unhitched the horse the same as we always do. She went inside and I led the horse toward the barn behind the house. I was telling Jack, the horse, about my day in Temple. He's good about letting me complain as much as I want to. When I thought I heard him say my name, I laughed and decided that I must be very tired. Then as we got closer to the barn, I heard another noise and jerked my head up to see something moving in the shadows. 'Who's there?' I called out loudly, sounding much braver than I felt. There was no answer, but the figure moved again.

I tried to hide behind Jack, to turn him between me and whatever was hiding in the dark. All I could think of was the panthers that sometimes come down from the hills. And the bears. I expected to hear an animal growl, but all I heard was my own racing heartbeat pounding in my ears. What was hiding in the darkness?

There was another movement and I could see the dark silhouette of a man. Pressing myself close to Jack's damp side, I closed my eyes and fought the urge to try to outrun the stranger. "Who's there?" I called again.

Suddenly, I sensed him standing right in front of me, but before I could scream, he put his hand on my shoulder. 'Shhh, Carrie, It's me, Robert.' All I could do was stare up at him, weak with relief.

I didn't know whether to laugh, cry or hit him. He pried the bridle from my hand and led Jack into the barn. I followed numbly. 'I have to talk to you, Carrie,' he told me as he poured out Jack's feed. 'But the whole house doesn't need to know I'm here.' I felt my fear melt away, thawed by the heat of anger that grew as I watched him calmly complete my chores. Then he took my hand and led me into the moonlight behind the barn. Outside, my words hit him hard and fast.

'What are you doing here? Why did you have to scare me like that? Tomorrow is Sunday. You know I'll be home and you'll be over for dinner. We can talk then.' I yanked my hand away and shook my finger in his face. 'Don't ever do that to me again.' I spun around and started toward the house.

'No, wait Carrie,' he said, grabbing my arm and pulling me back. I was fighting mad, but as I turned toward him to glare into his eyes, I realized something was wrong. Robert was holding back tears. I recognized his expression from years ago when his dog, Barney, got kicked by a mule, and he hadn't wanted me to think he'd cry about a pup. He's usually not afraid to let me see him cry, but for some reason, he was trying to be brave tonight. My anger evaporated as I saw the look of utter despair in his eyes. 'I'm sorry I frightened you,' he said. 'But we can't talk tomorrow because I'm leaving first thing in the morning. I waited for you to come home tonight so I could tell you goodbye.'

I wanted to believe that Robert was playing a mean trick on me, like he did when we were kids and he convinced me that the deer bones he found in the old Indian cave on the creek were the remains of a cannibal feast. But I knew instinctively that this was no trick. 'What do you mean "goodbye"? Where do you think you're going? Robert, you're my best friend. You can't leave me.'

He looked away and shoved his hands deep into his pockets. 'Mother is sending me to New York City,' he said quickly with little emotion. 'She's made arrangements for me to go with the piano salesman and work with him up there. I'm already packed and I'll be on the early train in the morning. I just had to see you before I left.'

164

I couldn't say a word. Although there had always been talk of Robert and Sam leaving Belton to work elsewhere, I thought that meant Temple or Waco or, maybe, McGregor. Why New York City? I couldn't picture Robert alone in that strange place. And selling pianos? Robert's not as big as Brother Matthew is, but he's a good carpenter, not a salesman. I put my arms around him and hugged his neck as tightly as I could, ignoring the tears I couldn't hold back.

Robert put his arms around my waist and his head sank to my shoulder. 'I couldn't leave without telling you that I love you, Carrie Henry,' he whispered. 'I always have.'

Determined to stop my crying, I held my breath, unbidden memories of our childhood together filling my head. He was in every scene, as I had assumed he always would be. I simply couldn't see myself without him, my best friend. As we stood in the familiar embrace, I wanted to hold on to him forever and never let go. But suddenly the fatigue from my long day and the overwhelming burden of emotion began to make me feel dizzy and a little ill. I let go of his neck and sat down on the pile of firewood behind the barn, leaning over to wipe my eyes with the hem of my apron.

'Would it help if I talked to your mother?' I asked as I looked up at his somber face, now bathed in moonlight.

Amused at the thought of me trying to influence his mother, he grinned, despite his sadness, and shook his head. 'She's already made up her mind, Carrie. I'm twenty-one years old, and she thinks I've been here too long as it is. She can't have me living with all of you women. That's what this is all about. It's okay. Mother says I can expect visitors often.'

He reached out to wipe away my fresh flow of tears, but I took his hands in mine so I could study them. I wanted to memorize the shape of his nails, the scar from the fireworks accident, the curve of his little finger, broken when he fell out

165

of the pear tree beside the smokehouse. 'Now what?' I asked as I turned his palms up and traced his carpenter's calluses with my finger.

'Now we pray, Carrie. Pray for a sign from God that He intends us to be together,' Robert said, his hands gently closing around mine.

Of course. Why hadn't I thought of that? 'Thou hast given him his heart's desire and hast not withholden the request of his lips.' After all, that's what the Bible says.

'Will you pray with me?' Robert asked softly as he pulled on my hands until I was standing to face him. I lowered my head and the tears fell again. Our hands locked together, Robert prayed. 'Our gracious heavenly Father . . .'

I heard his voice, but not the words. I was in the prayer, in the rhythm and warmth of it. It wrapped around me and through me, and I felt pure and light and good. I wanted to stay right there in the prayer, in that moment, for I had everything I could ever want or need. A joy that I could feel and taste and hold on to forever lifted me higher and higher. But too soon, the prayer ended. In the stillness after his 'Amen,' the comfort and confidence ebbed away, and I was left floating in the empty silence. Then I felt his face against the top of my head, and the gravel under my feet. He breathed deeply, slowly releasing my hands. I knew he was trying not to cry. Brave Robert.

Drained of energy and determined not to look into his eyes, I grabbed his arm and held on as he walked me to the back door. We parted in silence. There was nothing more to say. I didn't even watch as he walked away into the darkness.

As soon as I got into bed, I fell into a deep sleep, praying for a dream that would explain what was happening. This morning I woke in a panic as I realized that I probably would never hear from Robert by mail. As is our custom, all of his letters will be read to the whole church. And even if I did write to him, I couldn't buy a stamp. Sister Mac handles all correspondence, as well as our requests for personal spending money. If, like he said, he's being sent away in order to be separated from the women of the church, it's hopeless to think that his mother would allow us to communicate, even as friends. What now, Lord? Can I trust our prayer that somehow You will bring us back together? Will You grant us our heart's desire and not withhold the request of our lips?

CHAPTER 18

Emily opened Robert's letter and read aloud, " 'To all, I am writing, hoping all is well in Texas. You are my family and I feel I must write honestly. I miss you all and ask that someone in the church come to visit me here. I know I cannot leave at present because of my job, so I am asking that two or three in the church please come to New York as soon as possible. Love to you all, Robert W. McWhirter.'

"Here's another one he wrote a few weeks later." Emily scanned the page for something of interest. "He found a room in a nice boarding house, and the other boarders were helpful," she reported. "But he says, 'Sometimes I think they are friendly just so they can hear me talk, while I think it is they who are the ones with the queer-sounding speech.' Uncle Robert does have a drawl."

"And, of course, we don't," Emma declared with feigned sincerity.

"Not even a trace," Sarah agreed, pronouncing each word carefully.

Ignoring their comments, Emily opened another letter. "He wrote this one after he went to the unveiling of the pedestal for the Statue of Liberty. Let me see. Yes, that was on October 28, 1886. He went with new friends he had met at the boarding house. Listen to what he wrote: 'It was, unfortunately, a very gray and rainy morning on the day planned for the festivities.

But nothing stopped the grand celebration. The parade came right down Broadway, just blocks from my boarding house on Twelfth Avenue. In the parade, which was four miles long, there were a hundred marching bands and twenty thousand marchers. I got that information from reading Frank Leslie's Illustrated.'"

Emily continued reading from the Central Hotel stationery that Robert had taken with him to New York. "'Because of the rain, we did not follow the parade down to the Battery, but from there one could see the nautical revue which followed. President Cleveland and his party, including Mr. Bartholdi, the Statue's artist, boarded a ferry for Bedloe's Island. There, after speeches and songs, they unveiled the face of the monument, which had been covered with the flag of France. The Illustrated described the hundreds of ships and boats in the harbor around the island blowing horns and whistles for a full fifteen minutes. I will save the newspapers for you to see when you come to visit.'" Emily made a sad face. "Poor Uncle Robert. He was still hoping for a visit. I think it was years before anyone went up there."

Emma struggled to control her trembling hand as she reached for the letter that Emily held. "My brother was shamefully neglected. Not only was he sent away from home to live alone in a strange city, but he wasn't even told that Papa was ill. Look," Emma said, pointing to the letter's date. "He wrote this just three months before Papa died, and he had no idea his father was even sick."

"I remember when Grandpa's died," Emily recalled sadly. "It was right after my eighth birthday. He had been sick most of the winter. I'm surprised Grandma didn't write to tell Uncle Robert. Mama was worried about Grandpa and went over to his room pretty often to check on him. Sometimes I went with her.

"One time when he was sick in bed, he asked if Grandma had come with us. Mama said no, but suggested that she would come if he asked for her. He got angry and said 'I am not going to beg my wife to visit her own husband when he's dying.' Mama got mad then and told him, 'I wish you'd both stop being so stubborn. I know that you want to see her and she wants to come. Somebody has to give in or you'll both be sorry.' Grandpa Mac just shook his shaggy white head, and said, 'Nope. She's the one who'll be sorry. I'll be dead.' He just laughed and laughed." Oblivious to the fact that the older women saw no humor in the tragic scene, Emily continued. "Then he told Mama, 'Don't you tell that woman I asked for her, Ada, 'cause I won't do it.' That was the last time I ever saw him."

"My mother never went to him before he died, did she?" Emma asked.

Emily shook her head slowly. "You know the answer to that, Aunt Emma. Grandma said she wouldn't go to him until he asked for her. And despite the fact that she never came to his room, he still left her in charge of his estate."

"That surprised everyone, including Mother," Emma recalled. "Regardless, it was a very dignified and well-attended funeral. With the store and his other investments, he was a very important man in Belton trade. And since he was past Grand Master of the Masonic Lodge, he was buried with the full ceremony. The whole family was there. Except Mother."

"And Uncle Robert," Emily added. "He came down from New York a short time later, looking so different in his fancy city suit and his hair cut in a new style. I just remember how terribly sad he seemed." Emily took the letter Emma handed her, refolded it and slipped it back into the envelope.

Robert McWhirter
Belton, February, 1887

Even though I never expected Papa to last long living apart
from Mother, the news of his death came as a shock to me.
One thing that made it all the more heartbreaking was
knowing he always believed that Mother would come back to
him someday. I knew she never would. She once told me that
after she started having her revelations, a stone wall grew up
between them that rose higher and higher until they were
completely hidden from each other.

Although I could only imagine what sorrow awaited me
there, I was anxious to get back home, even if only for a short
stay following Papa's funeral. I've been in New York City for
almost a year and know my way around fairly well, but I am
still lonely for a familiar face. I have visited many churches
and find that they are still preaching the same old-fashioned
Methodism. Likewise at the Salvation Army.

On the train ride back to Texas, all I could think of was
seeing Carrie. If I could have one of the church members
come to New York to keep me company, of course I would
choose Carrie. We have been friends since childhood, and I
miss her terribly. She was sitting at the front desk of the
Central Hotel when I went there to visit Mother in her room,
but, under the circumstances, we didn't have a chance to
speak.

I stayed at the Pearl Street house, and that was fine with
me. It felt good to be back home, even though everything in
the big old house reminded me of Papa. He was so proud to
have been able to build the house just as Mother wanted it. I
know he always thought he'd live there with her again.

Being in the house also reminded me of Carrie and all the nights she and Ella came over with their mama when Mr. Henry had been drinking. The girls were there so often that they left their favorite dolls hidden under the stairs where they thought Sam and I couldn't find them.

It breaks my heart that I can't write to Carrie. She is always in my thoughts and prayers. As it turned out, the only time we got to be alone together during my visit was when she drove me to the train station the morning I had to return to New York.

Although I had left two feet of snow in New York and had on my heavy, new overcoat, the chill that last morning in Belton just about took my breath away. Carrie drove up in the hotel buggy before sunrise. After throwing my bag in the back, I took the reins. The warmth under the lap robe came as a pleasant surprise, as Carrie had gone to the trouble of putting a heated and wrapped brick on the floorboard at our feet. We hadn't spoken since the night before I left Belton last May, and after 'good morning,' the silence between us was awkward. Neither of us said another word until we were all the way up Main Street, past the new college road.

'Do you like New York City?' Carrie finally asked me. I opened my mouth to answer, but no words came out. At the sound of her voice, my throat suddenly closed and I had to swallow hard to get past the lump. The silence continued, broken only by the painfully familiar rhythm of Jack's hoofbeats on the dirt road. Carrie must have sensed my mood, for she said no more.

The beautiful quiet of my hometown only increased my sadness. It's never quiet in the city. Even at night I hear the sounds of traffic, trains and people, echoing on the bricked streets and sidewalks. The streetlights stay on all night in the city, too, I remembered as I noticed the morning stars shining in the predawn sky.

In a moment we were at the depot. A dim lantern in the window of the building was the only other light in the darkness. I stopped the buggy, put down the reins and turned to face Carrie. 'I hate New York City,' I told her through clenched teeth.

'But your letters . . .' she began. Then she looked at me. 'Robert, why haven't you said this before? You really hate it?'

By then, I was choking back sobs. I was so embarrassed. Carrie saw me cry lots of times when we were kids, but I certainly hadn't expected to leave her this way. It made me angry and I picked up the rough wool lap robe and scrubbed it across my face, determined to halt my embarrassing display of weakness. But when she put her hand on the back of my head, I couldn't stop the tears. Unable to contain all the emotion of Papa's death, leaving Carrie again and having to return to the city alone, I hid my face in the robe and wept like a baby.

'I don't know what to say, Robert,' she said softly as she soothingly stroked my head. 'You looked so nice in your new suit yesterday, I thought that you must be enjoying the city. I was afraid you might have already outgrown us country folks.'

My head was still down, but I could hear the familiar teasing in her voice in her attempt to cheer me She knew I had no choice but to get on the train and leave Belton once again. Remembering all the years we had managed to chase away each other's sorrows with good humor, I smiled in spite of myself.

I took a deep breath and lifted my head, although I knew I looked a sight. She put her hands in her lap. 'Robert, I'm truly sorry that you're so unhappy in New York,' she said in a more serious tone.

I had to look away from her to keep from crying again. 'I hope you've been thinking about what I said before, Carrie. I keep praying for the opportunity for us to be together. I have to find a way to get back home. God will bring me back. He has to. I can't stand it up there alone much longer.'

'You must be very lonely. Does your mother know how you feel?' Carrie asked.

I studied her face in the dim light, her expression sympathetic. 'I've told her I want to come home, but never in quite this way.' I tried to smile, but Carrie understands the control Mother has over my life. 'I feel so worthless when I'm up there, Carrie. I haven't made one friend. There must be something wrong with me. I can't even...'

She mercifully put her fingers over my mouth to stop the flow of self-pity, and this time I managed a smile beneath her touch. Before she could remove it, I caught her hand, and gently kissed her palm. She smelled so clean and good, it made my heart ache. I told her how much I missed her.

'I think about you all the time, too, Robert. You're in my prayers day and night. I . . .' Then we heard the train whistle.

I wanted to gather her in my arms and never let her go. I wanted to hold on tight to the one person who makes me feel I have value as a man. Instead, I took both of her hands as I had done that night behind the barn. 'Let's . . . pray now,' I stammered. In the closeness of the covered buggy, I leaned toward her until our heads met and instantly I felt joined to her. If only I could take that feeling of wholeness with me all the way back to New York, I'd be truly happy. Sitting together with her like that in the buggy, I realized how much I consider Carrie to be a part of my life. I've always thought that she could see inside my heart, things even I couldn't see. As I

174

poured out my prayer, I envisioned that our hearts had become one flesh. That vision filled me with new strength. And hope. Perhaps I can talk to Mother.

CHAPTER 19

"It fell to your mother to make Papa's funeral arrangements, since I was living in Salado at the time," Emma told Emily, not mentioning how uncomfortable she would have felt around Martha during the difficult period. "As it turned out, that was the beginning of a hard year for her."

"Yes, and a very complicated year as well," Sarah agreed. "Your grandfather died in February, and understandably, your mother was quite distraught. With Ben out of the country, she had come to depend on her own father for a number of things. His death was not only an emotional upset for her, but also left a huge void in her life. She didn't have long to grieve, though, before Ben suddenly appeared in Belton in October. After not seeing him for six years, I'm sure it came as a shock when he suddenly asked for the . . . divorce." Sarah said the last word hesitantly. Although the divorce trials that had plagued the tiny town for decades were inescapable public knowledge and the source of endless gossip, divorce was still not an acceptable topic of casual conversation among ladies. And although Emma had already gone beyond the limits of polite conversation with her mention of celibacy, Sarah still reddened slightly as she spoke the word.

Astonished that Sarah was the one to bring up the sensitive topic, Emma regarded her friend's flushed face. Deciding that Sarah's hesitation indicated she had surprised even herself, Emma filled the pause with what she learned at the trial.

176

"Apparently, Emily, your father had tried to contact your mother a few times and had even returned to Belton once, but each time a note came to the hotel from Ben, Mother intercepted it."

Without dwelling on Martha's interference, yet hoping Emily grasped what Emma had said, Sarah composed herself enough to continue. "Yes, that's right. But that day in October, Ben sent his lawyer instead of a note. When the lawyer met your mother at the front desk, he informed her that, as their father, Ben had complete control over the children. Your grandmother was there and had more than a few words with the lawyer, Mr. Boyd, insisting that you children belonged with your mother. According to the law, he told her, that was not the case. But the main reason for his visit to the hotel, Mr. Boyd announced, was to tell your mother not to worry about little George when he didn't come home for supper. Your father was back in Belton and saw your brother on the Avenue. It seems they spent the afternoon together, and when Ben left, he took George with him," Sarah explained.

"Took him?" Emily repeated, her eyes wide. "Is that how it started? Oh, poor Mama. What did she do? Where did they go?"

"Sadie told me that Ada was frantic," Sarah said. "I can only imagine how upset she must have been. George was ten years old at the time and hadn't seen his father since he was four. Not only did Ben virtually kidnap his own son, he took George all the way to his sister's house in Michigan."

Emily nodded her head. "So that's how he got to Aunt Mary's. All I remember is that we were separated from George for a time. I didn't know that he had been snatched off the street! It was a terribly confusing time, and Mama just wasn't herself. I know she must have been beside herself with worry, and it's no wonder. She's seen George only once since then, you know, although I couldn't begin to count the number of letters and telegrams she's sent and the telephone calls she's made to locate him through the years. But she never talks about that, either." Emily sat very still, reflecting on the burden of sorrow her mother carried in quiet, but painful resignation. As she bit a hangnail, she looked much like she might have as an eight-year-old that day, confused and worried about the turmoil in her family, and still not fully understanding all the issues involved.

Sarah's heart went out to Emily. "Well, just a few days later, when the divorce papers arrived, your mother had something else to cope with. In fact, over the next few weeks, several of us were officially served with papers regarding our depositions. The trial was scheduled for the middle of December."

"I didn't realize that you had to be involved in that nightmare, Mrs. Miller. Mama assured us that it would all be over quickly, saying that things would be back to normal again by Christmas. We tried to prepare for the holiday as if George would be back any minute," Emily recalled sadly.

"There's no good or convenient time for something like that to happen, but I'm sure it was especially difficult for Ada to deal with legal proceedings and to think about celebrating Christmas as well," Sarah continued. "No one at the Courthouse seemed to be concerned about such matters, though. All of the lawyers were men, of course, and every man in the county, including those who would serve on the jury, had already made up his mind on the subject of the women at the Central Hotel.

"I've often wondered whether your grandfather's death opened the door for what happened . . . if someone talked your father into attacking the church in that way. I always thought it strange that, after having been away for six years, he would

178

suddenly decide to divorce your mother. It just didn't seem like something Ben would do on his own. Major McWhirter was highly respected by everyone in town, even though he always defended the women. Without him, they were much more vulnerable, and it seemed like a very strange coincidence for the divorce to come so soon after the Major's death. No one would have dared go after the Major's own daughter while he was still alive.

"Looking back, it's obvious to me that the divorce trial, like the trials of the Dow brothers and Mrs. Johnson, was nothing more than an attack on the church. Your mother and you and Hattie and George just happened to be the most seriously injured. I am so very sorry, my dear." Her own eyes filling with tears, Sarah folded Emily into a comforting embrace.

Ada Haymond
Belton, January, 1888

The divorce trial is over, but I'm not really sure how I got through it. What I remember of that whole period is in pieces, like fragments of a dream in which nothing makes much sense.

The first piece I can recall was when I was told Ben had taken little George. I remember screaming at Mr. Boyd as I started toward the door to somehow reach the train depot and get my son. Then that despicable weasel of a lawyer calmly announced there was no use in trying because Ben and George had been gone for hours. When I told him I would get the sheriff, he simply stated that, since Ben had done nothing illegal, the sheriff wouldn't be able to do anything to help me.

I got hysterical and ordered him to leave the hotel. He is the same disgusting individual who has been intercepting the rent payments I was collecting on the farmhouse after I moved in with Mama. You would think Ben would be willing to let me have the fifteen dollars a month to help support his own children.

Then I got angry at myself, thinking it was all my fault. If only I hadn't sent George to the store to pick up the bluing. But he's been running errands like that since he was eight years old. The store is only one block away. Never would I have imagined that something like this could happen.

I soon realized there was nothing I could do to get my son back. Although he's ten years old now, he's still just a little boy. I wondered if he was frightened or lonely or cold. What is the weather in Michigan in October? He left without any of his own clothing or toys. The first few nights he was gone, I couldn't sleep at all and spent hours staring out the window of our room. The sight of his hairbrush or a little shirt would dissolve me into tears. I sat in a rocking chair, hugging the feather pillow he had slept with since he was a baby, remembering how his soft blonde curls had just begun to darken, wondering if he was eating well.

I ate almost nothing myself for weeks, but drank pot after pot of coffee, strong and black. Dr. Ghent finally gave me something from his black bag to help me sleep.

Mama read the divorce document to me when it came. In the impersonal language of law, it stated that in the early years of our marriage, Ben had 'discharged his every duty to his wife and children, supplying them with all the necessities of life and comforts that would add to their happiness.' But in 1879, 'there crept into his house a destroyer that lodged in the bosom of his family, that poisoned the atmosphere of the once happy and pleasant home and blighted his life from that time until the present, separated his wife from his home, alienated his affections, estranged his children, and made desolate all that was once pleasant, happy and comfortable.' He identified this destroyer 'as a religious body of fanatics calling themselves Sanctificationists.'

Having read the words so many times, I still recall the dreadful terms used to describe the breakdown of our marriage, and how he insisted on blaming it all on the church.

'I told you not to marry him in the first place,' Mama scolded me. 'I know he's handsome and charming, but in my opinion, he has always been spoiled and shiftless, and his brother was constantly bailing him out of trouble. Whatever happened in Fort Worth just proved my suspicions about him. You were involved with the church before you met him and should have known better than to be yoked with an unbeliever.' Her words struck me like knives. In her estimation, it was all my fault.

My lawyer, Mr. Montieth, told me that in the original petition, Ben accused me of withdrawing myself from his bed and board and refusing matrimonial duties. This, he claimed, was a result of the religious beliefs forced upon me by my mother. The petition stated that Ben would obtain depositions of family and friends who would support his claims. My family and friends.

I remember asking Mr. Montieth if taking care of his family wasn't one of Ben's 'matrimonial duties.' It was a well-known fact in Belton that my husband had abandoned me and the children. For six long years.

Another shock for me was learning from the divorce petition how many times Ben had tried to contact me by letter or in person and was turned away by my mother. While I will never be able to forgive Ben for taking George, I can see that when he got no response from me, he must have thought he would never see the children again.

On December 15, 1887, I found myself in the courtroom of the Bell County Courthouse facing the husband I had not seen since 1881. I hated that he appeared to be healthy and strong from his work on the plantation. I hated that I was so thin and exhausted. As I looked around the courtroom filled with people I've known my entire life, I felt as though I were about to be stripped naked before them.

I saw nothing but contempt when the black-bearded (and black-hearted?) Judge Blackbourne looked at me. Ben and his lawyer, with smiles on their faces, seemed to be celebrating before the trial had even begun, and the men on the jury would not even look my way. Despite having an attorney at my side, I felt vulnerable and totally helpless, almost invisible. What could stop this carefully coached team of men from completing their prepared agenda? I feared that this legal attack would be no different from the others that had been formulated against the church.

To build his case against me and his claim that my religious beliefs were the cause of the breakdown of our marriage, Ben's attorney had interviewed a series of witnesses in October whose statements had been recorded by the clerk. Then they were summoned to the trial where one after another, my friends and family members were called to the stand to publicly verify each word scrawled on the document in the lawyer's hand. Starting with dear Matthew Dow and including a couple of the Sisters, my precious friend Sarah Miller, and several others, each witness answered the same questions that had been asked in October. With heartbreaking detail, they described not only their impressions of my relationship with Ben, but also what they knew about my religious convictions as a member of 'the band known as Sanctificationists.' I sat in anger and humiliation as I heard the most personal details of my life and marriage revealed to the entire courtroom.

Mama was named by each as the band's leader who taught that it 'was sinful for a sanctified wife to cohabit with an unsanctified husband.' They acknowledged that this teaching had already resulted in the breakup of several marriages within our group. I was accused of refusing Ben's offers for reconciliation, offers which I knew nothing about.

Toward the middle of the day, Mr. Boyd called Mama to the stand. I listened to her familiar, authoritative voice as she contradicted the testimony made earlier concerning the Sanctificationist view on marriage.

'Our religious faith does not teach that it is sinful for a believing wife to live with an unbelieving husband if they were already married when the wife became sanctified. Our faith teaches us to be good and obedient wives and mothers, and to discharge our duties as such with perfection,' she told the court.

My face burned as disrespectful comments rose from the courtroom. I knew that public knowledge about the broken relationships in the town was much more real to the people of Belton than the actual teachings of 'the sanctified.' For the same reason, I knew that any mention of Ben's faults in our marriage fell on deaf ears, especially those of the men on the jury.

By the time the court was recessed for lunch, I felt completely drained. Mama hurried over to walk me out of the courtroom. The people of the town lined our path as we left the building, whispering and pointing as we passed. I saw Sarah's sad face in the crowd, and although we're not close friends anymore, I regretted that she had to be involved in this part of my life.

Mama and I walked the block up Main Street to eat lunch at the Central Hotel. 'I have a bad feeling about this, Mama,' I said. 'If Ben has built his whole case for the divorce on his opposition to the church, how can the jury let me keep the children when they all know that the children would continue to live here? I've never felt so helpless in all my life.'

'I hate to talk so plain, Ada, but you are helpless,' Mama told me. 'The men of Belton are in command of this court, as they are in every court throughout the country. Someday women will be able to vote and hold office, and only then will women have any control over their own lives. The members of the Sanctified have more power in that regard than most women in the United States. That's what makes the men of Belton so angry. You know that, don't you? This trial isn't just about the Haymond family. It's about men maintaining dominance over women. We have to trust that God is the one who controls all things. Whatever happens will be for the good of the church, Ada. We must be brave.'

I stopped walking and caught Mama's arm. 'What are you saying? That if I lose my children, it will be for the good of the church? How can that be good? How can you say that it would be God's will? How can you say that?' I cried out.

Mama looked at me coldly. 'Ada, you are thinking with your head, not your spirit. It's obvious to me that the devil is using Ben to attack the church. We have to realize that what's good for the church has little to do with our fleshly family. That's the lesson here. The Lord works everything for good. We just have to have the faith to trust Him.'

I said very little and ate even less during the lunch break. I haven't the heart to argue with Mama, but my family means a great deal to me. Surely Mama knows that she is the main reason I'm even involved with her church. As I sat quietly at the table, it occurred to me that I was the only member of

Mama's 'fleshly family' still living anywhere near her. Emma was banned years ago, as were John and Nannie. Poor Papa patiently waited years for Mama's heart to soften toward him, and it's starting to look as though Robert and Sam may never be welcomed home. She doesn't really love any of us, I realized. What kind of God, who calls himself 'Father' would require us to sacrifice our own family? If a loving God is not our guide in this church, then who is? Who is? It was too much for me to think about.

In the afternoon, my attorney called witnesses to refute earlier testimony. He immediately got the attention of the weary jury by first calling my dear Hattie to the stand.

I was so proud of my beautiful daughter, just beginning to look like a young lady at twelve years of age. With her flaming red hair, Hattie's resemblance to her grandmother was unmistakable. Gently, Mr. Montieth questioned her about the relationship between Ben and me. Avoiding her father's eyes, Hattie looked at me, and I smiled and nodded my encouragement as she answered the lawyer's questions.

I know it was difficult for her to talk in front of everyone like that. She was asked about the fight between Ben and me that occurred when she was just a little girl of six, the night he left us. The people in the courtroom could only imagine her fear as she was asked to relive the horrible experience. 'I thought he was going to hurt Mama,' she told the court in a tiny voice. 'I was afraid.' Hattie explained how her father had left the family and how I have worked to support us ever since. 'My mother has always treated me kindly,' Hattie stated bravely. 'I would rather live with her. I do not like my father.'

Though Hattie's courageous testimony is etched firmly in my mind, the remainder of the trial I remember only as a blur. Regardless of what Mama had told me, my children are the most important part of my life. Hattie's words kept repeating

185

in my head: 'I do not like my father.' Even though the townspeople disagree with my beliefs, the children belong with their mother. They are my responsibility and my life.

It was five o'clock before the judge gave the charge to the jury and the men left the courtroom. As soon as the jury rose to leave, the clerk began to light the lamps that lined the walls of the darkening room. I sat alone, praying for what I knew would have to be a miracle. Thirty minutes later, they returned their verdict, deciding in Ben's favor and awarding him custody of all three children.

Through the murmur of approval heard throughout the courtroom, I felt the air leave the room. My head was spinning and I sank into my chair. Months of anticipation of this, my worst fear, had not prepared me for the pronouncement of the jury foreman.

'Of course we'll appeal,' my lawyer said from somewhere that seemed very far away. 'And we'll ask for a separate meeting to decide the details of the custody decision.'

Back at the Central Hotel, I went straight my room. I didn't have the courage to tell Hattie and Emily what had been decided at the trial, so Mama broke the news to them. Although neither one fully understood the implications of the jury decision on their own lives, Mama's words frightened them, and they ran straight up to where I sat in the rocking chair in our room, and we all cried together.

'I haven't given up yet, girls.' I told them with much more optimism than I felt. 'On Monday, we're asking for a new trial.' I handed Hattie my crumpled handkerchief and pulled them both onto my lap. 'We have to try everything we can think of to stay together.'

Emily looked up at me with the same trusting eyes she had as an infant. 'And George, too?' she asked innocently. That was the last moment I remember having even a shred of hope

186

that the children and I would be together as I had always taken for granted.

On Monday morning, Mr. Montieth and I met with Judge Blackbourne to request a new trial based on the list of errors my attorney set before the judge. Barely glancing at the petition, the judge denied the new trial and went on to schedule the custody meeting.

'A week from today is Christmas Eve,' the judge growled as he thumbed through his calendar. Even the most black-hearted judge could not order that children be removed from their home on Christmas day. 'Come back on January fifth.'

I knew that without a new trial, there was no hope of changing the custody decision of the jury. Asking for the custody meeting was just a way to delay the girls' inevitable departure, if only for a few days, and to give me a chance to confront Ben about his plans for the children. I assumed that he would be staying in Belton, or making arrangements for them to live with his brother's widow, the children's Aunt Jo Haymond. At least I'll be able to see them regularly, I comforted myself.

Christmas the following week was a solemn occasion. I had made some new clothes for Hattie and Emily, and all of the other Sisters were unusually generous with their gifts for the two girls. George's presents lay off to the side of the room on Christmas day, making his absence all the more poignant for everyone. I remembered how much he enjoyed the holiday and wondered what he was doing and whether he was thinking of us. As for me, it was close to impossible to appreciate God's gift of His Son to the world when my own son was so very far away. I felt badly that the day was a sad one for Hattie and Emily.

On January fifth, Mr. Montieth and I met in the judge's office again, this time with Ben and his lawyer. Ben was dressed in a dark suit, and for some strange reason, I was reminded of that carefree night at the Christmas Cotillion long ago when we were so much in love. At the time, I had been amused when he compared life to a game of cards, but now I fully appreciated the analogy. Which card had been played to bring us to this point, I wondered, and when? Why is it so hard to predict the consequences of our choices? I wished I could gather up the pieces of my life and start the game all over.

I stole a furtive glance at Ben as we sat facing Judge Blackbourne. He didn't look like a monster. Did he really hate me enough to destroy my life in this way? Does he anticipate what this will do to our children? Certain that the tender heart that had loved him had turned to stone, I felt I would never be able to forgive him. The breach between us was too wide. Is this what Ben really wants, I wondered. Was Mama right about the whole thing being orchestrated by the men of Belton? Or is it a persecution of the church by the devil?

In the end, it didn't really matter. Judge Blackbourne pushed a folded slip of paper across the table toward me. 'This is for you, Mrs. Haymond,' he said quickly.

I felt my eyes fill with tears at the thought of being separated from my own children, but I blinked them away. If Ben's intention was to hurt me, I wasn't going to let him see me cry.

The judge continued. 'You are ordered to hand the girls over to the custody of their father on Tuesday, January 8, 1888. They have been enrolled in the same boarding school as their brother and their cousins, the children of Mr. Haymond's sister. The address is on the paper I gave you. You are permitted to contact them by mail only. Mr. Haymond's attorney, Mr. Boyd, will pick them up at the Central Hotel at eight o'clock in the morning and deliver them to Mr. Haymond to catch the train. Mr. Haymond will accompany the girls all the way to Michigan before he returns to his business overseas.'

It took just a moment for me to comprehend this unexpected information. Michigan. Boarding school. Train. Overseas. 'NO!' I shouted, jumping to my feet. 'You can't do this. We're not talking about a litter of kittens for Mr. Haymond's sister to feed while he's gone. These are my children and this is their home! Since he has custody of them, Mr. Haymond must return to Belton to raise them properly.'

Mr. Montieth put his hand on my arm as I sat down, seething with rage. 'Judge, my client is concerned that the court will not have jurisdiction over the welfare of the children if they are taken out of the state.'

'Mr. Montieth,' drawled the judge, 'I thought it was clear to your client that she is now divorced from Mr. Haymond and that he has been awarded complete care and custody of the children. He has made the decision that the boarding school is the best way to care for his children. This court supports his decision.'

'This is insane! What about visits?' I blurted out. "When will I see them again?'

Huffing impatiently, the judged responded. 'That will be between the two of you. This court supports all of Mr. Haymond's decisions.'

It's really the last thing I remember in any detail. The next two days passed in a dreamlike blur. I spent every minute I could with the girls. The usual work rotations at the hotel were altered as I went through the motions of washing and mending all of their clothes and packing a trunk for each girl. I also packed one for George and sent his Christmas gifts and the other things he had left behind, including his favorite pillow. In the evening, after praying with Hattie and Emily, I fell into bed, too exhausted to cry. Too tired to think of life without my children.

On January 8, 1888, the girls were taken away. My life has turned into an endless cycle of mind-numbing busyness followed by bone-weary sleep. Then I either see my children in my dreams, or I am blissfully unaware of their absence. Nothing else matters.

CHAPTER 20

Feeling self-conscious, Emily withdrew from Sarah's embrace. She sat stiffly, with her head bowed as she thought of the time she had been separated from her mother following her parents' divorce. Finding a wrinkled handkerchief in the pocket of her apron, she busied her hands with it, determinedly picking at the carefully stitched embroidery, then stopped to dry her eyes with the worn square of fabric. Her lovely tear-stained face concealed more of her troubled childhood than her companions even knew to ask about.

"I'm beginning to realize I'm more like Mama than I thought," Emily said with resignation. Knowing it was pointless to guard her feelings now, she continued. "Just as she shielded me through the years, I hid from her how miserable I had been in Michigan. Even though I was still just a little girl when I came home, I knew that talking about it would only make her feel worse than she already did about not being able to protect us.

"Now I understand a little more of what was going on at the time, but I still find it hard to believe that a court of law gave Hattie and George and me to Father and then approved his leaving us up there with his sister. We didn't even know her," Emily cried.

Deeply moved by her niece's pain, Emma shuddered. "I still get angry when I think about it. It was wrong, just plain wrong!"

"At least I'm beginning to find out more of the story," Emily said with an uncharacteristic harshness to her voice. She wiped her eyes once again and sat up straight.

"If the intent was to destroy the church, the divorce trial failed. It was my family that was destroyed. After Father traveled with me and Hattie to his sister's farm in the middle of nowhere, Michigan, he got right back on the train to Galveston to board the next ship bound for Central America. It was the last time I ever saw him, you know. He died of typhoid pneumonia just four years later."

Her anger spent, Emily took a trembling breath, and looked down at the handkerchief in her hand. "Mama told me that she wrote to the three of us in Michigan almost every day, but we never got any of her letters. Once, when I took out the trash to be burned, I saw a piece of one lying in the ash heap. And Aunt Mary never mailed the letters we wrote to Mama. To make matters worse, Aunt Mary told us hateful things about Mama and Grandma. Hattie and George believed her, but I never did, especially after finding her letter. I held on to that little scrap of paper for the longest time, just so I'd at least be able to remember her handwriting. Then a whole year passed with no word from Mama, and I missed her so much. I remember the day when I realized I had forgotten what she looked like. It was almost like she was dead," the girl whispered as she looked with alarm toward her mother's bedroom, her eyes expressing distress as memories from the past merged with present fears.

Emily wiped her nose with the twisted handkerchief. "I'm worried about Mama sleeping so long," she said as she stood abruptly and walked into the bedroom.

Emma rose to follow her niece, but Sarah motioned for her to stay. "I think she needs to be alone with her mother for a little while," Sarah said quietly as she got up and closed the bedroom door. She moved the empty food tray and placed it on the floor beside the outer door, then stopped to adjust the lamp on her way back to her seat. Just as she sat down and put the top back on the hatbox, there was a single knock before the door was opened by Carrie Henry.

"Oh, I'm sorry to intrude," Carrie said awkwardly. "I didn't expect to find anyone here but Emily. I just came up to see how her mother is doing."

"Carrie, you come on in and sit down. Emily is in there with Ada," Emma said, gesturing toward the bedroom door. "You may not remember me because I've been away from Belton for a while. I'm Ada's sister, Emma. You probably know Mrs. Miller." In spite of the strained relationship between herself and her mother, Emma was determined to remain on friendly terms with the other members of the Sanctified. Like her father, she had held out hope that someday Martha would recognize the importance of her own family.

Sarah knew with certainty that her testimony at the divorce trial had not endeared her to Ada's church family, but she was confident, at least, that she would be remembered for it. "Hello, Carrie," she said cautiously as she nodded her greeting. "We're just waiting for Ada to wake up. Won't you join us?" Sarah patted the settee.

"When I saw Emily earlier, she told me she'd be up here with her mother. She didn't say she had other callers," Carrie said hesitantly as she sat down. Her wariness over social interaction with the two women was clear. Although she was in daily contact with the general public through her job as manager of two busy hotels, personal conversations with the 'unsanctified' were strictly prohibited. Word of Ada's recently renewed friendship with Mrs. Miller had spread throughout

193

the church, and Carrie knew that Sister Mac was none too pleased.

"We were sitting here reminiscing about old times, and Emily started talking about the years she spent in Michigan. I think it upset her," Emma confided in a hushed tone, as she tried to ease past Carrie's obvious reserve.

Carrie looked toward the closed bedroom door with suspicion. What had Emily already told these women, she wondered? "That was a difficult period for the whole town, I know," she sympathized vaguely.

"Oh, the town has forgotten most of it by now, Carrie. People go on with their own lives, and other things come up in the newspaper for folks to talk about. But Ada and Emily will have to live with that terrible incident forever," Emma continued. "Of course Emily's been deeply affected, but she's young and has her whole life ahead of her. It's Ada that will never be the same. You may not remember how cheerful and trusting she was as a young woman. She and Ben were so much in love. I always thought the Lord meant for them to be together."

Emma's last statement took Carrie by surprise. According to Sister Mac, Emma was among 'the lost.' What interest or insight could she possibly have in the Lord and his ways? But Carrie had also been told that Emma had no feelings for her family members in the church. Surely, if that were so, she would not even be here to visit her sick sister.

"Does Ada ever talk about what happened back then?" Emma asked with gentle concern.

Carrie hesitated, pulling on the strings of the handbag in her lap. "No, not to me. She's never talked about Mr. Haymond. After the children were taken away, she was very quiet. She slept a lot, and everyone knew she wasn't eating. We were extremely worried about her." Her lips pressed into a

194

tight line, Carrie looked down at her bag, wondering if she had offered too much information.

"I felt terrible about having to testify at the trial. I know Ada saw it as a betrayal, but what else could I do?" Sarah said gently, trying to help Carrie see the larger issues. "I had to answer the questions under oath, but I've always felt partially responsible for what happened, even though I know it was out of my hands to help her. Did Ada ever talk to you about the trial?"

Again, Carrie was moved by the sincerity of the two women. Was it possible that Sister Mac had given her the wrong impression about people outside the church? She could see that Sarah and Emma truly cared about Ada, which made her wonder if a brief conversation with them would be considered out of line. Besides, she reasoned, Ada had been visiting with her friend, Sarah, for months, and Emma was, in fact, family, so Carrie decided she was safe to reply. "We never talked about the trial, but, as you can imagine, it took a terrible toll on Ada," she began cautiously. "I thought the separation from the children would destroy her, but although she seldom spoke to any of us, we knew that she started working on an appeal almost as soon as Hattie and Emily were on the train to Michigan." She stopped talking and resumed twisting the strings of the reticule.

"I heard that Mr. Tyler took her case to the Texas Supreme Court," Sarah said, prompting Carrie to continue.

Relaxing a bit, the young woman looked up. "Yes, that's right. She changed lawyers. Mr. George Tyler is probably the best lawyer in Belton."

Emma shook her head at her sister's plight. "I know all Ada thought about was getting those children back home. Every once in awhile, when I'd come to Belton to shop, I'd get a glimpse of her on the Avenue, although we never spoke. She got so thin that year I was worried for her health."

"We were all worried about her," Carrie said again. "Luckily, business at the hotel picked up about that time and she had plenty to do. Hotel work is good for keeping your mind off of whatever you'd rather not think about." Carrie paused as an unbidden memory distracted her. "Ada and I took turns working at the front desk of the Central Hotel when we were in the old building."

"Hopefully, she's not working that hard, but she's still very thin," Sarah remarked. "She looks even more frail than when I saw her last Wednesday. And Emily tells us she has an awful cough."

"Her lungs again," Carrie offered. "It seems that she gets sick whenever we travel. She had a terrible time on the first trip we took to New York City not long after Emily went to Michigan."

"Oh, I've been to New York City with Mr. Miller on one of his business trips," Sarah said enthusiastically. "We had a wonderful time. Did y'all enjoy your visit?"

"We sure did," Carrie replied, recalling the trip almost ten years earlier. She relaxed and leaned back on the settee, relieved to help steer the conversation toward a safe topic. "That was when I found out what country mice we really were. It was a good thing we went to Galveston first."

"Galveston?" Emma asked, confused at the mention of the bustling seaport town on the Texas gulf coast.

"Yes. Our first trip to New York City started from Galveston. There were about thirty women in the church then, and we traveled in groups of ten at a time so there would always be enough of us here to run the hotel and look after the children," Carrie explained. "Sister Mac arranged for us to travel by train and steamer, and Ada and I were in the first group that went to Galveston to board the ship for New York City. As soon as we arrived, we realized how old-fashioned we looked in our bonnets, so the first place we visited on the island was a millinery shop. Oh, my! Look at that. Ada has kept her hatbox all these years," Carrie said as she noticed the box at her feet.

"We stayed overnight at a hotel on the Strand. That's the shopping district near where ships from all over the world are docked. Galveston was a fascinating place to visit, and I could have stayed there longer, but we were anxious to continue the trip. Because it's such a busy international port, there are lots of interesting things to see and do. In fact, we went back to Galveston for a vacation a few years ago. I've enjoyed all the traveling we've done so far, and I can't wait to talk to Emily about Washington, D.C. My mother and my sister, Ella, are already there, you know."

"Yes, Ada mentioned that. I'd like to hear about the steamer you took to New York, Carrie," Sarah said. "I've only traveled by train. What's the steamer like?"

"Oh, that's my favorite way to travel," Carrie admitted, beginning to enjoy the friendly conversation, and the carefree way the two women interacted. Carrie was surprised that she felt almost as comfortable with Sarah and Emma as she did with her friends in the church. The difference was that in this conversation, she had information to share with a new audience, and Sarah and Emma seemed genuinely interested in what she had to say about her adventures. "The steamer is so smooth and clean compared to the train. Our cabins were small, but comfortable. I was amazed to find such a beautiful dining room on a boat! China, crystal and silver on damask tablecloths. And the food was delicious. Each evening a full meal is served including appetizers, salad, soup, a choice of entrees and vegetables, dessert and beverages. And we only spent seventy-five cents. The entire voyage was delightful, and I almost hated to see it end, but we were anxious to get to New York City. Of course the first thing we saw as we entered the harbor was the Statue of Liberty."

"Isn't it magnificent?" Sarah exclaimed. "It's so much bigger than I had imagined. Did you go out to the island?"

"Of course. That was the first place we wanted to go. Fortunately, Emma, your brother met us at the pier when the steamer docked. We sure were thankful to have someone to take us through that absolutely horrible traffic. Just getting from the pier to our boarding house was an experience I'll never forget."

"I know exactly what you're talking about," Sarah agreed. "It's terrifying. Streetcars, buggies, wagons, electric trolleys and full-sized trains right in the road! And those monstrous elevated trains. They make so much noise and throw coal dust and cinders everywhere."

"What was the boarding house like?" Emma asked.

"It was a nice house, a bit smaller than the old Central Hotel. We had all of the rooms on the second floor. They were comfortable and had the usual furnishings. One thing that was different was the gas light fixture in the bedroom. We had to ask the landlady how it worked. We didn't want to start a fire." Carrie laughed as she recalled their first encounter with the unfamiliar invention. The comfortable flow of the conversation among them continued, putting Carrie further at ease

"That's not the only funny thing that happened. I noticed that there was no chamberpot in our room. You should have seen how excited we were to find a real bathroom right down the hall, inside the house. Remember, this was almost ten years ago. The Central Hotel didn't have any indoor plumbing until these new buildings were constructed. Everyone used the bathhouse out here in the laundry building."

"So the new Yankee commode was one of the highlights of your trip! My brother must have thought y'all were easy guests to entertain," Emma said. "We were just talking about how lonely he was when he first moved to New York. I reckon he was glad to see you."

Carrie smiled absently. For just for a moment she let herself think about Robert.

"What did you do together?" Emma asked.

Suddenly called back from her reverie to the conversation in the sitting room, Carrie looked at Emma in confusion. "Excuse me. I'm sorry. What did you say?"

Emma noted Carrie's inattention. "What did y'all do with Robert in New York?" she asked again.

Carrie Henry
New York City, May, 1889

My first impression of New York City was that it was frightening and exciting all at the same time. I could hardly believe that so many people actually lived so close together, all frantically on their way to somewhere else. It was such a relief to find Robert waiting among the great rows of hansom cabs lined up at the pier. Soon we were on our way to find the boarding house Sister Mac had rented at the edge of Central Park. As we passed by the wide variety of citizens, it seemed we had worried needlessly over what clothes to bring. 'It looks like you can wear whatever you like in New York, as long as you're not naked,' Sister Mac observed.

199

SET APART

After we unpacked our trunks, Robert tried to hurry us out the door to go for a ride through the Park. He was excited for us to be there, and I was glad to see him so happy.

'Just a moment, Robert,' I insisted. 'We have to get our hats.'

'Hats? What happened to your lovely bonnets? I thought I was going to dazzle my country ladies with the sights and sounds of the big city. But if you're already wearing hats, I'm afraid you're all too sophisticated for this boy,' Robert teased us. I could tell we were going to have a good time in New York. Robert has always been so much fun to be with.

Although we were close enough to walk to Central Park, Robert insisted on a driving tour. As we rode in two open vis-à-vis carriages, he told us what he had learned about the lush, natural area, with its lakes, rolling meadows, trees and shrubs that were all part of a carefully designed landscape project.

'You mean this came about by men moving dirt and rocks? It all looks so natural,' I told him. 'But I did notice that the roads and bridges don't ever cross the horse trails or footpaths. It's not at all like driving through the countryside in Texas.'

Robert gave me a broad smile. 'It's certainly not Texas.' Farther along, he leaned close to point out a large pond, thoroughly enjoying his role as tour guide. 'This is my favorite place in the Park. In the summer there are boat races, art shows, concerts and lots of different events held around the water. In the winter, the water freezes hard enough to walk on, and they rent skates out of those little buildings over yonder,' he said, pointing again. 'I've earned quite a few falls and bruises, but now I'm a pretty good skater. You'll just have to come back in the winter and take a sleigh ride through the Park. There's nothing else like it.'

As Robert sat back in his seat, I admired the new sense of confidence he seemed to have developed. Though unmistakably Texan, his speech had lost some of its characteristic drawl. Encouraged that he seemed to be so happy in New York, I wondered if he still wanted to return home to Belton, or if our visit answered his prayer for us to be together.

The next day we were all up early, eager to continue our adventure. After taking the trolley to Battery Park, we boarded the ferry to Bedloe's Island, home of the Statue of Liberty. The crowded ferry seemed tiny after being on the luxurious steamer. Listening to some of the tourists speaking in strange languages, I remembered reading about the immigrants who come into our country at Ellis Island.

When Robert and I decided to climb the stairs inside the statue to the observation platform in the crown, his sister Ada volunteered to go with us. The view from the top was breathtaking, but in a different way for Ada. It worried me that she had such a difficult time catching her breath. She coughed and wheezed all the way back down the stairs.

'I suppose I'm just too old to do that kind of climbing,' Ada remarked casually. 'And reckon I haven't gotten used to this Yankee air.'

'Nonsense,' Robert scolded. 'You're not even forty years old yet, Ada. That's a terrible cough. You should see a city doctor while you're here, and I know just the one. We'll see about it tomorrow. You are right about one thing, though. There's a lot to get used to in New York.' He paused for a moment and I thought he was going to explain, but he didn't. 'For now, I'm just happy that you've come to visit. I've missed everyone so much.' At that, he leaned over and kissed his sister on the cheek in an uncharacteristically open display of affection. For the first time, I thought I saw a trace of sadness in his eyes, despite his air of big-city sophistication.

SET APART

He has been in my thoughts often in the three years since he left Belton. So much so, in fact, that sometimes I wonder if it is sinful to think about him so much. I've found that the best way to keep my mind off of him is to stay busy with my work at the hotel, the work that God has given us to do. Sister Mac once told us that anything that distracts us from our jobs has to be the devil trying to break into the church.

I tried to imagine what it must be like for Robert, living apart from the church like he does. Although I know he was lonely at first, it appears that he has adapted to a way of life vastly different from the one we have in Belton. The change is more than having grown accustomed to the activity of this busy city, though. Most of us who grew up in the church have no experience with making decisions like Robert faces here.

From the time we were children, almost every choice, whether important or trivial, has been made by someone else - usually Robert's mother - in the greater interest of the church community. We all wear a similar work dress and apron, and we never have to decide what to do, as our lives are conveniently scheduled, almost to the minute, within the church's various work rotations. Even our leisure time is carefully restricted. As a result, the very idea of having to make decisions frightens me.

Watching Robert talk to Ada about the Statue, I felt that his own newly earned liberty seemed to fit him well, like the stylish New York suit he had selected for our excursion. Proud of his adjustment and maturity, I immediately thought how closely his experience paralleled that of the immigrants who had left their homes and families to start over in this strange new world. Content with that comparison, I closed my eyes to thank God for answering our prayer to bring us together again . . . 'Then ye shall call upon me, and ye shall go and pray unto me, and I will hearken unto you.'

202

After busy days filled with excursions to every tourist attraction in the city, Robert asked me to go with him on one final walk through the Park. I looked forward to spending my last evening in the city with my best friend.

'So how do you like New York now?' I asked him as we walked the short distance to the Park, holding hands just as we had as children.

'Ha! I'm surprised you're brave enough to ask me that question again,' Robert said, laughing as he recalled our conversation in Belton on the way to the depot. 'I like it fine. Until tomorrow. Until you leave.'

'But you're happy here,' I insisted, certain that he was teasing me.

'Am I? Let me tell you something, Carrie. When I finally figured out that Mother never intends to let me come home, I decided to make the best of it here, and I've done some vigorous exploring of this fascinating city. But I still haven't made any close friends, and you don't know how I've looked forward to your visit.' He stopped walking and looked me up and down, as if he was trying to convince himself that I was really there. 'But as soon as you're gone, I'll be my same miserable self, and I don't want that to happen. I've thought a lot about it, Carrie, and I want you to listen to me carefully.' Robert gripped my hand tightly and his voice lowered just a bit. 'You know I've been praying for us to be together, and I think your trip here is our opportunity. I've decided to ask you to stay here and be my wife.'

Wife? Stunned, my casual smile turned into a frown. I dropped his hand and glared at him, my hands firmly on my hips. 'Robert, what are you saying? Did you hear yourself? Our prayer was to be together, and here we are. But marriage? That's insane! I miss you, too, but marriage is not an option for us, and you know it. Our lives are in the church, and there

203

are no marriages among the Sanctified. Your mother will let you come home soon. She's talking about buying another hotel in Temple, and I know she'll need you to manage it. Then we can be together again like before, like we prayed for.'

Robert slowly unclenched his fists and raised his hands, palms up in a pleading gesture. 'Carrie, don't you see? Nothing can be like it was before. We were children then. I've had to grow up here. Alone. I want you for my wife, Carrie. It's my only prayer now,' he said as he reached for my hand again.

'Don't touch me, Robert,' I snapped, immediately regretting my harsh tone.

Looking like he'd been slapped, he hesitated for only a moment. 'I love you, Carrie. Please marry me.'

I was bewildered by what I was hearing, and as I looked at Robert, his face seemed strangely unfamiliar. I had never known him to be impulsive. In all ways, he's the perfect carpenter: measure twice, cut once. Methodical. Deliberate. Sometimes he can even be a bit of an old man. But impulsive, never. This sudden talk about marriage was a complete shock and made no sense to me at all. 'I have to sit down. I can't think.' Reeling in confusion, I walked to a nearby park bench where I sank to the hard wooden surface.

As he sat down beside me, Robert put his arm along the back of the bench protectively and waited for me to regain my composure. Seeing that deliberate gesture, I instantly realized that although I had been surprised by his proposal, there was nothing impulsive about it. He had most likely been planning this moment for months.

'I love you, too, Robert. I could never marry anyone else or love anyone as I love you.'

'Then you'll stay? You'll marry me?'

'I didn't say that.' I felt his disappointment as clearly as I saw it in the immediate sag of his posture. 'I do love you, Robert, but you must know that I've never even thought about marriage, not ever. How could we be married, after the way we've been raised? Tell me what you're thinking. Where in the world did you get such an idea?'

Robert took a deep breath. 'Carrie, we were raised to know God. We're sanctified, and we have His Spirit, but God never meant for His children to live alone,' he said with great intensity. 'Now I know what "alone" really means, and I know God has something else in mind . . . for us to be together. As man and wife.' He moved his hand from the back of the bench to rest lightly but comfortably on my shoulder. "I see it clearly, Carrie." I said nothing, but suddenly I felt very light-headed.

'This is all very confusing to me,' I told him weakly, dropping my face into my hands. All I could think of was the verse so often repeated by Sister Mac: 'The unmarried woman careth for the things of the Lord, that she may be holy both in body and in spirit.' When I looked up, this unmarried woman saw a very dear friend, and wasn't a friend a 'thing of the Lord?'

'When you come back to Belton, Robert, we'll talk about it.'

'You still don't understand, Carrie. You know my mother better than that,' he argued gently. 'She's never going to let me come back. Never. And we both know that marriages don't last long in Belton, anyway. Look at poor Ada.'

'So what are you saying, Robert?' I sat up straight. 'You want me to live here? Leave my mother and Ella and everyone?' Robert didn't have to say a word because I knew what he was thinking. It was exactly what he had done. But I knew I didn't have the kind of courage that it required to be an

205

immigrant in this city. When he moved his hand from my shoulder to touch the back of my neck, I closed my eyes. My heart was beating so fast, I knew I was going to faint. His touch had never made me feel that way before. I was confused and a little frightened.

'It's not about leaving anyone, Carrie. It's about you coming here to be with me,' he said quietly. My eyes were still closed when he kissed me on the mouth for the first time since we were twelve. I didn't faint. In fact, I kissed him back.

'I love you, Carrie, and you just said that you feel the same way about me. If God intends for us to be together, He will make it happen. You know that,' he said as I opened my eyes to see the man I knew I would love for the rest of my life.

'I do love you, Robert, but . . . I'm a bit dizzy, and you must understand that I need some time to think. How will you explain this to your mother?'

'I'll think of something,' he promised.

When we got back to the boarding house, he walked me upstairs to the room I shared with Ada. 'Where's Mother?' Robert asked his sister.

Ada looked up from the book she was reading. 'She took some medicine for the pain in her face and went right to bed. The neuralgia seems to be getting worse all the time. Before she went to her room, she said something about staying here to see that doctor of yours and sending the rest of us on home tomorrow.'

'She did? Shouldn't she go to a doctor in Texas, closer to home?' Robert asked. I could hear the frustration in his voice. This was a complication he had not foreseen.

'She's gone to every physician within a hundred miles of Belton,' Ada explained. 'Surely there's one here in this big city who can ease her suffering.'

'I'll look in on her tomorrow. Maybe she'll be feeling better,' Robert said hopefully. As we parted, I sensed Robert's courage weakening at the prospect of having a face-to-face confrontation with his mother. During the years since he left Belton, he could not have forgotten how she has always directed the outcome of every situation involving the church.

The next morning Robert joined us for breakfast just as Sister Mac, her face still swollen from the previous night's episode, announced her plans to remain in New York. 'I'm counting on that doctor of yours, Bob,' she told Robert as he pulled a chair up to her table.

After breakfast, Robert dutifully carried our trunks down the stairs and placed them on the brick sidewalk near the cabs he had hired for the ride to the train station. 'I can't very well say anything to her now. Pray, Carrie. Please pray,' he managed to whisper to me before he walked over to stand beside his mother in the doorway of the boarding house.

CHAPTER 21

"What did we do in New York?" Carrie repeated awkwardly.

"Oh, just the usual tourist things as well as visiting a few other places Robert had discovered on his own. By then, he'd been in New York City for three years. Ours was the first group visiting that summer. If he spent half as much time with the others, he must have been exhausted by the time the third group returned to Belton. On the way home, our party stopped at Niagara Falls. Now, that was quite a sight. Have you been there, Mrs. Miller?" Carrie asked as she tried to direct the conversation away from Robert.

Before Sarah could answer, the bedroom door opened. "Carrie!" Emily exclaimed, hurrying to her friend. "I thought I heard laughing in here, and I knew it had to be you. I'm glad you came up to the room. Grandma and I plan to leave in the morning and I wanted to see you."

As Carrie stood, Emily clung to her in an affectionate embrace. After a moment, Carrie stepped back and gently took the girl's face in her hands. "You haven't been crying, have you, Em? Don't you worry about your mother. She's going to be just fine. Dr. Ghent sent a message to the front desk. He's running late, but he will be here and he'll take good care of her. Now stop worrying," she said, giving Emily another hug before they both sat down. "I've missed you, honey, but it won't be long until we're all together again. This time, you can pick me up at the depot."

Looking at the other women's puzzled faces, Carrie
explained. "I went along with Ada to pick up Emily at the
depot when she came back from Michigan." She saw no harm
in relating the story of the happy reunion.

"Now, how did that happen? I never was quite sure what
was going on," Emma admitted. "All I remember is that all of
a sudden Emily was back in Belton."

"Well, that's just about how it happened," Carrie said as
she grinned at Emily. "It was the summer of '91. After Mr.
Tyler worked on Ada's behalf for more than three years, the
Supreme Court of Texas finally reviewed the proceedings of
the Bell County Court and reversed the divorce decision. But
even though the divorce was nullified, Ben still had custody of
the children since the new opinion did nothing to change the
custody order.

"Next, Ada had to have what's called a 'cross-bill' in order
to be divorced from Ben and to, hopefully, regain custody of
the children. Her court date was set for the Monday right after
the Fourth of July weekend. You know what a busy time that
always is, not only for the hotel, but for the whole town. The
parade, fair, carnival, picnics and all. Now add the fact that it
was the weekend Professor George Garrison, from the
University of Texas, had chosen to come to the Central Hotel
to write his article about the church," Carrie continued.

"We had worked for weeks to be ready for the Garrisons.
He brought his whole family, you know. His wife, Anne, and
their three little girls. We were still in the old building then,
and in preparation for their arrival, every room in the hotel had
been thoroughly cleaned. Curtains were washed and starched,
and we painted walls. We cleaned windows and polished
silver. The animal pens and barn were swept clean, and even
the laundry equipment in the old Methodist church building
across Pearl Street was oiled and dusted," Carrie laughed as

209

she recounted all the extra work done to make a good impression on the professor.

"That Friday afternoon, Ada and I were working at the front desk of the hotel, and she was trying to teach me how to make a flower arrangement. She was having such a hard time concentrating that day. I'm sure that all she could think about was the court date on Monday. Then the boy came from the telegraph office carrying two envelopes." Carrie held up two fingers and smiled in anticipation.

"The first telegram said that the Garrisons would be arriving earlier than we expected, so I hurried to tell the Sisters who were supposed to meet the family at the depot. While I was away from the desk, Ada opened the other envelope, the one that said Emily was coming home!" Carrie leaned over and grasped Emily's hand as she experienced, once again, the joy of that day.

"I could hardly believe it when I read the telegram. We never have figured out what happened exactly, because when Monday came, the divorce was granted, while the custody decision was upheld," Carrie said. "Officially, Ada couldn't have the children, but, somehow, Emily was home!"

"I think it was a question of money. What my father had been sending to Aunt Mary suddenly stopped coming that summer," Emily explained. "She couldn't afford to keep all of us, and Hattie and George didn't want to come home. They were finished with school, though, and were old enough to go to work. George was fourteen and Hattie was sixteen that year. As I told you, they believed whatever Aunt Mary told them about Mama and Grandma, but I never did. I always wanted to come home to Mama."

"What was it like for you, coming back here after three years?" Emma asked.

"Well, in the excitement of getting back to Mama, I had forgotten that it was the Fourth of July weekend, so my first thought was that they had decorated the whole town just for me," Emily admitted. "The depot was so crowded, I was worried I wouldn't be able to find Mama. To tell you the truth, I don't know that I would have recognized her if Carrie hadn't been there. Mama was so thin." A shadow of concern darkened Emily's face momentarily. "It was a good time to return home, with so much going on. But best of all, I was with Mama again."

"What a happy story," Sarah sighed, touched by the deep friendship Carrie and Emily obviously shared. "Professor Garrison wrote such a nice article, too. I think it was just about the best one I've read about the church. Surely Ada kept a copy of it," she said, gesturing toward the hatbox.

Professor George Garrison
Belton, July, 1891

I have been aware of an experiment in communism in operation just up the road from The University for quite some time. When I contacted the Sanctificationists, as the press names the group, I received a reply from the head of their band, Mrs. Martha McWhirter. I explained to her my desire to study the community and was warmly invited to bring my family and spend some time at their hotel in Belton.

Arriving on Friday, July third, we got the impression that Belton is a very lively place to live. Apparently, as the county seat, it is the host town for the area's July Fourth celebration and was appropriately decorated for the event. We also found out that a child from the band had recently returned to the community after an extended absence, adding to the commotion.

The members of the community are all very pleasant women. Among them are a number who have been leaders in Belton society, universally respected and, some of them, quite wealthy. On the first evening of our visit, an elegant dinner party was planned in our honor.

The large dining room of the hotel reflected the good taste and refinement of the women of the commune. The tables were set with the best china and silverware on white linen tablecloths, as fine as the nicest hotel in Austin. Beautiful floral arrangements and patriotic decorations adorned the room.

Most of the women dined with us, while others served. I was surprised when wine was poured.

'This is excellent,' I told Mrs. McWhirter as I sampled the wine. 'I have to say, I'm surprised that you ladies serve this beverage at the hotel.'

'We are all free to drink wine or beer in moderation, for pleasure as well as for health reasons, Professor,' she replied. 'And we'll serve it to anyone who behaves.'

During the meal, I took no notes, but was intent on asking questions about the early history of the church as well as Mrs. McWhirter's personal family background. It was a story that she apparently is not tired of telling, and the evening passed quickly. Sensitive to our long day of traveling, she ended the dinner party early.

At ten o'clock the following morning, the Fourth of July parade began with the Belton Brass Band leading the way down Main Street toward the courthouse. It was a typically hot day for Texas in July, but our group sat under one of the shady oak trees on the property. The women had set up a table with iced tea and lemonade for guests of the hotel. 'Just think,' I remarked as I sipped a glass of tea, 'Americans all over this great nation of ours are celebrating today, just as we are.'

'I beg your pardon, Professor,' Mrs. McWhirter's adult daughter, Mrs. Ada Haymond argued, 'but we here in Belton prefer to think that we have a most superior celebration.'

I have enjoyed Mrs. Haymond's charming sense of humor. It was apparently her daughter Emily who has recently returned to Belton. Emily is the only one of her three children to return home following a bitter divorce and custody dispute. Hers is not the only divorce among the women resulting from their religious convictions. I was glad that I had thought to bring along my notebook, for I spent the remainder of the afternoon hearing of the family entanglements of the Sanctified Sisters. Divorce is not uncommon and, sadly, every woman in the band is well acquainted with her legal limitations.

Emily Haymond and other children of the community included my three daughters in their games and adventures of the afternoon. I learned that a school has been set up in the hotel for the youngsters, to instruct them in the elementary branches up to geography, grammar and arithmetic.

That evening after supper at the hotel, everyone went to the park beside the creek to enjoy the fireworks display conducted by the fire department each year.

The next morning my family went downstairs for breakfast, dressed for church. I asked Mrs. McWhirter whether the community attended services or held one of their own in the hotel.

'For years we held a weekly prayer meeting and Scripture lesson,' she told me, 'but we quit that about two years ago. We have found that each of us is led individually by the Spirit of

God, but all are in harmony with one another. God communicates with us in prayer and through dreams and visions. We openly discuss His revelations with one another at any time, so that scheduled devotion time seems unnecessary. We are also opposed to Sunday Christians, as every day is the Lord's Day. You could say that we are living the Bible, Professor Garrison.'

I admit I was surprised to discover that the women no longer have formal worship of any kind. In this, they have changed greatly from what they were at first when they held regular and frequent devotional exercises. Mrs. McWhirter's claim to be 'living the Bible' is, of course, according to her interpretation of the book.

The remainder of our visit in Belton passed quickly. The women did not seem to mind my questions or my presence as they attended to their tasks. The community is highly organized and efficient. It's no wonder that on his visit to the Central Hotel, Governor Hubbard remarked, 'The Central Hotel is equal to the finest hotel in Texas.'

In the Hotel, three Sisters work in the kitchen at a time. There is one cook for meat, one for bread and pastry, and one general assistant. The excellent food at the Central Hotel is popular with the regular boarders and travelers, called transients. The large dining room is used for catered affairs on a regular basis. Four children are also assigned to the kitchen to wash dishes, glasses and silverware.

Two Sisters are scheduled to work in the dining room. At each meal they set the tables, serve the food to up to sixty patrons and clear the tables, while keeping the room clean and tidy. Their promptness in refilling pitchers and platters earns the praise of each and every guest and boarder.

Six Sisters and three children are assigned to work in the steam laundry located in a separate building behind the hotel.

All of the sheets, towels and linens for the hotel, as well as the group's personal laundry, are completed in two days. The rest of the week, this crew works on sewing projects, chopping wood, and other necessary chores.

Two Sisters work as chambermaids. Each of the thirty-five rooms is serviced daily. Chamberpots are cleaned and the pitchers on the washstands refilled with fresh water. Rooms are swept and tidied daily, and clean towels set out weekly. Not every hotel in the area can make the same claim.

Two Sisters and four children live on and work one of the farms owned by the Central Hotel Company and located just two miles from town. They tend the gardens and livestock used to supply the hotel table. During the winter months, in place of gardening, they weave the rag rugs used in the hotel and sold in the stores in town. I am told that the Sisters look forward to this assignment in the job rotation because of the relative peace and quiet of the farm.

Each job area is rotated every month, and this arrangement has worked satisfactorily now for several years. Everyone is trained to do every job, and no one feels inequality of service. The Sisters seem to be proud of their ability to work together.

With the exception of the cooks, each Sister works about four hours per day. They enjoy the freedom of spending their leisure time in a variety of ways. The hotel subscribes to a number of periodicals including the *Forum, Frank Leslie's Illustrated, The Weekly Woman's Journal*, a dental magazine, and all of the local newspapers. A casually organized circulation library is available to the Sisters and their guests from the hotel's collection of books. From talented boarders, some of the women take lessons in drawing and music. The piano in the hotel parlor is in constant use for practice and entertainment.

SET APART

I was told that the Sisters have long since abandoned the activity of calling on relatives or friends outside their community, but they are clearly not adverse to travel. In the summer of 1889, the whole band visited New York City, making quite an excursion of it. I understand it is their intention to see the World's Fair in Chicago as well.

I observed that the Sanctificationists wear no uniform, though it is their custom to dress plainly. Black or dark-colored skirts and white blouses seem to be the popular selection. At work, neatly ironed aprons protect the clothing. Formerly they wore sunbonnets, but now hats are a part of their wardrobe.

The community also has its own dentist. One of the Sisters has learned the art mostly from books and with the instruction of a local practitioner. She does all of the dental work for the band, including extracting teeth, filling them, and putting in new sets whenever necessary. An office has been properly equipped for her to do work for the hotel boarders and the people of the town. As she has no license, she charges only the cost of materials used.

The net income of the community is about eight hundred dollars per month. Most of their earnings are derived from the hotel and the remainder from rental of stores, houses and dwellings. The women own real estate in the name of the Central Hotel Company valued at fifty thousand dollars.

At the present time, the growth of the hotel business demands an extension of the facilities. The present buildings must either be added to or replaced in order that the Sisters themselves may be comfortably housed during the winter.

At the end of our stay, we were almost sorry to have to go. The girls have grown close to their new friends, Emily Haymond and Anna Pratt. My wife, Annie, was presented with the recipes to some of the tasty dishes we were served at the Hotel, including Mrs. McWhirter's uncommonly delicious biscuits.

In response to my request for a final statement, Mrs. McWhirter described the community as 'the work of God, under whose protection the Sisters live and by whom a way will always be opened for them.'

From my conversations with the people of Belton, there appears to be a consensus that Mrs. McWhirter is the center and soul of the organization, and that its prolonged existence and success are due to her extraordinary powers and strange influence over her followers. They feel that when she is gone, there will be the end of it.

CHAPTER 22

"I remember playing with the Garrison girls, but I don't think I ever saw the article their father wrote," Emily said, picking up the hatbox from the floor and putting it on her lap.

"What's in the box?" Carrie asked, surprised to see something other than Ada's old hat when Emily removed the lid.

"Oh, just stuff that Mama has collected. Mrs. Miller and Aunt Emma have been trying to explain some of it to me. Here it is," Emily announced, pulling a magazine out of the box. "*Charities Review*. November, 1893. The article must have been published not long after we started construction on this new hotel building."

"And it was about time," Carrie said emphatically. "I remember how we were all mashed together in the smallest rooms because there were so many boarders in the hotel by then. We bought the rest of the block here next to the old building and started construction in January of '92. Do you remember what a good time your grandmother had designing and building this hotel, Emily?"

"How could I forget? Grandma was constantly climbing ladders and going in and out of windows to inspect everything. It scared Mama half to death, so she sent me up right behind Grandma every time. I don't know what I would have done if she'd fallen on me!"

"Poor Brother Matthew Dow was the builder, and I know she just about drove him insane," Carrie added. "I don't know how many walls and windows he had to take out and put back in order to make her happy. It seemed to take forever to finish this building. Of course, half of the time the work crew was over at the old hotel doing repairs or working on putting in the new bathrooms and plumbing. By that summer, I know he was relieved when she announced that she was taking a trip."

"A trip? She didn't go off by herself, did she?" Emma asked. "Although it shouldn't surprise me, of course."

"No, she was escorted by Eugene Scheble, Sister Gertrude's son," Carrie replied. "He was eighteen at the time, and I'm sure he got a real education that summer when they visited three other communes!" Carrie stopped herself when she saw from the women's astonished expressions that she had led the conversation in a precarious direction. As comfortable as she had become in talking with Sarah and Emma, she knew there was still sensitive information about the church that had to remain confidential.

Newspaper articles about the Sanctified Sisters of Belton had been published across the country, and, as a result, a number of celibate communities made contact with Martha McWhirter. One group from Chicago, the Koreshans, inquired about the laundry business run by the women. Their leader, a physician/alchemist named Cyrus Teed, told his followers he had proven that the inhabitants of the earth were living inside a hollow sphere instead of on top of the planet. He also taught that the celibacy practiced by the group would someday result in the development of a physically perfect human being capable of self-reproduction. Although irritated by his ridiculous beliefs, Martha had been willing to travel to Chicago to talk business with Teed before going to visit the

219

Harmonists in Pennsylvania and the Shaker community in New York State.

Sarah and Emma looked at each other with blank expressions. Clearly, they knew nothing of the Sisters' contact with other cults around the country.

"Well, it sounds like Eugene had an interesting summer," Emma said when it became obvious that Carrie would not elaborate further on the subject.

"Actually, we all learned something new," Carrie added, trying to minimize the awkwardness as she remembered the publication Martha had mailed from her trip. "You may have heard of the Shakers, a religious community in New York State. From a brochure that Sister Mac brought us, we found out that the men and women eat at separate tables and sleep at opposite ends of a shared house. They had written to Sister Mac with business questions, as well, so she made the trip up there to see how they operated. She told us that the country was beautiful up there, but it bothered her the way the men were in control of everything."

"I can see how *that* would annoy her," Emma exclaimed with a chuckle.

Carrie cringed at Emma's comment. Surely Emma hadn't gotten the idea that she meant any disrespect, Carrie worried as she glanced toward Emily just as her friend took one of Sister Mac's letters from the hatbox and removed it from the envelope. With a feeling of dread, Carrie knew that her casual references to Martha's travels had prompted Emily to want to read one of her grandmother's letters.

"Here's what Grandma wrote to Mama from that trip," Emily said as she flattened the letter on her lap. " 'I told the Shaker women that if they did not rise up and get the strength of character established in their own hearts to have their liberty, God would wipe them off the earth as a society. It's plain to me that I've been sent to give the women encouragement in freeing themselves from the bondage of their male members. The Shakers are a good people, and the time is at hand that they are going to be led up out of the wilderness where they have been hid for the last hundred years.'"

The women laughed as Emily imitated her grandmother's authoritative manner of speaking and her commanding voice. In spite of herself, Carrie was amused. But her laughter stopped abruptly as she felt a wave of guilt for her momentary lapse of loyalty to Martha. She knew that she was breaking more church rules the longer she lingered, but at the same time, she hated to end the conversation.

"After traveling the country that summer, they finally arrived in New York City," Carrie said, deciding the safest thing to do was to bring talk of Martha's trip to a close. "Sister Mac needed to order some furniture for the new hotel."

"Oh? Did they see Robert in New York?" Emma asked.

"Yes, they did. He was selling other furniture besides pianos by then," Carrie explained. "We had to buy a number of pieces for the rooms of the new hotel. Robert also helped your mother order that blue and gold carpet down in the parlor. In addition to his sales job, he was managing a boarding house in the city. She and Eugene stayed there with him."

Feeling her face grow flushed, Carrie took a piece of paper out of the hatbox on Emily's lap and began to fan herself. Why does everything keep coming back to Robert? she wondered.

SET APART

Robert McWhirter
New York City, September, 1893

I had been looking forward to Mother's visit for weeks, but I have to admit I was disappointed to learn that she was bringing only Eugene.

From what she told me, construction on the new hotel in Belton is coming along nicely. With my experience in managing this boarding house here in New York, I thought I could be of help in the expanded Central Hotel. But when I brought it up to Mother, she just patted me on the arm and said, 'You're right where you need to be, Bob. You'll get used to it here.'

I hate it when she calls me Bob. No one else does and she knows it annoys me. 'Mother, I've been here for six years,' I told her. 'I think I'd know if I liked it by now. Why won't you let me come home, or at least let some of the church join me up here?'

'You can come home to visit any time you want to, but you have a good job right here in New York,' she quickly pointed out. 'Don't you enjoy your independence and all of the things the city has to offer? Besides, you will never know the joy of self-sacrifice until you surrender every detail of your life. Look at the opportunity you have to live a life that is completely humble, pure and devoted to God.'

She is so manipulative. When I do as she asks and tell her everything that is in my heart, she somehow manages to twist what I say and use it against me. It makes me angry that, at twenty-eight years of age, I still seek her approval in everything I do. Knowing me as she does, she baits me with praise -- for her benefit, of course.

'You make all of your boarders feel welcome here, don't you, Bob? No wonder the house is full. Texas hospitality, that's what it is. Maybe the Central Hotel Company should think about buying a house up here for you to manage,' she suggested.

'Why, yes, Mother. That's a good idea,' I told her in my best sonny-boy voice and hated myself for it. 'Then you could send some other members of the church to work here. Sister Pratt. Maybe Carrie.'

She actually laughed at me. It made me wish I hadn't mentioned Carrie's name. 'We all have plenty to do, Bob. And once the new hotel opens next year, we'll really be busy. You belong here.'

I don't belong here; I'll never belong here. I want to go home. To my family. To Carrie. After spending six years visiting churches in the city, trying to find somewhere to worship, or even just someone to talk to, my only friend seems to be the saloonkeeper in the pub on the corner. I take most of my meals there now, just to have some company.

I still can't believe I let Carrie go home when she was here three years ago. She was really here, and I touched her and even kissed her once. She told me she loved me. I know I didn't make that up. I hate myself for being so weak. What am I afraid of?

On Mother's last night here in New York, she complained that the pain in her face was almost unbearable. I heated some wine and brought it to her room.

'Haven't you found anything that can ease the pain, Mother? I'm sorry the doctor here in New York wasn't able to relieve your suffering. I hate to see you hurting so,' the dutiful son in me said as I handed her the glass.

'I've found a new doctor in Temple who wants to do surgery, and I tell you, Bob, I'm about ready to let him cut me. It only gets worse,' she admitted, sipping the wine. 'I'll talk to him when I get home.' She moaned and held the warm glass against her face.

I had brought the wine bottle with me, so I poured a glass for myself and sat down in a chair across the room from Mother. At her mention of 'home,' I thought I was going to cry. I quickly drained my glass and poured another.

'Mother, I want to marry Carrie.' The words were out of my mouth before I realized what I had done.

The look on her face quickly changed from discomfort to distaste. 'What?' she asked as if she hadn't heard me.

'I want to marry Carrie.' The wine made me feel warm and comfortable. And brave.

'I know you miss the church, Bob . . .'

'No, Mother,' I said, actually interrupting her and feeling very courageous. 'It's Carrie I miss. I want to marry her.' Leaning forward in my chair and knowing I was taking a chance, I revealed my heart to her. 'I love her. I'm sure about that, and I want Carrie for my wife. I've met a lot of women since I've been here, and no one halfway measures up to Carrie. I will love her forever.'

'I see. Yes, of course you do. I love Carrie, too. She's a fine girl. Well, if that's what God intends for your life, Bob, it will happen. That's all I can say right now.' She sighed heavily and closed her eyes, dismissing me and my needs once more.

I sat back in my chair and slowly drained my wineglass again. Holding it in front of my face and looking through the glass, I tilted my head and closed one eye to view my mother's hideously distorted image across the room. 'That's what I thought you'd say,' I said, more to myself than to her. Then I took the bottle back to my room where I finished it alone.

CHAPTER 23

"Well, at least by staying in New York until the summer was over, Mother and Eugene escaped the Texas heat," Emma said. "That's another good reason to leave Belton in June."

"And, of course, the hotel was that much further along when she returned. It seemed like it took a long time to finish this building," Sarah commented. "Did you say it's been open four years now?"

"That's right," Carrie replied, relieved at the shift in the conversation away from Robert. "The fire set us back a few months. You remember it, I'm sure. We had hoped to move in around the first of January in '94. But when the laundry equipment caught fire and destroyed the old Methodist Church building in November, we were delayed." Carrie began to fan herself again as she spoke of the incident.

"Oh, I remember the fire, all right," Sarah said. "We could see it all the way from our place on the other side of town. When I realized it was in the direction of the hotel, I prayed everyone was all right. I knew the hotel construction was just about finished and hoped that wasn't what was burning. The old church made a huge blaze."

"It was pretty frightening to be this close to it," Carrie admitted, still fanning.

"Mama scared me half to death that night," Emily declared. "She had already started using the new office, so she ran over here to get the cash receipts and hotel ledgers from the safe and put them in a pillowslip. Meanwhile, I helped wet some blankets for the firemen to put on the roofs of the outbuildings, but mostly I just tried to stay out of the way.

"Grandma was grateful to those firemen for carrying the larger pieces of laundry equipment out of the building. When it was all over, the wringers and expensive steam mangle used for ironing the linens were all that was left. I know I was thankful for those big old machines whenever I was on the laundry rotation," Emily added sarcastically, rolling her eyes.

"Well! You might really mean that if you'd ever had to do the laundry in iron washpots like we did when you were a baby," Carrie scolded playfully. "Actually, it turned out for the best. The old church building burning down, I mean. We moved the equipment across Pearl Street onto the hotel property and built a nice, new laundry building and this lovely suite of rooms. We were so grateful the firemen had protected the new hotel building and rescued the laundry equipment, we invited them to our last Christmas banquet in the old Central Hotel the following month. Remember how pretty it looked, Emily?"

"Oh, it was lovely," Emily agreed. "The cooks really outdid themselves that night. The special menu included steaks, turkey and dressing, plover dressed with eggs, stewed corn, peas . . ."

"How in the world can you remember what was served?" Sarah interrupted, astounded at Emily's recitation.

"It was such a wonderful meal, how could I forget?" the girl responded with a mischievous giggle. "Ah, yes, and Irish potatoes, lettuce, corn bread, flour bread, coconut angel cake, white and chocolate cake, pound cake, ambrosia cake, and fresh fruits," she finished in one breath.

"Or maybe you're reading it off the menu in Carrie's hand," Emma said accusingly as she identified the paper Carrie had been using as a fan.

Laughing, Carrie examined the hand-written menu she was holding. "You left out the nuts, Emily. You know we always have nuts." She dropped the page back into the hatbox. "There are some interesting things in here," Carrie observed "Do you mind if I look, Emily?"

"Of course not. Go right ahead. I'm sure you know more about what's in there than I do. Here, just put it on your lap."

Carrie sorted through the box. "Well, look at this. Here's the certificate given to your grandmother the night she was the first woman asked to join the Belton Board of Trade," Carrie noted.

"At the first big banquet we held in the new dining room, right? One hundred twenty-five people, as I recall. I worked in the kitchen that night, but I'm afraid I don't remember the menu," Emily said playfully.

"Y'all served one hundred twenty-five people?" Sarah asked. "That's quite a crowd!"

"It was our way of thanking the boarders for staying with us during those two long years of construction as well as showing our appreciation to the townspeople for supporting the hotel," Carrie explained. "It felt so good to be able to lay to rest some of the bad things that had happened in the past." As she said it, Carrie realized she now felt that same satisfaction as she visited with these women with whom she ordinarily wouldn't have conversed so freely.

"Grandma was in such high spirits," Emily said. "At the banquet she gave a donation toward the construction of the new opera house, and then later, when we were cleaning up, she announced we were all going to take a vacation."

"Right when the new hotel opened?" Sarah asked in surprise. Emma shrugged and shook her head.

"I think she wanted to squeeze in some travel before we got too busy," Carrie replied.

"Construction had taken so long, we all thought the building would never be finished, and then it seemed like we worked around the clock to get moved in. We were all worn out and ready to get away from here," Emily added.

"Where did you go this time?" Emma asked, still bewildered at her mother's unconventional behavior.

"Well, I would have loved to have gone back to New York, but a trip of that distance would have taken more time than we could spare. It made more sense to take turns going down to Galveston," Carrie said, "and we had been wanting to go back there for years. This time we went in four traveling groups. Emily and I were in the last group and didn't get to go until almost the end of the summer."

Emily groaned. "It was so hard to wait, especially when everyone kept coming back and telling us what a wonderful vacation they had."

"That summer was the first time I ever worked at the front desk by myself," Carrie admitted. "After I got used to the new position, I found out I rather liked being in charge. I also enjoyed not having to work in the laundry or make beds or cook or anything like that. Of course, front desk management is all I've been doing in the Waco hotels. When our leases run out on the Royal and the Palmo, I'm sure I'll miss the activity, but I think we've decided we're all ready to make a change."

Emily thought she heard a note of regret in her friend's voice. "You're going to love Washington, Carrie. I just know it."

"Well, I am looking forward to our being together again."
But as soon as she had said it, Carrie once again thought of
Robert and the fact that he remained separated from them.

Carrie Henry
Belton, June, 1894

In the beginning, I was flattered when Sister Mac left me
in charge of the entire Central Hotel while she took the first
group of vacationers to Galveston. It didn't take long,
however, for me to feel overwhelmed with the complex task of
managing this business, especially since the recent completion
of the new building. Even though the old hotel was crowded
and showed clear signs of wear, I quickly found out that our
familiarity with it had simplified some of our jobs. In the new
building, boarders asked a thousand questions a day that I had
no idea how to answer. I, alone, was responsible for
scheduling the weekly work rotations, approving menus,
preparing shopping lists, paying bills, ordering supplies,
collecting rents, greeting transient residents, giving directions,
and remaining pleasant when someone stopped up the new
plumbing. Also included among my duties was a daily trip to
the post office to pick up the hotel mail. It was this simple
chore that led me to learn of something I shall never forget.

Along with the usual bills and a beautiful postcard from the
travelers in Galveston was a letter from Robert in New York
City. Lying on top of my desk, the envelope caught my eye
each time I walked by, and I ached to know what he had
written to his mother. Although it had been several years since
his proposal in Central Park, I prayed daily for his well-being,

230

since, at least for the time being, the marriage we had talked about was clearly an impossible dream.

Against my better judgement, I gave in to the unbearable temptation and steamed open the envelope in the kitchen that evening after I was sure that everyone had gone to bed. After all, 'Men loved the darkness rather than light because their deeds were evil.' My hands shook as I removed the pages from the damp envelope.

In the letter, Robert repeatedly begged his mother to let him come home or to send church members back to New York for another visit. It grieved me that he was so totally miserable. He admitted that in his loneliness, he was spending far too much time at a saloon down the street and pleaded for his mother's forgiveness. With feelings of deep regret, I recalled my own father's destructive drinking episodes and how the alcohol often turned him into a man I hardly recognized. My anxiety for my dear friend grew when I realized that the letter I held did not seem to be written by the Robert I knew so well. But it was the words penned on the third page that left their indelible mark on my heart:

'You remember that I told you a long time ago that I wanted to marry Carrie. You told me yourself that you loved her and that God intended us for one another. She once told me that she loved me and would never marry another. My dear mother, I am only writing what is in my heart, as you told me to do, and I must tell you that I am miserable without her. I love Carrie and always shall, and I am asking that you send her up here to me as soon as you can.'

The words haunted me, not only for their desperate message, but because I hardly recognized the careless, scrawled handwriting on the wrinkled, ink-smeared paper. This wild scribbling was nothing like the careful, even penmanship Robert and I had learned together in Sister

Rancier's classroom. Clearly, he had not only been drinking, but was also in tears when he wrote to his mother. Close to tears myself, I wondered how long Robert would have to endure his painful exile and whether we would ever be together again. It also made me question how Sister Mac could bear to leave her beloved son suffering such prolonged agony.

CHAPTER 24

"Let's not talk about you all leaving," Sarah said. "I want to hear more about Galveston. It's just a few hours away on the train, and I've never been there."

"Oh, Mrs. Miller, you really must go, if only just to see the ocean," Emily urged. "The Gulf Coast is so different from Central Texas. Grandma rented a beach cottage on Galveston Island that summer. Like Carrie said, she and I had to wait until almost the end of the summer until it was our group's turn to spend a week there. "Anna was with us. We were both fifteen that summer, and I was glad to be there with someone my age. The first thing we wanted to see was the Beach Hotel. Mama had sent us a picture postcard of it from her trip, and we just had to see it for ourselves."

"My only plan for the week was to relax," Carrie countered. "I just wanted to sit on the veranda at the boarding house and read all day long. I didn't want to pay bills, or order supplies, or run messages up and down the stairs, or beg boarders to pay their rent. It was heavenly. For a whole week, I was free."

"It was late when we got to the cottage," Emily said, "so we didn't get to see the Beach Hotel until the next morning. As it turned out, we didn't have to go far since the hotel was almost right beside the house. Mama hadn't mentioned that."

"I was surprised it hadn't woken us up. I've never seen such a colorful building!" Carrie exclaimed. "I believe Emily and Anna called it 'dazzling.'"

"Wait, there's the postcard," Emily said as she spied the card and snatched it out of the hatbox on Carrie's lap. "Listen to the notes Mama wrote on the back: 'three-story building, three octagonal pavilions connected by open porches. Queen Anne and gothic styles. Dome - 125 feet from the beach. Roof - red and white stripes, bronze and gold ridges. The rest of the hotel is mauve with green and gold accents. White grillwork along the galleries. American flag on top of the dome.' Look at this, Carrie," Emily said as she passed the card. "Mama underlined all of the paint colors. Do you think she wanted to copy the Beach Hotel's color combination on the Central?"

"I sure hope not," Carrie said, laughing as she tried to imagine the garish design on Main Street in Belton. "I think the Beach Hotel belongs at the beach. And what a hotel it was. We found out that it had two hundred rooms and an elevator run by a steam engine. Despite being on vacation, the first thing I thought of was how long it would take to clean two hundred rooms. With all that sand, can you imagine?"

"Did y'all go inside?" Sarah asked as Carrie handed her the postcard.

"We ate one meal in their dazzling dining room," Carrie answered with a wink for Emily. "Its three walls of windows made us feel like we were sitting out in the middle of the ocean. There was a gulf view in almost every direction."

"It was simply magnificent, to use a better word. We were disappointed when we saw in the newspaper that the entire hotel burned down this summer." Emily lamented.

"I thought I remembered reading about a big fire in Galveston," Sarah recalled. "I'm sorry that Mr. Miller and I won't get to see the Beach Hotel, but I'd still like to take a trip to the island. You've made it sound very enjoyable, and I'm sure we can find another place to stay. What else did you do while you were there?"

"Well, Anna and I spent most of our days at the Galveston Social Institute," Emily replied. "It's known as 'the resort for ladies and children.' Most mornings before it got too hot, we played croquet or lawn tennis, and then went back in the evenings to attend a concert or a sing-along. The ice cream parlor at the Institute had ten flavors! On our last night, Anna and I talked Carrie and the others into going to a concert at the beach pavilion."

"We listened to John Philip Sousa and his band," Carrie recalled. "You may have heard of him. He used to be the leader of the Marine Corps Band but has recently formed a band of his own, and now he gives concerts all over the country. We were fortunate he was in Galveston that week. The music was absolutely thrilling."

"I know you'll love attending the concerts in Washington, Carrie," Emily said. "Did I tell you there's one every Saturday night at the White House and every Wednesday night at the Capitol?"

"Please, no more talk about Washington, girls," Sarah begged. "I don't even want to think of y'all leaving."

"I do appreciate how much you care about us, Mrs. Miller, but I hope you understand that we're anxious to be reunited," Emily explained. "Remember, we're scattered from here to Waco to Washington. Uncle Robert may even move down from New York to be with us."

Emily's off-hand comment nearly took Carrie's breath away, and she quickly looked down into the hatbox, hoping her surprise had not registered on her face.

"Really?" Sarah asked doubtfully. "I heard awhile back that he had married a woman in New York and that they had a little girl."

Robert McWhirter
New York City, November, 1895

I am the most wretched of men. I see nothing in my future, no hope. Nothing can save me from this utter despair.

When Mother sent me here to New York almost ten years ago, I convinced myself that it was God's plan for me as part of His church. I viewed the painful loneliness as my struggle toward the maturity of my spirit, confident that someday my suffering would be rewarded and that someday my prayers would be answered. My prayers to be reunited with my church family. My prayers to be with Carrie.

But as the years passed, my loneliness only increased. Infrequent visits from church members intensified my desire to be with them. I looked forward to receiving their letters, but read and reread each one in tears. Every time I wrote home, I begged Mother to send some of the church to come and stay with me. My longing to be with Carrie ached like an open wound, and I imagined that I could actually feel the rough, broken edges of my heart. I felt that my prayers were being ignored. God was not listening to me. No one listened to me.

Except for Nate, the saloonkeeper on the corner. He listened night after night as I sat drinking his beer. After a while, I found I wasn't quite so lonely. After a few more drinks, I noticed that I stopped feeling the pain in my heart. And if I drank enough, I could forget that I would be going back to my room alone. Again.

Then one night, Nate introduced me to Laura. Beautiful
Laura. Perhaps he thought he was doing me a favor, or it
might be that he simply grew tired of hearing my same
complaints. It really didn't matter as long as Laura sat and
drank beer with me and listened.

And then she talked. Telling me the story of her divorce,
she revealed how she had come to New York to hide from her
former husband. He used to beat her, she told me, and it was a
familiar story. One night she showed me her scars. I couldn't
show her the scars on my heart, but I felt certain she could see
them. As we talked, it seemed as if she could see inside my
heart just as Carrie used to. I didn't want Laura to get that
close, but some nights as we sat and drank and talked, I got
her confused with Carrie. At least I wasn't alone.

Laura let me touch her the way I had touched Carrie. Then
she let me kiss her like I had kissed Carrie. Once, she bought a
bottle of wine and invited me to share it with her in her room.
She was sad and asked me to hold her because she knew I
wouldn't hurt her.

The next morning I woke up in her bed. And because I
didn't want her to be hurt again, I married her. I am the most
wretched of men.

CHAPTER 25

"Well," Emily began uneasily, "Uncle Robert is married. He has a little girl named Martha, but he says he's leaving his wife as soon as the new baby is born."

Carrie felt a tingling in her hands as she gripped the sides of the hatbox. Fighting to keep from crying out, she willed herself to breathe.

Sarah and Emma looked at each other in disbelief. "What?" Emma exclaimed. "New baby? He's going to leave a woman with two children? I can't imagine that my brother would do such a thing."

"Especially considering the way he was raised. He's had to live with the effects of divorces his whole life. Did he choose his wife unwisely?" Sarah asked.

"I don't know any details about his marriage," Emily admitted, "but I think Uncle Robert's been unhappy for a long time."

"Carrie, what do you know about this?" Emma pressed. "Why would Robert harm his own family? I don't understand."

"Oh. Well . . . Em . . . Emily seems to know more about it than I do," she stammered, shocked at how quickly the conversation had become so uncomfortable. "Not a lot of news makes it all the way to Waco. We're really quite busy up there."

"But you were in New York this summer, Carrie," Emily said. "Didn't Uncle Robert mention anything to you? Y'all have always been such good friends, surely he must have said something."

Carrie Henry
Waco, Texas, June, 1898

The letter came addressed to me at the Royal Hotel in Waco. Even before I opened the envelope, I recognized Robert's handwriting. Just seeing my name written in his hand brought back the sinking sensation I had experienced when Sister Mac made the announcement almost three years ago that he had suddenly married. In one moment, my whole world changed. I had been so sure that somehow, someday I would become Mrs. Robert McWhirter. While I understood how lonely Robert was in New York, hadn't we prayed that God would bring us back together? What happened? Why didn't he wait for God to answer our prayer? The instant I learned of his marriage, my heart shattered and my dream of a future with Robert dissolved.

The news had come about the time we leased the two hotels in Waco. In order to escape self-pity and to keep my mind off of Robert, I immediately volunteered for the management position of both hotels and made a solemn vow to God that I would spend the rest of my life in service to the church. I knew it was the only way I could escape the feeling of bitterness that threatened to consume me.

Nevertheless, I was disappointed that Robert never tried to contact me personally. When his letter arrived at the Royal almost three years later, it was so totally unexpected, I was almost afraid to open it. But, of course, I did.

'My Dear Carrie, I must go out of the country next month. Mother tells me that you are the only one she trusts to manage the boarding house here in New York while I am gone. We leave on May 5 and plan to be away until the end of the month. I would appreciate your coming to New York to help. All my love, Robert.'

A business letter after years of silence? With mixed emotions, I ignored the closing mention of love and resolved to respond to his request as an act of service. After all, I had dedicated my life to the church.

In a way, I had been disappointed by the letter. Sister Mac had told me months earlier about the situation that Robert described, and my schedule had been adjusted accordingly. I don't really know what I expected him, now a husband and father, to write to me. But realizing what courage it must have taken for him to correspond with me personally, without his mother's permission, I suppose I expected something other than an impersonal business letter.

Knowing he would be busy with travel arrangements, I made a point of planning my trip so that I wouldn't get to New York until the afternoon before Robert's scheduled departure. I didn't know if he would have anything of a personal nature to say that he didn't trust to put in a letter, but I wasn't planning to give him that opportunity. I hadn't come for a friendly visit. I was only there because of my vow to work for the church. I really couldn't imagine a personal conversation between us that would be appropriate, considering his marriage and our prior relationship.

I arrived at Robert's boarding house on the afternoon of May 4. Just as I was paying the cabdriver, Robert suddenly appeared at my side. Sensing his presence even before I actually saw him, I was overwhelmed by an unforeseen flood of emotion that weakened my knees. I took a step back and sat down hard on the trunk the cabdriver had just unloaded onto the sidewalk.

'You're as white as a sheet, Carrie,' Robert said as he reached out to steady me. 'Long trip?'

With an unexpected rush of panic, I trembled at the sound of his voice and the touch of his hand on my arm. Clearly, I had made a grave mistake in coming to New York. My stomach churned and my head throbbed. How I wished I could just jump up and run away.

'Yes, it was a very long trip,' I replied hoarsely, closing my eyes to avoid seeing his face. Gathering my courage, I stood so that Robert could carry my trunk up the steps and into the house. He showed me to a room on the second floor and set the trunk down, leaving the door to the hall open behind us.

'You got my letter,' Robert stated without expression. I knew he was probably anxious to know that his unauthorized communication had reached its intended destination. I nodded my answer. Not really knowing what the letter meant to me, but cherishing it nonetheless, I had hidden it in the lining of my handbag.

'I'm here as an employee of the Central Hotel Company,' I replied as lightly as I could, while still clarifying that the nature of our relationship had been irrevocably altered. 'At your service.' I even managed to come up with a smile.

A woman carrying a small, blonde-haired child came to the open door. 'It ees Mademoiselle Henry?' she asked as she entered the room. 'I am Madame McWhirter,' she said with a charming French accent, extending her hand to me in the European way. 'Zees is our leetle Martha. We thank you for coming. Excuse now, if you please. I must finish the packing.'

I had to close my mouth before taking her hand. Why had I never heard anything about the woman who was Robert's wife? She was so gracious. And so beautiful. I knew he must love her very much. I wanted to be happy for him. I wanted him to be happy. I wanted to cry. Little Martha waved goodbye as she and her mother disappeared down the hall.

'We leave first thing in the morning,' Robert explained. 'I'm taking Mrs. McWhirter to Paris to . . . visit her father, and to introduce little Martha to her grandfather. He's a physician.' There was an awkward pause as Robert appeared to be considering whether or not to elaborate on the details of his trip. I was relieved when he did not.

'Will you want me to show you the books before you unpack?' he asked as though he sensed my discomfort. 'They'll probably be familiar to you, since Mother set them up the same way they're done at the Central Hotel and, I assume, the ones in Waco, too, but I may need to explain some of the accounts.'

I told him that would suit me fine, then added that afterwards I would prefer to take my supper in my room. I knew there was no way I could manage to share a meal with Robert and his family. 'It was a long trip,' I said again.

I followed him down the hall, my gaze fixed on the familiar blue patterned carpet I knew his mother had selected. When we entered the small, airless office, I immediately walked across the room to open a window. 'Are you still uncomfortable, Carrie? We could do this after you've rested.'

'Oh, I'm fine, Robert,' I said with forced cheerfulness. 'Let's see what you have.'

As impersonally as possible, Robert showed me the books I would handle in the month that he would be away. As he nervously chattered about bills and boarders, I realized that this was the first time I could ever remember us trying to hide anything from each other. As clearly as I sensed his misery, I knew very well that Robert felt my distress, that he could see my broken heart the same way I saw his, and I wished I hadn't agreed to meet with him alone.

'The iceman comes on Monday, and milk is delivered around 6 o'clock, but don't let him leave any butter. We trade with the German grocer on Twelfth Avenue, Mr. Strauss. It's all written down right here.' Robert stopped talking just as a sigh slipped through my determined self-control. 'Are you sure you're all right, Carrie?' He closed the ledger and leaned too close to my face. 'Do you want to talk?' he asked more tenderly than was comfortable for me.

'No,' I said sharply, focusing on the closed book. I took a deep breath and straightened my shoulders. 'I'm okay. It looks like you're doing a fine job with the business, Robert. I think I can manage it while you're gone. If that's all the information I need, I'll go back to my room now. You'll send my tray?' He nodded and let me leave without another word.

In my room, I unpacked my trunk, wishing I were anyplace else. I took off my dusty boots and put them in the hall for the chambermaid to clean. After removing my traveling clothes, I hung them on the back of the door and, in my chemise and pantaloons, dusted off the suit and petticoats with a garment brush. At the washstand, I wiped my face and neck, purposely avoiding my reflection in the mirror on the wall. Although it was only six o'clock, I changed into a cotton gown, and, sitting on the edge of the bed, took the pins out of my hair. Uncoiled, it touched the bed as I furiously brushed through the waves, yanking the tangles until tears came to my eyes.

There was a knock at the door. 'Your supper, Carrie.' Recognizing Robert's voice, I quickly wiped my eyes and told him to leave the tray in the hall.

He was silent for a moment. 'I'm sorry, but we've had some trouble with, uh . . . mice lately. Can I just hand it to you?'

Reluctantly, I pulled on my wrapper and opened the door to take the tray from him. After setting it on the bed, I turned around to close the door, but Robert was still standing there, his hands frozen in the position of holding the tray, his mouth open to speak. I had to resist the urge to rush into his arms.

'Is there something else?' I asked. It was the wrong question. In his eyes, I saw what I knew could never be expressed.

'Carrie, I . . .' he began.

'I'm sorry, Robert. I'm very tired,' I interrupted. 'Can it wait until tomorrow?'

"No, I want to . . ."

Without even thinking, I reached out and put my fingers over his mouth to quiet him like I used to do when we were children. Horrified, I tried to pull my hand back, but he held it there, flattening my palm against his lips. He closed his eyes for a moment, then without another word, he dropped my hand, turned, and walked away down the hall. My heart pounding, I shut the door quickly, knowing it had been foolish of me to have come to New York.

I didn't leave my room the next morning until I was sure Robert, Laura and their child were gone. While they were away for the entire month of May, I was determined to stay too busy to think about him. But with the lingering scent of his shaving soap and having to face his familiar handwriting in the ledger books daily, the days and weeks dragged by. At least playing parlor games and attending the theater with the lively collection of boarders filled the evening hours.

Leaving plenty of notes to update him on the details, I left the same day Robert returned and was on the train to Texas before the McWhirter family got out of their cab. Every day I thank God for the busyness of my work in Waco.

CHAPTER 26

"No, I really didn't get to visit with Robert when I went to New York last summer," Carrie said matter-of-factly, managing to regain her composure. "But I met his wife and daughter. Their little Martha is an absolute doll. The reason I was there was to manage the boarding house for him while he and he went overseas for the month. It was only a business trip."

"Maybe it's just as well you didn't see much of him," Emily said, making a sour face. "I hear he drinks too much, and he smokes cigarettes, too. When he came to visit us in Washington earlier this month, Grandma wouldn't have a thing to do with him. I still feel sorry for Uncle Robert, though. He seems so lost. He told me that after his divorce, he wants to come live with us in Washington, although I doubt Grandma will let him. I think he hates his wife," she added in a confidential tone.

An awkward silence stilled the room.

"I'm sorry for bringing that up," Emma apologized, taking the blame for Emily's inappropriate candor. "It was rude of me. Please forgive me."

"I'm the sorry one, Aunt Emma," Emily responded as she realized she had revealed the kind of information only discussed among church members. She stole a glance at Carrie to try to determine whether any real damage had been caused. "I shouldn't have said what I did."

"That's all right, honey. We're all family here, but even so, we learn that there are some things better left unsaid." Emma paused to let her gentle reproof make its impression on Emily before changing the subject. "Are you very busy in Waco, Carrie?"

"Oh, yes," she replied. Her voice regained a measure of lightness as she closed her mind to speculation about Robert. "We've leased two hotels not far from the Opera House and they're almost always full. We're serving up to one hundred people at each meal, and some nights we even have to turn folks away. Actually, I prefer staying busy. And as much as I've enjoyed visiting with you all, I really should get back to my post." Grateful for the opportunity to leave before any more discomforting topics arose, Carrie placed the hatbox on the floor and stood up. "I've had such a nice time, I almost forgot that I'm here to work. I came to Belton to help out at the front desk until Ada's back on her feet." After carefully securing the drawstrings, she tucked the handbag containing the treasured letter safely under her arm.

"It was wonderful to see you again, Carrie," Emma said sincerely.

"Have a good evening, dear," Sarah added.

Emily rose and walked Carrie to the door. "I'm sorry I can't stay until your mother wakes up, Emmie, but just in case I don't see you again before you leave tomorrow, please give my mother and Ella a hug for me when you get back to Washington," Carrie said as they embraced once more. "Oh, Ella wrote that she's sewing new aprons for everyone."

"Yes. She intended it to be a surprise, but you know how Ella is about keeping secrets," Emily reminded.

"Yes, and I know how she is about keeping busy, herself. I'll wager she's shining shoes every day whether they need it or not! Well, I can't stand here chatting all night. I'll be up there with y'all as soon as those Waco leases are up in the spring. And no more fretting about your mother, Emmie. Dr. Ghent will be here soon. He'll know just what to do." After kissing Emily on the forehead, she pressed her handbag to her side and stooped to pick up the tray beside the door.

"Thank you, Carrie. Good night." Emily said as she closed the door behind her friend.

She returned to the settee. "Carrie was like a big sister to me after I came back to Belton," she explained to Sarah and Emma. "When Hattie finally came home last year, I had to get to know her all over again."

"I was just going to ask about my other niece," Emma said. "How is your sister? I heard that she . . ."

A soft knock at the door and the appearance of a bright red head of hair announced Hattie's arrival. Emily jumped up eagerly to greet her sister, who quickly put her finger to her lips, signaling for quiet. The child Hattie held was asleep, her head resting on the young mother's shoulder.

"I just passed Carrie on the stairs, but I didn't know Mama had more company," she whispered to Emily as she waved a greeting to Emma and Sarah. "Is she asleep?"

Emily nodded as she put her hand up to touch her niece's blonde curls. "Why don't you just put Wilma on my bed? I don't think it'll disturb Mama." Quietly, she opened the bedroom door for her sister.

In a moment, Hattie rejoined the women. After greeting Sarah and her Aunt Emma, she sat down. "How is Mama doing? I saw her early, early this morning, and I could tell she wasn't feeling well. I knew she'd never get a minute's peace with Wilma around, so I decided to take the baby out to the farm for the day. She's been asking to see the chickens, and you know, she's not a bit afraid of them. I was terribly afraid of chickens when I was her age. Actually, she's not afraid of any of the animals," Hattie said proudly. "But how is Mama? Is she still coughing?"

"She was before she went to sleep," Emily reported. "We asked Dr. Ghent to stop by and check on her. Carrie told us he'll be here soon."

"Sarah and I are anxious to hear what the doctor has to say, and then we'll be going," said Emma, explaining their presence. "But this is a treat, getting to see both of my nieces on the same night. And Wilma, too. Hattie, she's just as precious as I've heard. I'm sorry I haven't gotten over to visit with you two before now. Uncle J.J. and I have only been back in town for a few weeks."

"It's just as well, Aunt Emma. We've been here in Belton since last June, but it's taken us until now just to get settled, after being out of the country for so long. And it looks like we'll be packing up to move again," Hattie said with a shrug as she surveyed the disheveled room.

"Your mother has told me all about Wilma," Sarah said. "Since y'all got here, she's all Ada wants to talk about when we visit at the hotel desk every Wednesday. I think she's the proudest grandma I've ever met. That baby has purely stolen her heart."

"Yes, well, thank you," Hattie said, beaming with delight. "She's a handful. Two and a half last month, and talking up a storm. Ever since Grandma left for Washington on the train, all she talks about is 'Granny Choochoo.' And Sadie's taught her to call Mama 'Mammy.'"

"I know you're proud of her, Hattie. She's a beautiful child. Your mother is so happy you two are here. Were you glad to get back to Belton?" Sarah asked. "I've heard that a Central American plantation is a rough place to live."

"You can't imagine how rough, Mrs. Miller," Hattie replied, her smile fading.

249

SET APART

Hattie Haymond Weatherford
Nicaragua, June, 1897

I never in my life would have believed I would be so happy to be on a stinking banana boat, but I am absolutely thrilled beyond words to have a ticket on a vessel that smells like rotting garbage. When I get back to Belton, I will never, ever leave the country again. I have had enough of heat, mosquitoes, flies, spiders, scorpions and snakes to last many lifetimes. For the time being I am through with men, as well, so I will give in and seek shelter with my grandmother and her company of dry old maids for a short while. Just as soon as I can get a job and pay back my loan from the Sanctified, Wilma and I will be on our way.

I have no idea how I will be received by my mother when I return to Texas. After Father took George and Emily and me to Michigan, she never wrote to us. Not even once. I missed her so much when I first got there, but when she didn't write, I began to believe what Aunt Mary had always said about her and the others. For years, she insisted that Grandma and the women had started the church as a shrewd way to be rid of their husbands. No husbands meant no more children and that was the way they wanted it. My mother was glad we were gone, Aunt Mary declared. 'Accept it, Hattie,' she told me again and again. 'Your mother doesn't want you and she doesn't love you. You have to make your own way in this life.'

Well, I've certainly done that and made a big mess of it. Less than a year after my father's death, I married the despicable Mr. William Weatherford. I was just a child, barely eighteen years old, so how was I to know that he saw my inheritance of the fruit plantation as his personal gold mine?

250

At first, my brother George and I saw the trip to Nicaragua to claim the plantation as a great adventure. But when we arrived in Bluefields in December of 1893, we discovered that most of the property had already been sold to pay off the debts and taxes owed by our father's estate. Instead of living in the grand plantation home we had envisioned, George and my easily disillusioned husband and I lived in the same tiny, bug-infested huts occupied by the native workers. With the few laborers who remained, we struggled to support ourselves on the small part of the fruit farm that was left of our grand plantation.

Within a year I had a child, with only a Creole medicine woman to help me through the frightening birth. As if dealing with solitude, snakes and a sickly child weren't enough, within months I was expecting again. On April 2, 1896, two days after my precious firstborn died of some horrid jungle fever, I delivered Wilma. Immediately, she became the joy of my life.

When Wilma was but three months old, the rainy season began. What little that was left of our plantation was soon destroyed in a horrendous flood. Our deliverance came in the form of a kind man on a neighboring plantation who invited us to share his home and offered my husband a job. George left to find work elsewhere.

In the six months that we lived with him on Mango Plantation, Mr. Brown was a perfect gentleman and offered nothing but kindness and friendship to our little family. Instead of being grateful, though, William responded to Mr. Brown with suspicion. After hearing William repeatedly call me a 'damn fool,' Mr. Brown approached my husband and suggested that he stop treating me so cruelly. Our neighbor's courteous treatment of me caused William to accuse us of being intimate. It was an embarrassing situation for poor Mr. Brown, and I felt badly for him. I decided that I could not

251

continue to live with my husband's brutish and irrational behavior, so I borrowed money from my brother George and made preparations to go to the United States. When my husband learned of my plans, he threatened to kill me, and I had to postpone my escape.

On the morning of February 19, 1897, I was up very early and sat sewing as the baby slept. Mr. Brown was on his way to bring fresh water to my room, as he did each day. While he was still in the front hall, I heard my husband begin to argue with him. At the sound of a gunshot, I cracked open my door and was horrified to discover that my husband had shot Mr. Brown in the head and apparently killed him.

Before I could close the door and lock him out, a crazed William pushed his way into the room waving the gun and yelling, 'I'm going to kill you, too!'

I snatched up the baby from her pallet on the floor. 'If you kill me, what will become of my child?' I screamed.

His eyes wild, he raced around the room, stuffing a straw bag full with his clothes. Heading straight to where I thought I had so cleverly hidden the money George had given me to get back to Texas, he took every cent. When the authorities arrived, having been summoned by the workers, William was long gone. I was unable to be much help.

Feeling certain that Mother would not be interested in helping me, even in my desperate situation, I wrote to my grandmother, asking for a loan. 'It is a small amount to you,' I wrote to her, 'but it will do baby and me lots of good.' The Sanctified sent enough money for the boat and train tickets, for which I am eternally grateful.

As soon as we get to Galveston, Wilma and I can get off of this sickening boat and board the train to Belton. All I want is a bath and a bed and someone to hold Wilma for a while so I can rest.

CHAPTER 27

"After I was married, my husband and I and my brother George went down to Central America to claim our inheritance of the fruit plantation after Father died. It didn't take long for me to discover that I wasn't cut out for plantation life," Hattie declared without amplification, determined not to discuss a part of her life she was trying hard to forget. "I won't bore you with the details, and that's really all I want to say. I left that place as soon as I could."

Although Sarah and Emma respected her reluctance to talk, they could not help but wonder what Hattie had experienced aside from the facts of the murder investigation they had read about in the newspaper. Even Ada had been unwilling to share with Sarah many of the details of her older daughter's life in Central America. Nevertheless, the women let the matter drop without so much as a raised eyebrow.

"Well, I know your mother is glad to finally have you here," Sarah told her. "You can't imagine how hard she worked to get you and Emily and George back home after the divorce. It like to killed her. I know she considers Wilma to be an extra bonus for having to wait so long. Now that you're a mother, you can appreciate that nine years is a long time to be separated from your daughter. Ada is just tickled to death that y'all are back. Now if she could only get George to come home, too."

"I don't know if she'll ever be able to do that. That one visit back to Belton a few years ago was enough for him. He's been able to buy his own plantation in Mexico, and he actually likes it down there." Hattie shuddered.

"George was *here?*" Emma asked. "I never heard he was back in town."

"He wasn't here for long. It was just before this hotel building was finished," Emily said. "I remember exactly when he came. That January, the girls of Belton had their annual ball and reception. Actually, we had anticipated being in this new building by then, but since it wasn't quite ready, we decorated the old dining room especially nice for them. We didn't want the girls to be disappointed to be over there when we had told them we'd be in the new hotel for their party. The photographer who was taking pictures of the girls that evening was very impressed when he saw the new hotel was almost finished and told Mama how nice it looked. She asked him to come back in the morning and take a photo of the building."

"Emily!" Hattie teased her younger sister. "Aunt Emma asked about George."

"I'm getting there, Hattie," Emily said, not used to having to share her attention with a sibling. "I had to explain why we were all standing out in front of the hotel for a photograph when George walked up."

"Oh, my goodness!" Emma cried. "You mean he just walked right up the same street he had disappeared from? Didn't anyone know he was coming?"

"No, it was a complete surprise, and at first, no one recognized him. He was almost seventeen years old and looked very different than when he left at age ten," Emily explained.

"Why didn't he stay?" Sarah asked, finding it unusual that a reunion so long in coming would be so brief that some people never knew George had returned. "And why weren't you with him, Hattie?"

Hattie quickly formulated a response that revealed as little as possible. "Actually, George came to Belton hoping to get a job here at the hotel to make some extra money for supplies we needed. He didn't get back to the plantation until the end of May, so you can be sure I was as glad to see him as the folks in Belton had been. As it turned out, living on the plantation wasn't exactly what I had envisioned, but then Wilma was born and I had to stay until she was old enough to travel. I'm just glad we had someplace to go. Since we've been in Belton, everyone here has made us feel so welcome. To tell you the truth, I didn't know what to expect after being away for so long. I got acquainted with everyone a little at a time as everyone began to come back from the trip to Mexico that summer. I'm glad they all had a good vacation, but you won't catch me leaving this country again."

"Oh, Hattie. I enjoyed Mexico," Emily said. "I'd go back any time."

Hattie rolled her eyes. "Surely Mexico can't be that much different from Nicaragua. What in the world could you have possibly enjoyed about anything in that horrid jungle, Emily? It's completely backward and totally uncivilized. I've never seen such squalor and misery." As she spoke, Hattie wrung her apron through her hands, as if to wipe away the disturbing memories of her plantation ordeal. "I find it hard to believe that George is happy to be living in Mexico. I'll never leave the country again. Surely there are more pleasant things to talk about. There's a new calf out at the farm."

"Mama?" a small, anxious voice called from the next room.

"Oh, dear. It's Wilma." Hattie announced unnecessarily as she stood and walked toward the door. "I'll go put her to bed in our room. I don't want her to wake Mama." Hattie slipped

255

into the next room and reappeared carrying the sleepy-eyed child. "Aunt Emma, Mrs. Miller . . .I'm sorry I can't stay and visit. Emmie, please stop by later and let me know what the doctor says. I hope it's nothing serious." Wilma waved shyly over her mother's shoulder as Emily closed the door behind them.

Crossing the room to light another lamp, Emily struggled to banish the worrisome thoughts about her mother's health. She looked around for an easy task to occupy her hands and picking up a fallen quilt, she began folding it.

Sensing the need to distract Emily from Hattie's mention of the doctor, Sarah spoke up. "What a darling niece you have, Emily. I know you must enjoy having them back. You and your sister seem to have completely opposite opinions of life across the Rio Grande, though. She evidently had a very difficult experience, while it sounds as though you had a grand time. I have to tell you I'm still amazed at a group of women vacationing unescorted in Mexico City," she exclaimed. "Four groups, actually. And it sounds like you're ready for another visit. Y'all must have really enjoyed yourselves. What was the best part of the trip?"

Emily sighed with relief as she put down the quilt and returned to the settee. "The best part? Oh, my, how do I choose? We went to museums, the cathedral, a pyramid, a bullfight, and an opera. It was a busy trip. But if I have to pick my favorite thing, it would have to be the president's birthday celebration. What a party! The closest thing I can compare it to here would be the Fourth of July. There were huge crowds of people, but we, of course, stood out from the barefoot Mexican women with babies strapped to their backs." Emily couldn't help but smile as she recalled the colorful scene.

"Mama and I were in the last group to take the trip, and by that time, our party was easily recognized by the way we were dressed. When Mama showed a card that said, 'The Central Hotel, Belton, Texas,' the guards moved us to the front of the crowd, where we were invited into the palace to meet President Diaz himself. A translator was there so we could tell the president what a nice time we were having in his country. He told us how he had enjoyed meeting with Mrs. McWhirter earlier that summer. Goodness, we felt important! Mama was bold enough to ask if we could meet his wife, Mrs. Diaz. To our surprise, they gave us passes to visit the private palace in Chapultepec. We had our Kodak with us and even had our photograph taken with her. I wish I had thought to bring my album."

Almost out of breath with excitement, Emily recounted her adventures. "As we left the reception, we were approached by several people who recognized our clothing. One was a reporter from the *American Herald*, and another was an American woman who wanted to invite us to the fancy ball she was giving for Mr. and Mrs. Diaz in honor of the president's birthday."

"A ball! What fun. No wonder you have such fond memories of your visit. Do I understand that y'all were seriously considering moving to Mexico?" Sarah asked.

"Oh, yes," Emily replied. "That was one reason it was so easy to get in to see the president. He's actively encouraging American investors. While we were there, we met many Americans who are living down there already. We figured that with twenty American colonies in Mexico, before too long we wouldn't even have to bother learning Spanish. We all loved the climate, especially Mama, because the most amazing flowers grow there all year round. If you asked her what she liked the best, I think it would have to be the trip out to the floating gardens. Flowers and vegetables were growing on both sides of a large canal system, so it looked like gardens actually floating on water. We ate lunch on the boat as we rode out to see them. It was quite impressive. Mama couldn't resist bringing home some seeds and those gorgeous orchids."

"It sounds lovely," Emma commented. "Your mother's orchids are already legendary in Belton. What made y'all decide not to move there after all?"

"Well, to tell you the truth, I believe that was Ella Henry's doing," Emily confided. "She was travelling in our party, and when she wrote Grandma and told her that Mama was coughing again, Grandma put an immediate end to any talk of moving to Mexico. Actually, I believe the drier climate there would have been good for her lungs, but they didn't ask me."

Aware that once again, their conversation had returned to Ada's health, Sarah chose not to acknowledge Emily's comment. "Well, I still think it was adventurous for a group of women to travel on their own."

"Oh, Mrs. Miller, we weren't a bit afraid. The railroad travel agent planned the whole trip, including hotel reservations, and he traveled with us on the train. Women are doing lots of things these days that couldn't be done years ago. Why, in Washington, we all move around as free as you please, with no escorts at all."

"What's this I hear about your grandmother going to Colorado? Did you get to go on that trip, too?" Sarah asked.

"No, just Grandma and Carrie's mother, Sister Henry. They were in Colorado while our group was touring Mexico. Grandma wrote about how much she enjoyed what she called the 'rugged scenery' and the cool, dry weather. But when it snowed on them in August, that was the end of moving to Colorado. In one of her letters, she said that the climate made her nerves 'toned so high they would make good fiddle strings,'" Emily said, amused at the traces of Tennessee still found in her grandmother's colorful language.

"After that, she went to visit Uncle Robert again. When he realized she was serious about moving the church, he tried to get her to move us all to New York since we already own a boarding house up there. But Grandma never even considered it. I doubt whether she and Uncle Robert could ever live in the same city."

Avoiding any more uncomfortable talk of her brother, Emma ignored the comment. "So how did she finally decide on Washington, D.C.?"

"I'm not really sure," Emily admitted. "Grandma went up there in June of this year and immediately fell in love with the city. I just saw the letter she wrote to Mama when she first got there. Here it is."

Emily pulled an envelope from the hatbox on the floor and opened the letter to read, "'Washington is a beautiful city with wide streets bordered with trees. The little birds were singing this morning when I awoke, and I felt as though I was in the midst of a forest. It's the most home-like city I was ever in. Everybody nearly looks like they want to say howdy. I have to watch myself to keep from bowing to them all. The outside of the Capitol is just the same as the one at Austin, only larger, and the grounds are beautiful. You feel as free as you do at the Central. When you walk into the Capitol, a very pleasant Negro man meets you at the door, and they tell me it is the same at the White House. I think I am going to ask to see the President and Mrs. Harrison. I feel as free as if it all belonged to me.' " Emily sighed again as she put the letter back into the box.

"But this is your home," Sarah insisted. "I wish you all would stay. One of the things I like best about coming to the Wednesday Club each week is being able to see Ada and spend the afternoon in this beautiful, home-like hotel. We love you," Sarah said with genuine feeling.

SET APART

"Oh, Emily, before I forget, I wanted to tell you an amusing story about your mother and the Woman's Wednesday Club," Sarah continued with a mischievous twinkle in her eye. "You know Mrs. Tyler, the club president. Well, Ada told me that on the day Mrs. Tyler came to the hotel to reserve the parlor for the first meeting, she was so excited she could hardly talk. She whispered to Ada that an organization for women was being started right here in Belton. Your mother thought that was so funny because Mrs. Tyler seemed oblivious to the fact that she was speaking to someone who had belonged to *a woman's organization* in Belton for the past eighteen years.

"But it was when Mrs. Tyler told her with great pride that the club would meet for programs on literature, art, current events and *women's* issues that Ada had to bite her tongue to keep from laughing out loud. Women's issues may be a new idea for the rest of the female population of Belton, but certainly not at the Central Hotel. After all, your grandmother wrote that letter to the Texas legislature about women's property rights. And Ada herself has had to deal with several women's issues throughout her lifetime. I don't think you can realize just how courageous your mother is, Emily. I'll miss her so much when she moves away," Sarah frowned as her mood quickly darkened at the prospect of permanent separation from her friend. "She's always in my prayers."

Emily looked curiously at Sarah. "Really? Do you pray, Mrs. Miller?"

Sarah smiled kindly, touched by the girl's child-like question. "Oh, yes, Emily. I pray quite often," she replied. "Every day, in fact. Prayer is the way our spiritual life is nourished, much the same way food nourishes our physical bodies. The real business and privilege of a believer is prayer. I've prayed for your mother and all of you for years."

Emily paused for a moment to reflect on the possibility of being the subject of Sarah's spiritual attention. She lowered her head and spoke softly. "I can't remember the last time I said a prayer. Certainly not since I was a child. I think I told you that we don't even have our prayer meetings anymore. Grandma says the Sanctified are always in harmony with the Spirit of God. Sometimes we're directed by dreams, but usually we just rely on her sense of guidance to determine whether we're doing the right thing or not. I don't think anyone in the church prays or reads the Bible on her own."

Over Emily's bowed head, Sarah and Emma exchanged expressions of sadness as they considered the tragedy of so many women having devoted their lives to what turned out to be nothing more than a business by sacrificing their own families at the altar of one woman's twisted dream. At what point, they wondered, did the women stop reading the Bible on their own and start accepting Martha's pronouncements as God's truth? When did the busyness of their lives and the success of their business replace the personal holiness they once sought? Both Sarah and Emma hoped that Emily could see the "church" for what it was before her young life was spent.

"Emily? Is that you?" Ada's unexpected voice called out from the next room. The women looked at each other in surprise.

"Yes, Mama." Emily called, hurrying to the bedroom with Emma and Sarah close behind.

All three women were delighted to find Ada sitting up in bed. Despite being pale and gaunt, she was bright-eyed and smiling. "I thought I heard someone talking. Sarah! Emma! What are y'all doing here? Have you been here long? Were you talking to Ben? He was just here," she chattered cheerfully, then coughed, wincing at the pain.

Emily rushed to adjust the pillow behind her mother's back. "Mama . . . are you talking about my father?" she asked in alarm and confusion. "No, he's not here. You must have been dreaming. I'm sure that's it. You've been asleep almost all day."

Ada was adamant. "No, honey, he was right here. Sitting in that chair. We were talking about Mexico and the beautiful flowers. He's been to Mexico City several times, you know. It's a wonder we didn't see him when we were there."

Emily stooped to open the door of the washstand beside the bed and pulled out the bottle of elixir she had given Ada earlier. "You took some of this medicine for your cough, Mama. Maybe I gave you too much. It must have made you dream about Father." She put the bottle on the washstand and dropped into the chair beside her mother, weak with fear. "Have you forgotten, Mama? He died six years ago."

Ada put a comforting hand up to Emily's face. "I think you're a little confused, sweetheart. Of course I know that your father's been away, but he's come back. Now we can all move to Mexico like you and I talked about. He just stepped out for a moment to find a deck of cards, but he's coming right back. Do you want to play? Your father's an absolutely amazing card player."

"Well, no, I . . ." Emily stammered, looking to Sarah and Emma for help.

Emma immediately stepped up to the bed and took Ada's hand. "I'm so glad you're awake, Ada," she said, smiling tenderly at her sister. "I heard you were sick and came right away, but you've been asleep. We thought you might sleep clear into next week. Feeling better now?"

Ada's frail body shook with another spasm of painful coughing. "Except for this cough," she responded weakly, but with determination. "It sure is good to see you, Emma. I'm sorry Mama's been so strict about unsanctified visitors. I really don't think you can defile me now. I just hope Ben got past her on his way out. He always could make her fur fly."

Growing alarmed at Ada's mental confusion, Sarah quickly moved up to the bed to stand next to Emma. "Ada Haymond, did you know that you slept right through the Woman's Wednesday Club meeting? There are twenty-four women in Belton who had to go home still wondering how in the world you can manage to grow orchids in Central Texas. Twenty-five, if you count me. How will we be able to sleep tonight? What on earth will we do in the morning?" she said with mock severity.

"Oh, dear," Ada moaned. "I guess we'll just have to address that mystery of plant life at a later date. I'm awfully sorry about missing the meeting, Sarah, but when Ben and I get back from Mexico, I'll have some more orchids to show the club. I'll be sure to get some different colors. Won't that be nice."

"Mama, I don't . . ." Emily began before she was interrupted by a heavy knock at the door of the sitting room.

"Mrs. Haymond? Anyone here?" a man's voice asked.

"Ben?" Ada called.

"In here, Dr. Ghent," Emily replied in a choked voice.

"Oh, good," Emma said with obvious relief. "Ada, the doctor is here to see you. Sarah and I will go in the sitting room for now." She squeezed Ada's hand and kissed her sister on the forehead.

After Emma stepped away, Sarah took Ada's hand in both of hers as the doctor entered the room. "Get well, my friend," she whispered.

"I'll be right back, Mama," Emily said, hurrying out behind the women.

In the next room, Emily's eyes filled with the tears she'd kept from her mother. "What's wrong with her, Aunt Emma?" she sobbed. "I've been so worried all day, and then she looked so much better, but she's not. The way she talked about my father. She's . . ."

Emma put her arms around the weeping girl. "I wish I knew what to tell you, Emily. The best thing is that Dr. Ghent is finally here. He'll know what to do for her."

"I'm frightened. I can't lose her again." Emily fought to regain her composure so that she could explain her fears. "You don't understand. I know about dreams, Aunt Emma. You heard her, she was dreaming about Ben, my father." Emily looked from Emma to Sarah, alarm in her eyes as she found no comfort in their stricken expressions. "And he's dead," she whispered, hiding her face on Emma's shoulder. Emma held the sobbing girl until she caught her breath.

Unsettled by Emily's fears and emotional collapse, Sarah placed her arm around the young woman's shoulders. "You have to be strong, Emily. Go back in there and listen to everything Dr. Ghent has to say. He'll tell you how to take care of her. You'll see. She'll be up next week talking about her orchids and packing for Washington. Don't forget the hatbox." Sarah's voice softened as she focused on Emily's tear-streaked face. "I think there's still more your mother wants you to know. Just listen; she'll tell you."

Emily hugged Sarah, then dried her eyes with a corner of the crumpled handkerchief. "Thank y'all so much for waiting with me. I didn't realize how much I needed someone to talk to."

"Well, we love you, darling. Now go on back in there. We'll just wait out here if that's what you want us to do."

"Oh, yes. Please wait," the girl pleaded.

"And we'll be praying for you." Sarah said as she gave Emily an encouraging nudge toward the bedroom.

Although Ada was sitting up in bed again, the girl noticed that her mother's eyes had lost their earlier sparkle. Emily stood quietly at the foot of the bed while the doctor completed his examination. Turning to the young woman, he shared his concern.

"Your mother's lungs are badly diseased, Emily. She's having a great deal of pain with the coughing, so I've given her an opiate. If you can, get her to eat something before she goes to sleep. She needs to get her strength back before she can even think of taking another trip to Mexico."

"Did she say that? Did she tell you she was going to Mexico?" Emily asked, her eyes brimming with new tears.

"Not until I speak to the ladies' club, sweetheart" Ada called weakly over the doctor's shoulder as he wearily bent over to gather his things. "And not until I take a nap." She settled back down on the bed again.

"I'll come back in the morning, Emily," Dr. Ghent said as he patted her shoulder on his way out of the room.

"Thank you, Dr. Ghent," she said, watching him leave.

Emily looked back to see that Ada had already closed her eyes. "Wait, Mama," she pleaded. "The doctor said you need to eat something. Here's some chicken broth I brought you. It's still a little warm. Have a cracker. Water? Mama, please don't sleep yet. Please." Tears streamed down the girl's face.

Ada opened her eyes and, smiling, looked at her daughter. "Emily, baby, don't cry." Weakly, she lifted her hand to wipe the girl's tears. "And don't you worry. I've seen them. I've seen the great cloud of witnesses. When he gets back, tell your father it's a full house. He'll understand," she said with a weak laugh.

Fixed on her mother's face, Emily's eyes were wide with fright and her heart pounded. "Mama, what are you talking about? What cloud?" she sobbed.

"I have to tell you this, too, sweetheart," Ada continued. "Without faith, it is impossible to please him. Did I ever tell you that?" Ada closed her eyes.

"No, Mama, you never told me that. Impossible to please who? Tell me more, Mama. Stay with me," Emily begged tearfully. "Please don't leave me alone. I need you!"

EPILOGUE

Martha McWhirter and granddaughter Emily Haymond stayed in Belton long enough to bury Ada two days later on Friday, November 25, 1898. As recorded in a letter, Emily took her mother's death "so hard," while "Hattie feels it but can't cry at all."

Ada may have suffered from tuberculosis, then called consumption. Ironically, the opiate administered by the doctor for her chest pain actually made breathing more difficult. Opium is now understood to act as a respiratory depressant. Ada was forty-eight years old when she died.

Emily, Hattie and Wilma moved to Washington, D. C., to be with the rest of the church community, which was fully reunited by the spring of 1899 when the leases on the Waco properties were up.

In 1900, Sam McWhirter, who was in New York working with his brother Robert, wrote of extreme fatigue, coughing and severe weight loss. He died in May, possibly of the same affliction that struck his sister Ada. In 1901, Robert McWhirter separated from his wife, Laura, and went to Washington with his two small children in June of that year. In the same year, Hattie moved to Pennsylvania and worked in medical sales, leaving Wilma in Washington with Emily.

Although Emily lived with the group in Washington, she made plans to leave as soon as she figured out a way to get some money from the community. Apparently not expecting help from her grandmother, she asked her Uncle Robert for advice on this matter in a letter which he promptly shared with his mother. Martha's indignant response was to write that Emily "has managed to become blind to what our mission is" by linking up with Hattie who "shows every way that she has no use for any of us." In 1902, Emily was paid five thousand dollars to settle all claims against the community. At that point, Martha declared Ada's children and grandchild, "could never come in our house again except that they were changed."

In May of 1902, Emily, Hattie and Wilma visited Uncle Robert in New York and then traveled to Mexico to stay with their brother, George, on his plantation. Finding it far different from Hattie's experience in Nicaragua, the women felt completely comfortable there. In September, Emily wrote to Uncle Robert: "This plantation life reminds me of the stories that Grandma used to tell us about when she was young. People will come down the river and, if they are in a canoe, they stop at whatever place along the river . . . and spend the night. No one is ever charged but instead, you are always glad to see them . . . the Superintendents of all these places are Americans, so you feel like they are one of your own family."

In October 1902, the group was officially organized as the Woman's Commonwealth of Washington, D.C. In their constitution and by-laws, the Holy Scriptures are named as the "measure and guide of our lives and the touchstone of truth and falsehood, and that all our other principles arise out of these and rule our conduct in religious, spiritual, and natural life." The "true Christian life" is described as being non-sectarian, purely celibate, communal, politically responsible and in adherence to the Golden Rule. In Article III, Section 4, Martha McWhirter, as founder and promoter of the organization was named "president for life."

Emily, Hattie and Wilma returned to Texas in the summer of 1903 to visit relatives in Waco. Wilma, then seven years old, stayed to attend school while her mother and aunt returned to Mexico. Some time after 1903, Emily married a wealthy Mexican man, Ricardo Mestres and moved to New York. They had a son, Ricardo Mestres, Jr.

By then Robert was a serious alcoholic, still seeking a divorce from his wife. He turned up in Oklahoma, apparently having a nervous breakdown, and Ella Henry was dispatched to bring him back to Washington, where he later worked for the Sisters as a carpenter.

Martha died in April of 1904, one month before her eighty-seventh birthday. After Anna Pratt left to be married in 1908, membership in the Commonwealth began to drop rapidly. Margaret Henry died in 1910, and her daughters Ella and Carrie left the group two years later. They both moved to New York City where, interestingly enough, Ella Henry and Robert McWhirter were married in 1915.

The six remaining Sisters operated the huge Washington home as a boarding house for two more years, after which they moved to a full-time farm they had bought in nearby Maryland. They ran the farmhouse as an inn for many years and built a boarding house on the property in 1934.

After two more deaths, the four surviving Sisters purchased a home in Florida where they spent many winters. It was operated as the Commonwealth Guest House until it was sold in 1945.

By 1956, Sister Martha Scheble, the child Sister Gertrude Scheble named after Martha McWhirter, was the last member of the Woman's Commonwealth. Having lived frugally, she died in 1983 at age 101 leaving an estimated worth of $250,000. Although the Washington Orphan Asylum was named in the 1902 constitution as the beneficiary of any remaining assets of the Commonwealth, it had closed in 1972. Ms. Scheble had chosen a home for emotionally disturbed children to benefit in its stead.

Resources

Bell County Museum, Belton, Texas

Exhibit file, The Sanctified Sisters of Belton
Exhibit file, Going up the Chisholm Trail
Resource file, Haymond vs. Haymond divorce trial
Resource file, Salado
Resource file, Ex-slave narratives
Personal journals of Belton residents, circa 1860 –1890
Photo collection

Lena Armstrong Public Library, Genealogy Room – Belton, Texas

Microfilm of Texas census - 1860, 1870, 1880
Tennessee census -1850
Original minutes of Woman's Wednesday Club
Sanborn Fire Insurance maps of Belton city buildings and improvements circa 1880-1900
Photo Collection

Temple Public Library

Microfilm of the Belton Journal and other area newspapers, circa 1870-1900
Microfilm of Texas Census -1910

SET APART

University of Texas – Center for American History – Austin, Texas

Woman's Commonwealth archives – newspapers, diaries, photographs and personal correspondence between the Sisters
Robert Alexander Collection – handwritten sermons of a Methodist circuit preacher who visited Belton in the late 1880s Methodist Annual Conference agenda records for regional conventions, 1877-1879
George P. Garrison Papers
Personal journals of Belton women circa 1860-1870

Baylor University - The Texas Collection - Waco Texas

Waco City Directories for 1895 -96

The Rosenberg Library, Galveston, Texas

Galveston City Directory for 1894
Photo Collection

First Baptist Church of Belton Library

Minutes of deacon's meeting documenting heresy charge of March 17, 1877
Rev. Martin Vanburen Smith biography

Estate of Dr. Eleanor James

The Sanctificationists of Belton magazine article manuscript

Books

This Strange Society of Women
By Sally Kitch
Ohio State Press, Columbus, Ohio

History of Bell County, Texas
By George W. Tyler
The Naylor Company, San Antonio, Texas

The Story of Bell County
By The Bell County Historical Commission
Eakin Press, Austin, Texas

The Methodist Excitement in Texas, a History
By Walter N. Vernon, et al
The Texas United Methodist Historical Society, Dallas, Texas

Trail Drivers of Texas
By J. Marvin Hunter
University of Texas Press, Austin, Texas

The Indians of Texas
By W.W. Newcomb, Jr.
University of Texas Press, Austin, Texas

SET APART

The Workwoman's Guide
By a Lady
Simpkin, Marshall & Co. London, England

The Galveston That Was
By Howard Barnstone
Rice University Press, Houston, Texas

The Sunny Slopes of Long Ago
Wilson M. Hudson, Editor
Southern Methodist University Press, Dallas, Texas

Marxists and Utopias in Texas
By Ernest G. Fischer
Eakin Press, Burnet, Texas

Forth Through Her Portals
By Eleanor James
University of Mary Hardin-Baylor Press
Belton, Texas

ACKNOWLEDGEMENTS

The story of the Sanctified Sisters was a book waiting to be written. *Set Apart* is the result of much encouragement and cooperation on the part of many friends and neighbors, and I wish to give particular thanks to the following folks: Stephanie Turnham, Holly Mathis, and Jodi Gidley of the Bell County Museum; the late Lena Armstrong and Josslyn Jenkins of the Lena Armstrong Public Library; Vada Sutton, Bell County Clerk; Rick Miller, Bell County Attorney; attorneys Barbara Young and Gini Coyle; Andy Davis, pastor of First Baptist Church, Belton; current McWhirter House owners, Bob and Vyone Kimball; friends and encouragers, G.K. Merrill; Laurie Jackson; Ann Wildy Carpenter; computer support, Dottie Brooks; my editor extraordinaire, Kay Walter; and, of course, my wonderful family who had to accommodate the Sisters in our home for so long: the Most Patient Howard Lufburrow, Blake and Erin.

Printed in the United States
27232LVS00003B/1-54